Up in a BLAZE

POLISHED P&P SERIES

LILA ROSE

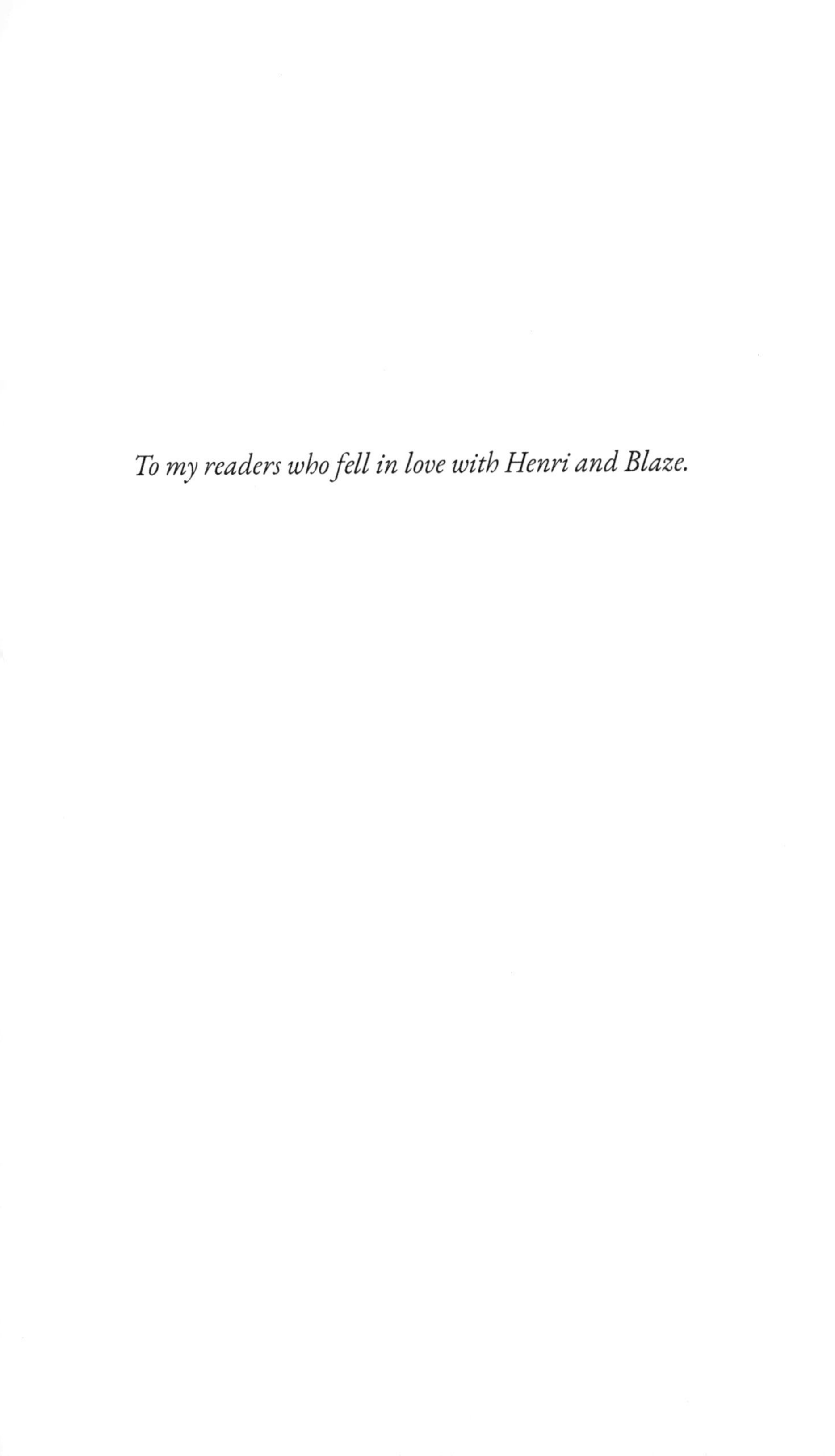

To my readers who fell in love with Henri and Blaze.

CONTENT WARNING

Violence, kidnapping, foul language, derogatory slurs, and
homophobic language

BLURB

Years ago, Blaze chose his shady business over me—Henri Doulle. Fool. Even then, he couldn't shake his fascination for me.

When we finally reconnected, he admitted he'd learned his lesson. Gave it all up and claimed me like he never meant to let go.

He knows he messed up, and now he keeps me close, like he's afraid I'll slip through his fingers again.

Not that I'd even try. He's stuck with me for good.

And if anything ever happens to me? God help whoever's in his way—my beast won't stop until I'm safe.

CHAPTER ONE

HENRI

Once again, I sat in the common room at the Diamond MC surrounded by bikers and their better halves. If my *maman* had asked me years ago if I would set foot in a place like this, I would have laughed heartily and told her I likely would have been killed if I even tried to enter their territory for being my wonderful gay self.

To be truthful, I was quick to judge people. But still, I think their acceptance of me had a lot to do with my ex-employee and best friend, Dusty. She was now married to their president, Country, and they had a little boy *bébé* named Seth. I had begged for them to use my name, but Country kept shooting down my dreams.

There were little monsters popping up here, there, and everywhere. Lucas and Wreck had their girl, Opal. Death's woman, Raya, would spit one out in a couple months' time.

And Courtney had two of them. I was sure there were other members in the club with children, but I wasn't as close to them as I was Dusty, Lucas, Raya, and Courtney.

Being around all these bundles made me crazy for a bébé of my own. However, I wasn't sure my stomach could handle all the dirty diapers. I wondered if I could find an older child who needed my love.

A child in their teens.

Hmm, maybe that wasn't good either. I had been moody throughout my teen years.

Maybe it would be best if I got a puppy.

But that would be if I could get a certain someone on board with the whole idea.

Warm arms slid around me from behind and pulled me back against a big hard chest. "When're you coming back?"

Tipping my head to the side, I smiled up at Blaze. The only man who had ever had my heart.

And he *was* mine.

M. I. N. E.

"Are you missing me already, *mon amour*?"

"Just your face, not the attitude."

Huffing, I pushed at his arms, but the big oaf wouldn't move. He chuckled in my ear before I bent my head and nipped at his forearm, then stated, "I do not have attitude."

Since Dusty was sitting next to me holding her bundle of joy, I heard her soft peals of laughter as she murmured, "Yeah, right, Henri."

Glaring at her, I sniffed. "I do not."

She reached out and patted my hand. "Sure, okay."

She didn't sound sincere, though. Not that I could

blame her. I was fibbing. I'd been born with attitude, but at least Blaze liked it. He called me his firecracker.

"I will come out to you soon."

He growled in my ear, "Be good." With a pinch to my nipple, which had me squealing, he walked away.

There was no guess to where he was headed. If I wasn't in his life, he would live with his little computer toys. Although, the room he was going to wasn't his and Tech's main setup. This smaller computer room was just for when he and Tech were here at the compound. Their main office had been moved to the Polished P & P escort, a brothel agency where I worked the front desk.

A job I had begged for.

A job I thought would bring me the happiness and excitement I'd lost when I owned my own florist shop.

But over the last few months nothing thrilling had happened. I even worked the busiest hours, from six to midnight, and yet, there was zero action.

Where were the shoot-outs, the asshole customers, the creeps?

All the customers I had met so far were regulars and seemed like nice men and women. I wasn't sure how long I could continue working there if something didn't happen.

Hopefully things would change in the coming days, because if I ended up leaving, the guilt would eat at me since Blaze and Tech moved all their equipment there when I started working.

Then again, it wasn't *my* fault Blaze was an overprotective ogre who didn't trust any other men around me since I was hot.

Dusty bumped my shoulder. "You still can't believe he's here, right?"

Looking to her, I noticed her man, Country, talking to another member, Death, who was Country's third-in-command at the club. Both men had an unsavory past with my Blaze, but at least now they were civil to one another.

Although, the animosity at the start had been understandable. It was also the reason Blaze and I had parted ways many years ago after I found out he was involved in selling organs on the black market. The drug dealings I could have handled, as I was sure Country and Death would have as well. We just wanted no part of those shady dealings, and since he wasn't ready to give that part of his life up, we went our separate ways.

Until now.

It may have taken years, but after we'd spoken, he had finally seen his mistake in letting me go, and of course, he quickly snagged my scrumptious self up. I mean, I was irresistible.

Smiling softly to Dusty, I shook my head. "*Non, chérie*, I cannot. It is a lot to me that he is here and had been willing to give those things up for me."

She reached out, squeezing my hand. "I know. But you are a catch."

"I really am."

We cackled together.

Since shutting down his illegal activity, he was now paid by the Diamond MC—much to my surprise that Country had agreed—to assist their computer guy on anything the club needed.

Compared to those two, my knowledge of the digital world involved minimal information about my cell and laptop.

In the past, I had even employed someone for my florist shop to do the accounting for me. That was until Blaze took over the position. Blaze told me he didn't want me to pay someone who had been, apparently, "ripping me off" in the first place because it was a simple task he could do with his eyes closed.

He only had a few IRS forms to complete now since I sold the shop.

His wisdom could be why Country didn't pass up on the chance of having Blaze work under the MC. Not only could he keep an eye on my man, but the president would use Blaze's smarts to his advantage.

"Darlin', you want another drink?" Country asked as he and Death stood from the table. If I didn't have Blaze, I would have continued to drool over many of the men in this club, but my attention was now and forever focused on Blaze.

Besides, a lot of the brothers in the club were big balls of intimidation.

When I'd first met Country, I'd lost count of the times where I thought he was going to kill me after I'd pretended to be Dusty's man.

"I'll take one, honey." She smiled up at him.

He bent and pressed his lips to hers, then against her neck when I heard her sigh. He straightened with a smirk, taking Seth into his arms before he flicked his gaze to me.

I stared back.

He kept looking at me like he expected I knew what he wanted.

I did not read silent biker man.

Dusty laughed. "Want a refill, Henri?"

"Oh, non. Thank you. I have work later."

See, you hired a responsible man for your business, Mr. President.

But all Country did was tip his chin up and leave for the kitchen.

"I know I asked this at the start, but how are you finding working the late hours now?" Dusty asked.

"The hours don't bother me. The boredom might."

Dusty groaned. "Oh no."

"Yes, chérie. There has been no excitement. I am afraid I will have to bring in a book to read."

She laughed. "You read?"

"I do not, but I am willing to try. We can't tell Blaze any of this, of course."

She nodded. "I hope things change soon. Not that I want drama to happen just for your sake. But it'll help a lot of other people's lives."

"*Oui*, it will. Tech would murder me if I up and quit since Blaze moved their toy room there, and I think my man would help him."

Dusty snorted. "Their toy room?"

"Oui, they play and play and play on their little screens." I picked up my glass and drank the rest of the soda.

"You're not really salty over them working, right?"

"Non. I get jealous with the time he pays his work. But when he gives me *all* his attention, that makes up for ignoring me."

She grinned. "You get jealous over computers, and he gets jealous over anyone looking at you."

"We are a fiery couple that go well together. Most days." Leaning in, I kissed her cheek. "Have a good night, chérie."

"Talk to you later. And, Henri, try to have fun."

I winked, standing. "I will make fun somehow." Worry pinched her brows, and I quickly reassured her with "Do not fret. No harm will come to your man's business."

"Or you," she called as I walked off.

Turning back, I blew her a kiss and loudly said, "*Au revoir.*"

What I loved about this biker place was that I wasn't treated as an outsider—like now when many returned my farewell.

Outside the computer room, I tapped on the door and said, "Stop stroking those keys. I am coming in." I pushed through and stepped in. Neither of them looked over at me and continued to tap, tap, tap away. Sighing, I glared at the back of Blaze's head. "Mon amour, if you don't stop, I will strip naked and—" I smiled when he spun his chair around to me. "Better. We don't want to scare your friend."

"I agree," Tech muttered.

Blaze scowled at him. "You'd be fuckin' honored to look at him naked."

Tech stopped typing and groaned. "Yeah, yeah. Your man is a god."

I preened. "Why, thank you. I can give you a sneak peek."

Tech stood, hands up in front of him. "I don't wanna peek at anythin'. Stop tryin' to get your man to kill me."

Chuckling, I shrugged. "But I think if you were not here, I would have more of his attention."

Blaze let out a deep huffing sound and stalked toward me. When he stopped in front of me, he wound an arm around my back and with the other he gripped the front of my throat to pull me close. "Stop being greedy, firecracker. You get the best of my attention."

Melting against his chest, I glided my hands up over his hard muscles. "You like me being greedy, mon amour."

His gaze softened and heated as he remembered how greedy I had been by swallowing his cock and seed twice before we'd come to the compound.

The hand around my throat tightened, and he watched me closely as he deprived me of oxygen.

He'd wait until I was nice and red in the face and marked around the neck before he allowed me to breathe.

He loved how needy I got when he controlled me and my body.

Releasing my throat, he said, "Let's get you to work."

After catching my breath, I pouted, pushing my hips forward to run my erection against him.

He smirked. "Later."

I glared. "I hate you."

He kissed me rough and hard, forcing his tongue in to roll with mine. Another thing he knew I loved.

Blaze pulled back, his gaze roaming over my face. "No, you don't."

He was right. I could never since I loved him completely.

There was a sigh before Tech said, "Can you two keep your romance to a room I'm not in?"

"Non," I said without looking away from Blaze, whose lips twitched.

"Let's get you to work," he said.

And let us also pray something happened tonight before I bashed my own brains in on my desk from boredom.

HENRI

Hours later, when the doors opened again, I looked up from the computer and through the clear protective partition in front of my desk and smiled. Moving closer to the gap so I would be heard, I called, "Welcome to Polished P & P. How may I help you?"

As the man walked over, I took him in and easily guessed he was a businessman. He still wore his suit and had probably just come from work. He seemed around my fabulous thirties age.

He smiled friendly. "Hey, gorgeous. I have an appointment with Pixie."

Ah, sweet little Pixie, real name Sawyer. He was a newbie and freshly turned eighteen. It made me uncomfortable to see such a shy, young man entertaining men. But I was sure he had his reasons for choosing this path.

It was something I wanted to know, but Blaze said I wasn't allowed to question the employees.

"One moment, sir. I'll see if he's ready." I hadn't seen him arrive. However, some employees entered via the back. I brought up his name on the computer, and it was high-lighted green, which told me he was here. There was a room number allocated next to his name. "Please make your way to the elevator. He's on floor two, room 209."

Some workers liked to collect their customer and then others preferred the client to be sent up to the room.

"Thanks." He grinned and leaned closer. "Have you ever thought about—"

"No," a cold and dark voice clipped from close by.

A voice I loved.

The man paled, straightened, and nodded to my man before he walked over to the elevator.

Heat hit my side, and I grinned when a warm hand gripped my hair to tug my head back. "I don't like this job."

"Mon amour, they can look and try, but I am not inter-ested in any. *You* are the one I go home with."

He growled under his breath, which made me tingle all over as he dipped to claim my mouth.

It was a brief kiss but one that still left me panting for more when he pulled away and tugged at my hair once again before he walked back over to his office and slammed the door after him.

Of course, the broody ogre couldn't have an office away from me. It was lucky Country, State, Saint, and Wreck allowed them to change the break room into their computer room. They resituated the break room and bathroom to the back of the ground floor, where there were also another couple of offices off to the right of the building. Though the main area of the ground floor held the waiting area with a few sitting spots and bathroom. On the second and third floor, there were a couple of offices, bathrooms, a meeting room, and a couple of additional break rooms but most were bedrooms where the employees entertained clients.

Tech had shown me and Blaze around the place when I first started. But he didn't let me witness any happenings inside the rooms.

Boo.

When the doors opened, Saint strode in and walked over to me. "Henri, what's happenin'?" He was another brother to the Diamond MC, and I was closer to him and his lover, Gun. They were born with different names, but only their significant other was allowed to use it.

Not like my Blaze. His parents gave him his cool name when he was born.

The memory of the first time I met him and heard his name flashed through my mind.

Walking out of the nightclub, I turned left to go down the alleyway to get to my car when I stumbled across a big, scary-looking man sitting with his back to the wall and bleeding from a wound on his stomach.

When I stopped, he glared up at me.

"You're bleeding," I pointed out.

Of course, he said nothing, just stared.

Any other man would have run from just his look, but I was still a little drunk and a lot stupid since I also thought he was the handsomest man I had seen in a long time.

Even with blood coating his fitted gray tee.

Reaching for my phone in my back pocket, I told him, "I'll call for help."

"No."

Even his sharp, rough tone should have put me on edge. Instead, I slapped my hands to my hips and glared. "Non? You are bleeding. You need assistance."

"Don't call anyone," he warned. "Just fuckin' leave."

In French, I spewed, "I am no saint, but I will not leave a good-looking, scary idiot to die in a dirty alleyway. Even when they are acting like a growling beast."

To my utter shock, he replied in French, "You think I'm good-looking?"

I harrumphed. "And a beast. Let me call for help."

"No. You do it and I'll make your life hell."

"You won't be alive to treat me to this hell, idiot." When he said nothing, I sighed and looked up to the sky for guidance. Of course there was none, and I could not leave the fool to bleed out. "Fine. You probably know more about these wounds. You come home with me, and I'll stitch you up."

His gaze flared. "You'd have me in your home?"

Glowering, I told him, "It is either that or let you die, and I refuse to allow that to happen."

"You don't know me."

"Non, but if you try anything, I will shout out to my cop friend next door. He will come running."

He shifted and winced but then nodded.

Reaching down, I tried my best to help him to his feet. He wobbled and groaned and did most of the work because the man was built like an ox.

"I am parked on the street." I glanced at the blood.

"Maybe you should stay here, and I will bring the car to pick you up."

"You just helped me stand. I'll be fine."

I doubted it. He was very pale, and if anyone saw him, they would think I had done something. But I wasn't wasting time arguing. I had a feeling, from the doctor shows I watched, that this man needed to be stitched up as soon as possible.

"Come then," I ordered, looping his arm around my shoulders while I placed one of mine around his waist.

The injured man stared down at me for a beat but then shuffled forward, and together we made it to the street and car without an incident. It was lucky I had driven that night and been able to park so close to the club.

As soon as I had him strapped in the passenger seat, I rushed around to the driver side and got in.

I started the car, pulled out, and drove off while wondering if I was doing the right thing.

I could just drive him to the hospital and drop him off.

"Don't even think about it," the beast warned.

Scowling over at him for a moment, I cursed at him in French.

The man snorted before he asked, "What's your name?"

"Henri. You?"

"Blaze."

Rolling my eyes, I pulled into my driveway and looked around. It was late, and no one seemed about. When I looked back at the man, I said, "You could just say you would prefer not to tell me your name instead of lying."

"I ain't lying. Grandfather's name was Blaze after the poet and writer Blaže Koneski." He blinked slowly at me. "Why the fuck did I tell you that?"

"Relax, la bête. I do not spread secrets." Just my legs, and if he wasn't an asshole bleeding all over my car, I would have given him a chance.

Maybe.

"Let's get you inside before you pass out."

"I won't," he grumbled.

Muttering under my breath about the foolish, sexy man, I got out of the car and went around to his side to assist him. I searched our surroundings as we slowly made our way to the front door.

Once in the living room, I asked, "Can you stand there for a moment?"

When he grunted, I raced off to grab my sewing kit and first aid box, as well as the shower curtain in the downstairs bathroom that I yanked off its rail. I was not letting him ruin my couch.

I lay the curtain down on the seat and told him, "Sit."

Surprisingly, he did without a word, and then he managed to lead me through removing the bullet, stitching him up, and covering his wound before he passed out.

Sitting back on my knees, I stared at the half-naked man before me. It had to hurt when I patched him up, but he hadn't cursed at me or threatened me in any way.

I could call for help now. The police. An ambulance, since I wasn't sure I did a good enough job. What happened if it became infected? How would he get antibiotics?

Should I pick the brain of my neighbor who had been on the force but had retired ten years ago?

Sighing, I stood and removed all the mess. Before I cleaned myself up, I placed a few towels down on the couch and kind of pushed and shoved Blaze down to pull the curtain out from under him. With a lot of cursing and grunting, I picked up his tree-trunk legs and placed them along the couch so he was lying flat.

Why did I help him?

I could have walked away.

Then again, I liked helping. I liked knowing I was able to do something.

Taking a smaller cushion, I placed it under his head and took the throw blanket off the back of the couch to rest over him.

"What am I thinking leaving a man in my house?" I asked myself. He could kill me. Obviously, he'd done something that someone didn't like since they hurt him. With unease, I placed the curtain in the washing machine and grabbed a spare from the linen closet to hang.

I took one look at my guest before walking out of the room to lock the front door. Once upstairs in my bedroom, I showered quickly in my en suite. I would usually slip under the sheets naked, but I dressed in sleep clothes. I made sure my phone had enough charge in case I needed to call for help. Though, I already had a feeling I wouldn't. He could have lashed out at any time or left, but there was some part of me that thought he wanted to stay. He wanted my help and company.

Or I could be reading it all wrong and die through the night.

After that charming thought, it took me a while to get to sleep. When I woke six hours later, I gasped, remembering my guest downstairs.

It was early, but I felt the need to check on him. For all I knew, he could have stolen all my things while I slept.

With a robe on, I made my way downstairs and saw

Blaze sitting up on the couch, watching television on low. He followed my every step as I moved closer.

"Would you like pain meds?"

He tipped his chin up.

Crossing my arms over my chest, I cocked a brow. "Does that mean yes?"

"Please," he forced out.

Smiling, I nodded. "That is better." Turning, I headed toward the kitchen. When I returned with the medication, he opened his eyes and lifted his head off the back of the couch. I held out a bottle of water and after he uncapped it, I placed the two tablets onto his palm. "They have pain relief and anti-inflammatory in them."

He grunted and swallowed them down.

I wouldn't mind watching his throat work while he swallowed around my cock.

Said cock twitched under my sleep pants.

I shouldn't be thinking of him like that. For all I knew, he could be homophobic.

Then why was he outside a gay club? Unless he'd just been in the area.

"You gonna stare at me all day?" he asked.

"Since you are in my house, chéri, *I can do whatever I like."*

"Then you wanna stare at me while I shower?"

My mouth dropped open as my stomach tingled.

Was that really an option, or was he teasing? It was hard to tell with his straight face.

"I might need to in case you fall over."

Baiser, *am I really flirting with a dangerous man?*

Did I really want to see him fully naked?

Oui, I honestly did, and if he was willing to show me, who was I to argue against his choice?

With a groan, he stood and pressed a hand to his wound. Bruises marred his big build, but they were less of a worry than the gunshot I'd stitched up.

"Show me the way," he said, still without any facial expression so I didn't know if he was uncomfortable with me tagging along or if he really was teasing me.

"Fine." I turned and took him to the guest bathroom downstairs. Not that I had guests who slept over. The acquaintances I had all lived in the same area and went to their own homes on nights out.

I reached into the shower and started the water while I waited for Blaze to confess he was messing with me and wanted me out of the bathroom.

He could be into guys, but I doubted I was to his taste. I probably mouthed off too much. He looked like he was used to a docile partner—someone who didn't argue back. That would never be me.

And why would I even think about being with a man I just met who had been beaten and shot for some reason?

That was just asking for trouble.

Although, trouble could bring a bit of fun to my life.

"The water is warm, not too hot," I said.

When he didn't reply, I turned and swallowed my tongue.

He was naked. Completely naked.

My gaze slowly ran over his form and ate up every delectable inch of this beast of a man.

That was a nice cock. A cock that twitched under my stare.

Quickly, I looked up at the man in front of me.

"You gonna get outta the way or join me in there?"

Holy fuck. *Had I died? Had he actually killed me?*

His lips kicked up in the corner for a moment before he schooled his features again. "At least I know what makes you silent."

My feathers ruffled, and in French, I snapped, "I will never stay silent for long, so don't enjoy it too much."

"Get in the shower, Henri."

I flicked my gaze to his hardening dick, to his wound, and back up to his eyes. "It seems you don't like me silent."

"Shower. Now."

"And if I say non?"

"Then you can leave. I'd never force someone."

Liking his words a lot, I sighed like I wasn't really into this, when it was the complete opposite, and removed my robe.

"I suppose you will need a hand in the shower."

He snorted. But he didn't argue with me.

Saint rapped his knuckles against the partition, and I blinked back into the now as he said, "Henri, you okay?"

Nodding, I smiled. "Yes, and I was just getting to the good part of a memory."

Saint chuckled, waving a hand my way. "Is that what the drool is about?"

Rolling my eyes, I leaned forward, resting my chin on my hands, elbows to my desk. "The only time I drool, *mon ami*, is when Blaze has my mouth stuffed full."

Saint groaned. "I walked right into that one."

Grinning, I winked. "You did. Are you here taking over from Wreck?"

"Yeah, and I'm gonna head to my office now before Blaze shoots me for spending too much time around you."

With a scoff, I shook my head and leaned back in my seat. "How will he know?"

Saint grinned and glanced behind me. "Hey, Blaze."

There was a grunt before Saint walked off. Next, my hair was snagged, and my head was tugged back. He nipped at my chin with his teeth. "Time to eat."

Smiling, I then licked my lips. "I could use a meal."

Shaking his head, he kissed me quickly and pulled back. "Food, firecracker."

"I'm here," Isobell announced, racing across the waiting area. She was one of the sex workers but also filled in at the reception desk when I needed my time away.

I blew her a kiss and stood, taking my man's hand. "Feed me then, *mon amour.*"

CHAPTER THREE

BLAZE

As we walked into the break room, I looked down at my little firecracker once again while he smiled, waved, and greeted every person in there. The man was too damn good-looking for his own good. Too nice. Too charming. Drove me fucking crazy with the amount of attention he got. But at least I could say he was *mine*.

At least I could tell any fucker looking at him that he was taken.

And if they didn't get the message, I would remove their eyes and make them eat them so they were clear that he was mine.

All fuckin' mine.

Although, if I was still in the business of selling body parts on the black market, I would have thought about keeping the eyes for the money.

I gave up Henri once because of the shit I dealt in. I'd be a damn fool to lose him again. The first time had nearly broken me, and the only thing that kept me from going mad was watching him from afar.

I'd stalked him on the days I was desperate to see and hear him. I'd also installed a couple of cameras around his place.

It was just luck that no other fucker had been with him at his house or those times I followed him through the streets. If there had been, I wouldn't have been able to stop myself from ending them in one way or another.

He'd been an addictive hobby. My obsession.

I wanted to know he was always safe, which was why I had to move the computer room here to Polished. To be close in a place where shit could go down. Thank fuck nothing had happened since he'd started.

When we stopped in front of the buffet line to grab some warm food, I thought again about how well this place was set up. The brothers of the Diamond MC knew how to treat their employees.

"Mon amour, what are you having?" Henri asked as he picked up a tray.

I took another one and set it beside his on the rails. "Just put on mine whatever you wanna try." I'd eat about anything, and I knew Henri liked to pick or try different things.

He beamed up at me, and went to his toes to kiss my jaw. My gut danced. It always did.

He'd been the only man to get that type of reaction out of me—just another reason I'd become infatuated with him.

As he grabbed food, he called out to the cooks in the

back, telling them, "Bonjour, everything looks amazing like always. Harriet, how's the little one?" After she answered, he went on. "That's great. Bruce, did Audrey get that part in the musical?" Bruce grinned and told Henri all about it.

The light of my life didn't care we only had so long to eat. He made sure everyone around him knew he saw them.

Like he'd seen me.

And that was after he'd saved my ass.

Hell, I'd fallen for the guy the moment he glowered down at me as I bled out.

I'd been damn blessed when he stumbled upon me and was brave enough to take me back to his place.

I moved over to a table, placed our trays down, and pulled out Henri's seat for him. He slipped down into it before I took hold of the chair next to him and moved it closer to his side to sit.

"You know I love you," he said. When I looked at him, I grunted. He smirked. "And you know you're stuck with me forever and ever."

I wouldn't want it any other way.

"What do you need?" I asked.

He laughed. "What would you say to someone else joining our family?"

Dropping my fork, I gripped his throat and pulled him close. "I share you with no one."

"Not even your computer bestie?"

"No. One," I bit out. "Did Tech say something to you? Did he suggest something?" I stood, ready to fold Tech's body into a pretzel shape, when Henri's hand wrapped around my wrist as he cackled like a madman and others looked over at us.

"Relax, mon amour. I did worry that you had fallen for Tech since you spend so much time with him, but I know I don't have to. I am, and will always be, only yours."

Sitting, I cursed under my breath and asked, "Then what the fuck you talking about?"

"A puppy? I want to be a papa. To dote on another like you do me."

The ache in my chest eased, and I felt foolish for it to begin with.

Henri wouldn't step out. He was completely committed to me, which he'd proved time and time again when women and men tried to get his attention.

I should do to him what he threatened to do to me. Piss on him in front of everyone so they knew he belonged to me.

"Are you thinking of peeing on me?" he questioned before taking a bite of the pizza slice on my tray. He chewed a couple of times before his nose screwed up, and he put the slice back down on my tray.

"I'll do it if I have to," I told him, taking a sip of his iced coffee.

"So," he drew out. "What are your thoughts about a little *chiot*?"

A puppy.

I cringed.

He wanted a puppy that'd whine, pee, shit, bark, and chew everything up. "You know what they're like to train?"

"Non, but I know you and I will make perfect papas together."

Shit.

"It could chew up your shoes and clothes."

He shrugged. "Then I will buy more."

"When did you start thinking about wanting a dog?"

"Earlier at the compound."

Groaning, I rubbed at my forehead. "Can we think about it for more than a few hours before we decide?"

"Sure, mon amour."

A tray set down across from us, and I narrowed my gaze on Loyal, a Diamond MC brother who worked as security here.

He tipped his chin. "Hey."

"Bonjour, Loyal. How is work?"

"Good," he said around a mouthful as he eyed us. "Don't you two get sick of seeing each other at work and home?"

Henri laughed. "Non, chéri. Besides, my Blaze spends more time looking at a screen than me."

"Henri," I warned. He was talking bullshit.

He rolled his eyes. "However, I know it'll always be me he seeks out when his love affair with a computer is finished."

Damn right.

I loved coding, hacking, investigating, and all the other shit Tech and I did on the computers, but Henri would always come first over everything. I'd sworn it to myself when he'd reached out to me after years of no contact.

When he asked for my help, I knew I wouldn't be strong enough to walk away for a second time.

It probably wasn't good to be thankful since Henri had only reached out to get me to help find Dusty.

At first, I didn't think the Diamond MC would want an assist from me, but Country's fear of losing Dusty meant he quickly accepted my help. I knew Country and Death back in school. We'd been friends for a while, until I'd started dealing in shady shit and they'd wanted no part of it. But it was also around the time my sister was brutally murdered, and the vengeance that burned inside of me overtook everything in my life.

A slim hand squeezed my thigh. I glanced to Henri, who quirked a brow, silently asking me if I was okay. I nodded once.

He went on eating, as did I, but Henri also asked Loyal, "Has there been any drama happening in your area?"

Loyal snorted. "If I was to guess, you're itching for something to go down."

"Moi? I would never."

Shaking my head, I grinned for a moment.

"Sure, Henri," Loyal said. "Hey, did you happen to see Pixie when he came in?"

"Non, why?"

"He didn't look too good."

Henri cocked his head to the side. "He is with a client right now, but I will check on him."

Loyal tipped his chin up. "Knew you would. Thanks, Henri."

In the time Henri had been here, he'd become somewhat of a mother hen to the employees. He lived to gossip and help where he could, and the brothers knew he was always willing to be there when certain employees needed a gentler hand.

Pixie was shy and quiet, and Wreck had told me he'd spoken to Henri more than anyone else in the building, but even with the times they'd talked, it wasn't much.

The kid needed help. There was something troubling

him, but it was up to him to reach out. We couldn't interfere. Not yet at least. I had a feeling that if we moved too fast with him, he'd just up and quit.

Henri laughed at something Loyal said. I fucking loved watching him. Everything he did I was obsessed with.

The way he moved and talked....

I still remembered the first time I'd seen him naked. My lips tugged up in the corner briefly as I thought of the shocked look on his face when he'd turned around in the bathroom to find me naked first.

As I stared at the beautiful man, I was sure he thought I'd tell him to fuck off.

But I couldn't.

The need to see him naked in the shower clawed under my skin. My cock was already hard, desire pushing me to palm it as he said, "I suppose you will need a hand in the shower."

Fuck yes.

Even when pain radiated all over my body, I blocked it when he started to undress.

Inch by inch, he revealed his sweet skin that I wanted to lick, bite, and claim.

I'd wanted to make him mine when I'd seen him, when he'd spoken to me and cursed me out in French.

"Mon bête, you look at me like you want to devour me," he said.

My beast.

Yeah, I wanted to be his beast.

"I do," I admitted roughly.

He clamped his teeth into his plump bottom lip as he pushed his sleep pants down. His erection bobbed free, ready for my hand to wrap around it. But I stopped myself, ordering, "In the shower."

He cocked a brow. "You," he challenged.

"If I had the energy, I'd spank you. Please get in the shower. I want to look at your ass."

His whole face lit up as he winked. "You should have started with that, chéri." He spun around, and looked back over his shoulder to me, eyes shining.

I followed right after him into the steamy shower, shutting the curtain behind me.

He moved beyond the spray of water, crooking his finger at me. I stepped right under the water and brushed my hair back with a hand, watching him through the droplets.

Henri scraped his top teeth over his bottom lip, running his gaze down over me. "It is lucky, mon bête, that I placed a waterproof patch over your wound."

With a grunt, I nodded once.

"Will you allow me to wash you?"

Fuck. I'd give up my own kidney to have that. "Yeah."

He reached around to grab the soap and slid it over my flesh, starting at my shoulders. I dipped my head, closing my eyes, enjoying his gentle hands on me.

I hadn't been with anyone in a long time. Hadn't realized I'd missed the touch of someone. But Henri's was different to anyone else's.

It was more welcomed. Wanted.

Henri hummed when my dick jerked from his touch.

Opening my eyes, I kept my gaze lowered to see his hands. One brushed over my balls. The other that held the soap stroked my cock. Unfortunately, he didn't linger. But still, his next move had me gulping when he crouched in front of me to clean my thighs and calves.

As he looked up with a seductive smile, I took a step forward and curled my fingers through his hair.

He cocked a brow. "What is it that you want, mon bête?"

"Your mouth."

"Then take it."

Desire burned hot under my skin. I dragged him to his feet and heard his gasp, saw his surprise, and heard the soap drop just before I claimed his mouth with mine.

He moaned into my mouth when I forced my tongue in to play and tease his.

Fuck, fuck, fuck.

His mouth was made for me to take. I wanted more. I wanted to devour him in ways where he wouldn't be able to forget me.

And I felt all that from one kiss.

He tore his mouth from mine, staring at me while we caught our breath. "Baiser." He breathed out the word fuck *in his thick French accent. "You can kiss." He dropped to his knees again, and before I could say anything, he swallowed my cock, sucking like a goddamn vacuum.*

"Fuck," I grunted.

His dark gaze lifted to lock with mine as he bobbed up and down on my dick, licking and sucking it in ways that drove me crazy.

His hand cupped my balls, slowly rolling them, tugging them.

"Can I come on your face?" I wanted to mark him, paint his face with my cum and rub it into his skin.

He hummed and nodded slightly. My gaze flared in surprise. As far as I'd figured, not many would allow it with a man they'd just met. Then again, I'd never wanted to do that to another before.

Having his trust, his approval, was a rush to my body. My climax tickled down my spine. "Christ," I clipped, pulling free and wrapping my hand around my dick to jerk.

Henri sat back, smiling, gazing up at me like a devious devil.

Or my French firecracker.

Groaning, I released all over his face, on his chin, forehead, cheeks, swollen lips.

Reaching up, I quickly moved the water spray away so my seed lingered on his soft flesh. Want burned inside me to have my essence soak into him in a way it never had before. Leaning down, I gripped the back of his hair in one hand and used my fingers on the other to gently massage my cum in.

After, I dipped my thumb into his mouth and out again. He just kept smiling up at me.

Gripped with need, I reached down, wincing as my wound pulled, and grabbed his wrist, yanking him up. Turning him, I blanketed his body and wrapped my palm around his hard dick.

"Yes," he moaned when I started jerking him off. He pushed his ass back against me.

Taking the front of his throat in hand, I squeezed. "Still," I ordered.

His breaths panted out as he stopped moving against me and let me toy with his body.

Grazing my teeth against his neck, I then sucked his skin into my mouth, marring his flesh in another way that would show he was taken.

He quivered and whimpered. "Blaze, baiser. Coming," he shouted.

I didn't stop milking his cock until his body ceased shaking. He let out a noise that sounded a lot like a purr.

After turning him, I pinched his chin. "I'm keeping you," I warned.

His lips quirked, and he rolled his eyes. "We will see how this goes."

"I'm keeping you."

"As long as you tell me why you were bleeding out in an alleyway."

"It was the brother of a man I killed in revenge."

He gasped, but he never moved away from me. That gave me hope. "Why did you kill his brother?"

"He beat, raped, and murdered my sister."

His jaw clenched and gaze narrowed. "Then he deserved it."

Fucking hell. He was my ideal partner already.

"Oui," I answered.

His smile had my heart clenching. I wanted to bury myself into his goodness. Forever.

How had this man captured me in such a short amount of time?

I didn't care. I wasn't walking away.

"How do you know French?" he asked.

I brushed my nose up and over his temple. "My grandmother taught me when I was young. She passed away, and I kept learning for her."

He shared another smile with me before he ran his hands up my chest. "You need more food and rest, mon chéri."

"You're still willing to have me here? To take care of me?"

"Oui."

Christ, my heart had ached with the swarm of warm emotions flooding it. "Then I promise to take care of you too," I told him.

In French, he said, "You may be a beast, but I can see your soft side. I am not promising anything, but I would love to get to know you. To spend time with you."

"Affaire," I replied, committing to the deal.

What he didn't know was that he'd just signed himself up to be mine.

CHAPTER FOUR

HENRI

A figure dashed by the waiting area to my left and took my attention away from a very busy game of solitaire on the computer. When I saw Sawyer rushing toward the break room, I stood and moved toward the tech room. After a quick knock, I poked my head in. "Mon amour, can you please watch the front for a moment?"

His fingers stopped flying over the keys, and he pushed his chair back to stand. No questions were asked as he made his way to me. I rocked up to my toes and kissed him quickly.

"Thank you."

His reply was to kiss me again, palming my ass.

I skipped off to the break room and entered. Sawyer had just sat down with a tray in front of him. He didn't look up at I approached. He was too busy hiding the packets of food he picked out from under the table in the bag he held between his feet.

My heart broke.

The poor boy was hoarding food for a reason.

"Bonjour," I called loudly to one of the escort girls, who waved in return with a smile while she ate. I saw Sawyer jolt and pull his hand up onto the table, picking up a spoon. He stared down at the table while he slowly ate the hot dishes.

Pulling out the chair opposite him, I sat. "Bonjour."

His cheeks flooded with heat as he glanced up and down quickly. "Hi."

How could one as shy as him be in the sex work industry?

"I never asked, but would you wish for me to call you Sawyer or Pixie?"

He shrugged. "Either."

"How are you settling in, chéri?"

He watched his spoon as he slid it through the stew. "Fine."

"I wanted you to know that if there was anything you ever needed, I am willing to help. If you do not wish to speak to any of the big burly bikers, who are pussycats deep down but can seem scary, I will always lend an ear to listen."

Even when I saw how stiff he was, there was still a small smile on his lips when I'd called the bikers pussycats.

Finally, he nodded once. "Thanks, Henri."

"You are welcome, chéri. You can also let me know if you have any clients you wish to never see again. Like the managers here, I won't allow anyone to hurt you, Sawyer. In any way."

He bit down on his bottom lip just as it trembled, and he cleared his throat.

My stomach churned at the thought of someone already hurting him. "I have my own security who I can count on if you need backup." I smiled gently. "He may look like a handsome but grumpy ogre, but I have him wrapped around my pinkie."

It was true. My Blaze would do absolutely anything for me.

"I, um, I'll let you know."

I nodded. "Do you still live at home, Sawyer?"

He nodded, then shook his head, then shrugged.

I smiled softly.

"I...." He blew out a breath as his gaze flicked up to me and down to his plate. I really wondered how this boy took clients to have sex with when he was so nervous having a conversation.

Then again, there were a lot of men who liked the timidness from others.

He shook his head, lips thinning. He wasn't ready to talk, and I worried if I pushed anymore, he wouldn't eat and would instead leave.

Slowly, I reached over and brushed my fingers against the back of his hand. "I'll leave you to your meal, chéri. But please do remember we are here for you."

"Thanks," he whispered.

My stomach tightened when I turned and left the poor boy there, knowing there was something going on in his life that I believed wasn't good for him.

Would it be wrong of me if I asked mon amour to trail him?

I didn't know what best suited in this situation. Did we push to help and risk losing him altogether or wait for him to come to someone?

Loyal stood at the front counter talking with Blaze, but I knew it would be Loyal doing most of the talking. Blaze preferred to speak when necessary, and it was never much.

When we'd first started dating years ago, he'd been worried I would end up annoyed with how little he spoke. But I learned I did enough talking for the both of us and that when Blaze did speak, it was always meaningful.

Well, that was most of the time, except when he teased me in some way about my attitude. The little liar liked everything about me.

"How'd it go with Pixie?" Loyal asked.

Sighing, I ran a hand through my hair. Blaze stood from my chair and ushered me into it. "He's not ready for help, but I do worry there is something happening." I frowned. "He was hiding food in his bag."

"Shit," Loyal bit out. "Doesn't look like his home life is good then."

"I tried to ask if he still lived at home, but he didn't give me a straight answer."

"Don't the managers do a background check on all the employees?" Blaze asked.

I hummed. "Maybe it would be good to speak to one of them."

Loyal tipped his chin up. "I'll go talk to Saint. Catch ya later."

Nodding, I spun my chair to my man, pouting. "What?"

"He is so young to be walking around here with the weight of the world on his shoulders, mon amour."

His finger slid under my chin and tipped my head back a little, and his thumb glided over my bottom lip. "Tell me what you need, and I'll do anything to deliver."

My heart galloped. This man was so intimidating to most. Too scary and silent. But he was my world.

And I was very grateful I reached out to him when Dusty had been kidnapped or else I would have lost my chance to be with the love of my life.

"Mon amour," I whispered.

He ducked down, pressing his lips to mine, and there he said, "You're mine, Henri. Mine to tease. Mine to fuck. Mine to mark. But also mine to take care of in every damn way."

The need to have him fuck me right then and there pushed at me and had my cock fattening.

"When we get home, I need you to tease and fuck and mark me as soon as we're through the door."

There was a deep sigh, but we didn't look away from each other when Tech said, "And it's a few hours until that time, so can we get back to it, Blaze?"

My man didn't move or say anything.

"Henri," Tech whined.

Smiling, I kissed Blaze's jaw. "We will talk more at home, mon amour. Go to your friend. He misses you and craves your attention—"

"Fuck off, I do not," Tech snapped.

I loved taunting that man. It was easy rile him up. I knew nothing would happen between either man. Tech was very much heterosexual. I just knew Blaze enjoyed his company as they worked side by side on their devices.

Blaze made a noise in the back of his throat, kissed me hard, and left to follow Tech back into their computer room.

It still amused me that Blaze had forced Tech to move their toys here. However, I was sure Tech knew that Blaze would be a horror to work with if he wasn't close to me when working the front counter at the escort agency.

Honestly, my beau's possessiveness was such a turn-on. But I was just as fiercely protective and needy about Blaze as he was me.

The front doors opened, and I looked over with a smile. "Welcome to Polished P & P. How may I help?"

The gentleman made his way over with a blush to his cheeks. "I have a booking." He must have been new since I'd never seen him before. Unless he only visited infrequently.

"Certainly. Who are you seeing, chéri?"

His gazed flared. "No. I'm, um, I'm not seeing a Sherry. I...." He blew out a breath, and the blush spread. I wanted to hug the man.

"Non, I am French. When I say chéri, it means sweetie or darling."

He winced. "Oh, sorry."

"No need to be. Your name and who are you seeing?"

"Brody Mullock, and Carnal," he whispered.

Surprise had me blinking up at him. Carnal was a femboy with attitude, and this gentleman radiated anxiety. Winking, I grinned. "Perfect." I added that Brody had arrived in the system, since it didn't show Carnal was ready. "Your man will be down to see you shortly. Just wait over there for him."

He nodded. "Thanks." With his gaze low, he made his way over to the waiting area. He dropped down into a chair and hunched his shoulders.

The doors opened again, and a woman swayed her way up to the desk.

"Hey, honey. I have an appointment with Hunter."

"Of course, chéri." After clicking a few buttons, I said, "I've let him know you're here. Just take a seat, and he'll be down shortly."

She winked and went over to a couch to sit. I watched her take out her phone to scroll through some things.

The doors opened again. It was another client. Obviously, the previous customers had left when I was speaking with Sawyer.

What I liked most about the job was meeting all the different people who wanted to spend time with our prostitutes. I would love to know if they were different from the other clientele that just wanted an escort for a date or company. I didn't get to meet any of those, though.

For the next while, I was busy greeting people and taking calls. I was able to schedule recurring clients with their favorites, but if there was anyone new contacting the agency, I passed them over to a manager. There was a lot of screening before they allowed someone new to enter the premises.

Clients used to be able to book for home visits, but that stopped a while ago because management didn't want to risk the employees any longer. It was a good call as I'd heard there'd been a few incidents that could have been disastrous if it wasn't for the security they had with them.

I took a sip from my water bottle as I glanced to the

waiting area. Carnal's guy was still sitting there. He should have been down here half an hour ago to collect him.

Picking up my phone, I pressed the button for Saint's office.

"Yeah?"

"Carnal's client is still waiting. Do you know why?" If Carnal got too far behind, it would mess up his next couple of appointments.

"There was a situation with the previous client. It's been handled, so he'll be down shortly."

I supposed it would be bad if I asked what happened. Probably. Instead, I said, "I will inform this man down here."

"Thanks, Henri."

After hanging up, I stood and walked over to the gentleman. "Excuse me, Mr. Mullock."

"Brody, please." He straightened in his seat.

"Brody, I am sorry for the delay. Carnal shall be down in the next few moments."

"Okay." He nodded, and his gaze flicked to me and then the elevator just as I heard the doors ding open. I turned to take in Carnal strutting out in a short leather skirt, a mesh top, and ankle boots. He smiled over at Brody as he walked over, running a hand through his black hair.

"B, it's good to see you."

Brody stood in a rush, blushing. "Yeah, um, you too."

Carnal bumped his hip against mine as he came to a stop. "Thanks for minding him, Henri."

"It was no trouble, chéri. He's a cute one."

Brody's blush spread down his neck.

Carnal snorted, reaching out and taking Brody's hand to

drag him close. "Don't let your man hear you say that, or he'll get cranky."

I cackled. "But I like it when he gets cranky."

Carnal grinned. "Of course you do. Later, Henri."

"Au revoir."

Brody waved awkwardly before Carnal led him to the elevator. I cocked my head to the side, watching them. Carnal said something to Brody that made him grin and blush, ducking his head down until Carnal threaded his fingers in Brody's hair and forced the man to look at him. Carnal said something else, and Brody's reply had Carnal smirking.

If they were strippers and offered a private dance together, they would make millions. Everyone would want to see them together.

I gasped at my own thought.

Strippers.

The club was already involved in prostitution, so why wouldn't they venture into exotic dancers as well?

An excited thrill rolled through my belly.

I wanted it.

I would invest money into the business, and I was certain with my guidance we could make it thrive. After all, I'd owned and run my own stores, but I also had dancing skills from school, and then when I went to college, I did pole dancing to keep fit.

There was also my natural talent for makeup and design. I could already picture how I wanted the place to look. Blaze did say I always had a vivid imagination. Oh, we could do themes like college students, cops, paramedics.

Gasping, I widened my eyes. We could do role-playing

taboo shows, pretend the dancers are step-related while they put on a show together. If anyone wanted a private dance with that type of theme, we could charge so much more.

My mind spun with all different ideas, and I was sure some of the employees who worked here would be interested. Stripping could also be something they prefer over attending to clients.

When the doors opened, I turned and waved. "Bonjour." I made my way over to the desk and asked, "Welcome to Polished. Can I take your name and who you're here to see?"

For now, I had work to do, but later, I would bring my idea up with Blaze.

Hopefully he loved the idea, because I really wanted to be involved and not just as an investor.

I could sew some costumes, help with makeup, and help them with moves to seduce the customers. I excelled in all fields.

There would be much to organize, but the possibility was exciting.

CHAPTER FIVE

*H*enri was bouncing in his seat as we drove home. He was bursting at the seams to tell me something, but he wanted me to wait until we were home. My lips twitched. I knew why he wanted me to wait. He'd try and seduce me to give in about something he wanted.

The man should know that I'd do anything for him.

Henri dragged me to the front door, and once inside, he slammed the door behind him to lean against it as I removed my shoes.

"Porn," he said.

I cocked a brow. "You want to watch it?" Wouldn't be the first time we'd done that. With the porno noises in the background, Henri liked to pretend there were others in the room, watching how we made each other feel. Witnessing our love as we fucked. He got off on the thought of people watching but knew that could never actually happen. The thought of someone seeing what was mine naked and lost with the arousal that *I* made him feel made me want to kill.

A red haze filled my vision for a beat and had me clenching my fists.

Soft hands cupped my cheeks, drawing me back. I blinked down at Henri. "Mon amour, stop thinking bad thoughts and concentrate on me."

I grunted.

He smiled. "Good. I didn't mean porn. I was just seeing if you were listening."

This man.

He winked. "What are your thoughts about exotic dancers—"

"No."

He groaned. "Not me, mon amour. I already know you would go on a murdering spree if anyone saw me dance in that way." He was right. "I would be the same if you wanted to strip in front of others. I am meaning we could start a strip club business and give this option to the sex workers at Polished. Ask the bikers if they would want to go in with us. Think, this could be a safer option for those who want the stability of the money but are tired of dealing with the risks they take."

The eagerness in him was clear to see.

"When did you think of this?"

"This afternoon when Carnal came down for his shy client."

With my hands to his waist, I squeezed. I loved seeing him enthused, and this wasn't a bad idea. It would bring us money. Not that we needed it.

"We can talk to Country."

He squealed.

"However," I added, "I'm not sure he'll go for the idea, since it'll mean losing employees for his other businesses."

Henri waved me off, beaming up at me as his hands slid to my chest. "But we will ask?"

"Yes, firecracker. We'll talk to him."

He jumped and wrapped his arms around my neck and legs around my hips. I curled an arm under his ass, holding him to me with one at his waist too.

"You give me so much, mon amour. I truly love you."

My dick thickened. "You'll always have my fuckin' love, Henri. You're mine forever."

"Oui, forever." He rolled his crotch against me. "But it will be best if you show me too."

A sound dropped from my mouth as I pushed his back against the wall, kissing him, claiming him, making sure he knew he was mine.

As I trailed my wet lips down his neck, he worked his hand and fingers into my shoulders and neck.

"Blaze, mon amour. Bedroom, please."

Latching my mouth to his neck, I sucked, needing to mark him as I straightened with him in my arms. At his moan and the roll of his hips, I quickly walked down the hall while I kissed and licked over the bruise I'd made.

Not everyone craved a person as much as I did Henri.

I wanted to hear every breath, touch every inch, and taste every inch of him. He used to be squeamish about having sex before he'd prepped, but now, thank fuck, he understood I wanted every part of him. I'd grown addicted to his smells, even his sweat. And every time I buried my face into his ass as I devoured his hole, I drank in his scent and taste. Each time I did it drew me closer to my own release because I got off on his reactions, his noises, his movements. Him.

I craved and loved the man to the point it was definitely an obsession.

Utterly besotted by *my* French firecracker.

Kicking the bedroom door wider, I stepped in and stalked to the bed, then bent to gently laid Henri down. He got to his elbows and smiled up at me.

My damn heart lurched at the sight of him, knowing he was actually mine.

With his legs still hanging off the bed, I crouched to remove his shoes and socks. His fingers went to work on the button and zipper of his jeans as I trailed my hands up along the outside of his legs, stopping when I gripped the waistband of his denim. He lifted his ass, and I slid his jeans down along with his boxers. His hard cock called to me.

When I threw the material to the floor, I yanked my tee up and off, then dropped it too.

Starting at his inner knee, I licked and nipped up the inside of his thigh before I pressed my nose against his neatly trimmed pubes and inhaled. A rumble dropped from my lips as I closed my eyes.

Christ, his scent had my dick throbbing.

His cock twitched. "Mon amour, please."

I wound my hand around his erection and slowly ran it up and down. My little French firecracker spewed some threats my way.

Chuckling, I sucked him down until the tip of his cock hit the back of my throat, and when I swallowed around him, he hissed out a breath. As I bobbed over him, he lifted to yank his shirt up and off, running his hands down over his chest as he rested back down with a moan. Fingers threaded through my hair and tightened.

"I want to come with your cock buried in my ass, mon amour. Make that happen before I spill into your mouth."

With a low groan, I popped off his cock and picked up his legs, baring his hole for me to eat. I kissed, licked, and toyed with his hole, flicking my tongue over and around and in.

The sounds he made were a high that drilled adrenaline into me. I made him needy, wanting more from me.

I spat on two fingers and ran them over his pink hole before pushing one in.

Henri arched, planting his feet to the bed edge, and pushed his body up the mattress so he didn't slip off. I followed, dribbling saliva over his hole and my digits. I curled my finger, pressing, rubbing.

"Mon amour," he cried. "More."

Demanding little creature.

But I would give him anything he asked.

With more spit, I added another finger, pushing them in and out, playing with his prostate. When his cock leaked onto his stomach, I leaned down and licked it up to dribble it over my fingers and his hole.

"Baiser, mon amour. Give me your cock," he demanded.

Removing my fingers, I straightened and pulled a packet of lube out of my back pocket. I always wanted to be prepared to have Henri whenever we could, and thank fuck condoms were long in our past.

I loved the feeling of sliding in bare and painting his insides with my cum.

My chest expanded at the thought. Knowing I got to mark Henri in ways no one else would was heady.

As I undid my jeans, I kept my gaze on my firecracker as he went to his elbows to watch my hands while he dropped his legs wider, waiting for me. Slowly, I reached in and pulled my cock free, stroking over it while I tore the packet open with my teeth and spread the lube over my length.

"Come on, mon amour. I need you."

A noise rumbled out of me. I shoved my jeans all the way down and kicked them off with my boxers. I went to my knees on the bed, between his legs.

He smirked. "Oui, my big beast. Come, get inside me."

Gripping his legs, I flipped him over to his knees. Henri squealed then laughed, but that faded when I covered his body with my own.

Our size difference was always a blessing and aphrodisiac. The intoxicating feeling of dominance it gave me was a rush to the cock.

I licked and nipped at his shoulder. "Want my dick, firecracker?"

"Oui."

"*Beg me.*"

He glanced back and snarled, "Get in me."

I tsked. "That wasn't nice."

"I am not nice when my lover holds back. Fill me. Fuck me. Prove I'm yours."

With a growl, I set the tip of my dick against his slicked hole and edged in. The head slipped through the tight ring, causing Henri to moan.

"Yes, mon amour," he breathed as I pushed in. As soon as I was embedded deep, my firecracker grinned, glancing back up at me for a moment. "Where you belong."

"Fuck yes," I told him. Latching my teeth onto his shoulder, I pulled all the way out and slammed back in.

"Yes, mon bête. *Harder.* Make me feel it even tomorrow."

His words always did something to me. I thrust back and forth—harder, faster. His sounds encouraged me to dominate him.

His ass squeezed around me, the lube making it easier to pound in and out of his tight, wet heat.

A thrill rolled down my spine. I licked and sucked over his shoulder before I went to the other side, marking that one up as well while screwing him into the bed.

He was mine.

All fuckin' mine.

I'd keep him forever.

Fuck him, love him, and protect him.

Mine. Mine. Mine.

"Basier oui, mon amour. So good, mon bête. So good."

Christ. I was close. Sliding my tongue over the bite, I told him, "Come, firecracker. Fuckin' come for me."

His body stiffened for a second before he moaned and shook through his release onto the blankets.

"Fuck," I clipped, hips stuttering as I emptied inside him.

I slipped out of him as he slumped to the bed, breathing heavily like I was. Standing, I picked him up, bridal style, and carried him into the bathroom. My body was lax from coming hard, but the need to take care of Henri outweighed my own wants.

He rested his hand to my chest and patted there, all mellow after coming.

I had him stand beside the shower, making sure he would be fine, while I opened the door and slipped in to turn on the water. I adjusted the temp until it was perfect.

When I stepped back out, I wound an arm around Henri's waist and led him in, smirking at the thought that if I ever needed to shut Henri up, I just had to fuck him.

"Good, firecracker?" I asked when he stepped under the spray.

"Perfect like always, mon amour." He hummed under his breath. "You take good care of me."

My chest expanded. It was all I wanted in the damn world, to make sure he was taken care of.

After cleaning, I helped dry him and applied the balm to the marks I made—proving I owned him.

Henri lifted his head and snorted. He must have read my mind because he said, "Oui, mon amour, I feel very owned."

"Good." Dipping, I kissed him. "I'll change the covers on the bed."

"I'm going to get a drink," he said, pressing his lips to my chest before walking out of the bathroom as I finished drying myself.

When Henri hadn't come back to the bedroom by the time I did what I had to, I went to search for him. I found him in the kitchen at the counter, wearing a silk robe and waiting for the electric kettle to boil.

Moving up behind him, I rested my hands to his slim waist and leaned down to kiss his neck. "Hot chocolate?"

"Oui."

"I thought I'd have made you tired."

He grinned, staring down at the counter while I nibbled on his earlobe. He hummed before saying, "Mon amour, you wore out my body, but my mind is still running." He turned in my arms. "Do you truly believe it was a good idea?"

"Oui," I answered him. "I'll set up a meet with Country ASAP tomorrow. But I'm already sure the club will want to join your business venture."

He reached up, linking his fingers together behind my neck. "Remind me again how lucky I am to have you."

I nipped his chin and kissed his lips. "Very fuckin' lucky."

"Non, *you* are lucky I found your stalking cute."

That was damn true. I'd been worried when I'd admitted that over the years when we hadn't talked, I was still aware of everything he did because of the cameras I'd set up.

He'd been silent for a while, just watching me while I ate my tongue for being honest in the first place, especially since there'd been a chance I could lose him.

But after a while, he'd asked, "Did you watch me sleep?"

I'd nodded.

"Did you touch yourself when I played?"

Once again, I'd nodded, gut twisting in fear, but I'd needed to be completely honest if we had a chance to make this work.

"You're lucky I am more turned on about you watching me than peeved."

It was then I knew I fucking adored the man and had to make him mine once more. Only that time, there'd be nothing to stand in our way. Earlier that day, Eve had told Henri she'd overheard me telling Country at the compound that I was ending my career in trafficking organs. He'd been ecstatic, but even then, he didn't understand how far I would have gone to have him back brightening my world.

So, after I'd told him about the cameras, I'd added, "If you give me a second chance, I'll not only give up trading in body parts but all other illegal activities you hate. Anything to keep you in my life."

His brows had shot up. "You would do that for moi?"

"Yeah, Henri." There wasn't anything I wouldn't do for him.

"You still want me?" he'd asked.

Snorting, I'd said, "What? My cameras didn't give me away?"

His laughter had filled me with damn joy. He'd smiled. "Chéri, you love me."

I had felt the heat hit my cheeks and had braced for teasing, but instead, Henri's smile softened, and he'd stepped close, stopping in front of me. "You have seen that no one has held my interest, Blaze. No one has amounted to anything because I have always had you on my mind, and I knew that I cared for you too, mon amour."

A deep groan dropped from my mouth as I'd lunged at him.

Thinking of that now had a smile tugging at my lips. I nodded down at Henri. "You're right. I'm damn lucky."

Henri huffed, smiling. "Now, do you wish to talk about a puppy?"

Groaning, I rested my forehead to his and closed my eyes.

"Or," he added, "we could put a pin in this subject until this strip joint is up and running?"

Kissing his temple, his cheek, and grazing his lips with mine, I then told him, "Didn't know you could be reasonable and smart at the same time."

It drew the reaction I wanted. He smacked my chest, and he ranted at me in French.

Once he was done, he crossed his arms over his chest and glared up at me. Smirking, I said, "Drink your hot chocolate, and I'll suck you off again. We need some sleep, firecracker."

His glare narrowed even more before he rolled his eyes. "Fine."

Christ, I love this man.

CHAPTER SIX

HENRI

Nerves turned my stomach to lead as Blaze and I sat across from Country in his office at the compound. I'd just finished telling him my idea and how I would love to invest and be hands-on in some way with this venture.

But all that would only be if he agreed. I mean, I could do it on my own, but it would be bad form for me to steal the employees from Polished. This way we could share the responsibilities, and I wouldn't feel guilty if anyone quit Polished to work at the strip club.

Country leaned back into his chair. "Huh."

What did that mean?

Was it a good or bad huh?

"Since I will be a partner, I will help in any way I can," I told him again.

He leaned forward to pick up the phone and pressed a few buttons. "Yeah, come in here."

Why was he holding back from saying anything?

Why did he need someone else in here?

I shifted on my seat, wanting to climb onto Blaze's lap and have him hug me tight. My nerves kicked up even more.

When the door abruptly opened, I let out a strangled sound. Blaze reached over and grabbed the armrest of my seat to drag the whole thing close to him while glaring at State as he entered.

"Hey," he greeted, tipping his chin our way.

"Bonjour, State," I replied while Blaze grunted, tipping his own chin up.

I looked to Country and found him already staring at me. "Tell State your idea."

So, I did. All while I could feel Blaze's warm gaze on me as he rubbed circles with his thumb on the back of my hand.

When I fell silent, State's reply was "Huh."

"Huh? What does this mean?" I questioned, frustration bleeding out in my sharper tone. I glanced to Blaze as he ducked his head, lips twitching. I let out a growl. "You men need to speak clearly. Is it a good idea or bad? Do you think it is something we can work together on?"

State and Country shared a look. They tipped their chins up at each other and then Country picked up the phone again.

"This biker language is upsetting me. I understand none of it. Mon amour, what are they saying?"

"Come back to the office and grab Saint on your way," Country said into the phone before he hung up and placed it back on his desk.

"I swear you are only dragging this out to annoy me."

Country smirked. "I'd never do that."

"You're still getting back at me for pretending to be Dusty's boyfriend that night."

His gaze narrowed at the reminder. It probably wasn't the best time to mention it.

"He's calling in all the owners of Polished to hear your idea. Country and State like it but need to see if Wreck and Saint will. Then they'll talk business," Blaze supplied, glaring back at Country.

Smiling, I relaxed.

Country's glower shifted to my man. "You used to be fun."

"Not when it comes to Henri."

The door opened, and there was Wreck and Saint. "You need a bigger office," Saint suggested.

"Nah, brother, I'm good." He looked at me. "Tell them."

Once more, I spoke about my idea. When I ended, Wreck's expression hadn't shifted once from his serious pinched one, but Saint grinned like a maniac.

"I fuckin' love it," Saint said.

Country and State chuckled.

I clutched my hands to my chest. "You do?"

"Hell yes. Imagine the money we could make. We won't just be a female strip club but men too. We'll need outfits, makeup, employees for the bar, servers, strippers, security, and someone to teach the strippers to dance. Shit, there's a lot to organize."

State nodded. "We'll try and keep security and bar staff to members, but if we have to hire outside, we have to make sure they won't get distracted by the dancers."

"We'll need to find a building first. Somewhere that'll have showers, changing rooms, and a break room," Wreck said, which meant he was on board too.

Blaze grunted, and all attention went to him. "The place next door just went up for sale. It's a three-story building. Could have one level for the women dancers, one for the men, and the top for offices and security. There are a few elevators inside, but it has an outside access at the back that can be used for the second level and underground parking. Plus, more can be added at the side of the place."

Everyone blinked at him while my heart spasmed. He'd already been looking for somewhere, supporting my idea. I wanted to drop to my knees and show him my appreciation.

Instead, I leaned over and smacked my lips to his in a quick kiss.

"It would be the perfect place," I said. It had been a printing warehouse that already held many separate rooms we could use for private dances, but two massive main areas on each level that would work for the bar, seating, stage, and poles. We just had to check if there were showers and enough bathrooms and a break room.

"And you think some of the workers we already have would be interested?" State asked the room.

"I think some would be keen to go into this instead of escorting," Saint said as I nodded. "Hell, we could hire new people. We've always got interest in working here."

"I'm happy to help in any way I can. I want to be hands-on as much as I can. I would like to still work part-time at Polished too, if possible."

"Be good to go into business with you, Henri. Who else wants in?" Country asked.

Oh goodness, this is happening.

It was going to happen.

"In," Wreck said.

"Kylo and me are in."

"Count me in," State said. "Quake said he wanted to branch out with his bar. He might want in so he can manage the bar for the strip joint. Death's probably got enough going on with his businesses and the baby coming. We could check."

"I'll call church," Country said.

"How about we leave it as us in the room and Quake, if he's interested, as owners? It'll get too confusing to add more." Blaze rested his hand to my thigh, squeezing. It was the perfect idea. Too many interested could get messy.

The brothers shared a look, but it was Country who answered, "Saint and Henri, will you two be happy with running things for now? Buy the building, get permits, work out who can do what from the members within the club and then source outsiders if needed. State, put out an email to our employees at Polished to see if they'd want to join this team."

I clapped, excitement rolling through me. "This is happening." I reached out and shook Blaze's leg. "It's happening." He grinned at me, cupping my cheek.

I gasped when a thought popped into my mind.

"What?" Blaze asked.

"What, what?" Saint said.

"He's had an idea," Blaze supplied.

"Don't you get scared when he does?" Country questioned.

Blaze snorted. "Never."

I loved my man so much.

"Jesus, I would," State mumbled.

"What's your idea?" Blaze asked me.

"What about if we call it Polished Playhouse so it's a branch off from Polished P & P?"

"Fuck yes," Saint cheered with a clap of his hands before he pointed at me.

State grinned. "It's one of your better ideas."

Wreck grunted, tipping his chin up.

"Done," Country stated.

"This is amazing! Thank you," I cried out. "Saint and I will sit down and work things out. We'll keep you all updated with everything, and do not worry, I will still be working hard at Polished P & P."

"Might have to cut some of your hours back once things get started with the Playhouse," State suggested.

Nodding, I told him, "Oui, whatever works." Standing, I looked to Saint. "Do you have time now?"

"Sure do."

"I gotta hit the road before people figure out I'm not behind my desk at Polished," State said, moving to the door first.

"Later," Country called to him, before saying, "Right, I got shit to do here, so the lot of you get the hell out."

"Thank you for listening and agreeing, Country. You're a good man."

Country rolled his eyes and shook his head, but he did it grinning.

With Blaze's hand in mine, we followed Wreck and Saint out into the common room. There were a few members lingering around, same with the amount of club girls, but it was quiet.

"I'm goin' to see Opal," Wreck said. "Let me know if you need anythin'." Opal would be, no doubt, in the day care center the club now provided in the compound.

"You got it," Saint said. "Give my niece a kiss for me."

"No," Wreck answered before he walked off.

We sat at a bench seat. Saint was opposite Blaze and me as he quickly typed something out on his phone. When he looked at us, he grinned. "Just tellin' Kylo to get his ass down here."

"I'll get drinks," Blaze offered. When I went to open my mouth, Blaze gave me a look. "I know, just a soda. You've got work later."

"I love you," I told him since that was exactly what I was going to say.

Blaze's cheeks tinted a little before he glared and walked off.

Saint snorted. "I'd shit myself ten times over if he glared at me like that and yet you look at him like you'd eat him up."

"I really would and have." I winked.

Saint chuckled, shaking his head. His gaze went to the stairs where his man walked down them with a slight limp.

"You do know you look at him the same?"

Saint grinned. "Hell yes, I do. That guy is mine, and I'd shout it to the fuckin' world if I had to. I never thought about pissin' on anyone until it came to him, and I see the interest men and women have for him. They eye him like they want to lick him."

"Oui, I know the feeling, but at least we are the only ones who get to do the licking."

"Do I want to know what you two are talkin' about?" Gun asked.

Smirking, I looked over at him as he sat beside his lover. "At least you missed the talk about urinating on you."

He sucked in a sharp breath and choked on his saliva. "What?" Then his hand shot up. "Nope, don't fuckin' tell me."

Saint and I grinned at each other.

"Guess what, boo?" Saint said to Gun.

"What?"

"We're branching out into a different business."

Gun's brows pinched. "What type of business?"

Saint grinned. "Strippers."

Gun froze for a moment before he started laughing. "Why doesn't this surprise me? All right, I'm in to help. What do we need to do?"

I wanted to burst out of my skin with how excited I was.

BLAZE

*A*s we walked through the cold warehouse, Henri nodded at something the real estate agent said. Saint appeared from a room off to the side and joined them, adding his own opinion.

Gun and I trailed a bit behind, taking in things as we went, until Gun's phone rang. He stopped to answer, but I kept following the others because I didn't like the way the agent's eyes kept running over Henri's body.

"May I ask what you're thinking of running in here, Henri?" the agent asked.

The fuckface turned toward what was mine, and once more his gaze swept up and down.

I moved up behind Henri, curled an arm around Henri's neck, and pulled him against my chest. The agent gulped from my stare. Henri shook his head and patted my arm but didn't step away from me. "I am sorry. For now, the information is top secret," Henri told the guy.

"Blaze, Saint, a word," Gun called.

After another stare down with the agent, where I hoped my look read that I'd kill him if he flirted with Henri, I yanked Henri's head back and kissed him hard before stomping off with a chuckling Saint.

"At least the agent didn't piss himself," Saint commented while I wished the guy had. "What's up, lover?" Saint asked as we stopped by Gun.

"Country's at Polished. He wants us there right now."

"What for?" I asked.

Gun shrugged. "Something about a phone call from the Hawks MC."

"Shit, what the fuck happened now?" Saint said.

"Henri," I called.

He faced me. "Oui, mon amour?"

"We gotta go." I wasn't leaving Henri alone.

"But—"

"Now, firecracker."

He studied me for a moment and then nodded. "Nathaniel, we love the place, and we'll be in touch very soon. Thank you for your time."

"We've had a lot of interest. It could get snapped up quickly," Dickthaniel said to Henri.

When I shifted my stance, his gaze came to me. I stated, "Then it'd be best if you put it on hold until Henri talks to you again."

He licked his lip nervously. "I can't—"

Saint snorted. "Dude, you can. Just give us until

tomorrow since something important came up. We'll be in touch."

He looked around at all of us before nodding.

Henri clapped excitedly. "Thank you, chéri." He blew the man a kiss and swayed his hips my way. I'd tan his ass later for the air-kiss.

But then he stopped beside me and pushed to his tiptoes to press his lips to my chin and cheek. "You are my world, mon amour."

"Fuckin' better be."

He cackled and walked away. "Come. You can tell me outside what the rush is, oui?"

Gun moved to keep up with Henri while Saint and I trailed behind them. Since we'd come from the compound earlier, we'd driven into the warehouse parking lot. We climbed back into the car out front and took the short drive to the underground car park at Polished right next door.

In the elevator, Henri bit down on his bottom lip. "I hope nothing bad has happened." He glanced up to me. "You go with Saint and Gun. I'll be in the break room."

He didn't start work for another few hours.

I hated that he'd have to wait, but he also knew I'd want to help if there was a situation.

Cupping the back of his head, I kissed him quick and hard. "I'll collect you after."

"Okay, mon amour."

The doors opened to the second floor. I pressed the ground button. "Behave," I ordered.

He crossed his arms over his chest, cocked his hip, and glared. "Mon amour, I am but an angel," he said as the doors closed him in.

Saint snorted. "An angel with devil horns."

A small smile slipped onto my lips as I grunted.

At Country's door, Gun knocked. We waited until Country ordered us in.

Death, Quake, Tech, and Wreck were already there, so it was lucky this room was a lot bigger than Country's office at the compound.

"What's goin' on?" Saint asked.

Country's hand shot up just as the phone rang. Saint, Gun, and I stopped behind the men sitting—Tech, who held an iPad, and Quake. Death and Wreck stood off to each side.

"Country here," he answered.

"It's Talon, and you've got Dodge." Both presidents in the Hawks MC, but Talon was the founding member. Dodge looked over a different chapter of the club.

"What are you after, Talon?" Country asked.

"We're ringin' about that favor," Talon answered in his Australian accent.

"All right," Country replied, glancing around at all of us.

Something was said in the background, and after it, there was a smash through the phone. "Shit. Dodge, fuckin' calm down."

Someone roared something I didn't catch. Then there were more voices and noise before we heard a woman say into the phone, "Hey, this is Low. I'm Dodge's old lady. He ain't coping right now and isn't in the mood for small talk. You see, our girl was kidnapped. Romania Monroe. She's just twenty-three. We need help finding her, please." She sniffed, and then shouted, "Dive, you tell them to shut the fuck up so I can hear in here."

Some of the brothers smirked from her words, but I'd already stilled.

Memories of my own sister's disappearance flooded my mind.

Jesus Christ. Fuck me.

"Low, name's Country. What can the Diamond MC do to help?"

"Hang on. Talon's back. He'll let you know. But please, I'm on my knees begging, please do anything you can to help find our girl. She's a special one. A sweet and kind one with a big heart."

Fuckin' hell. Fuckin' Christ.

"We'll do what we can, Low," Country said.

She whimpered, and "Thank you" was whispered into the phone.

"Country, we managed to get one of the guys. The fucker said she's been put on a ship to the US, but he doesn't know where it'll stop. We're looking into it." Talon made a deep, gruff sound in the back of his throat. "Dodge lost it now because we just got delivered more information. These cunts are traffickin' people. We'd seen stories on the news about kidnappin' but nothin' about sellin'. We've been doing our own work to find these motherfuckers but were comin' up empty-handed. Thought it was only women they gunned for, but it's men too. We're not sure if the US will be the boat's final stop either."

Would it be too late by the time we got to her?

Did he know how much time it took to get here by boat?

Hang the fuck on... they were selling them, which meant they'd at least keep them in one piece.

Unless they acted up.

Images of Emily's beaten body flashed through my mind. If it hadn't been for the tattoo she got behind her ear, I wouldn't have recognized her.

That could happen to Romania. A young girl like my sister had been.

Fury ignited. I ground my teeth together. My gut clenched, almost painfully, from the fear building for this unknown girl.

"Talon, I'll get my men onto this situation now. We'll find out where the boat will stop and intercept it. But you know a trip like that could take a month and then some?"

"Yeah, we fuckin' know," Talon bit out.

It was too many days and weeks for something else to happen. For the abuse they'd receive.

Fuck. Fuck. Fuck.

Rage stabbed at my temples. I sucked in a breath through my nose. I wanted to hurt someone. We had to find them.

End them.

A soft hand touched my back, I looked over my shoulder, ready to tell whoever it was to fuck right off, until Henri moved around in front of me.

Country and Talon spoke some more, but it all drowned out as I focused on the man before me.

His presence calmed me.

Slowly, Henri ran his hands up over my chest to my cheeks.

The thoughts of hurting and hunting cooled. Whoever thought to get Henri in here knew me better than I thought anyone did.

Henri winked.

"You got it, Talon. Talk soon," Country said and hung up. "Blaze, you good?"

I grunted.

Henri patted my chest. "Mon amour, you should use your words."

Letting out another grunt, I tugged Henri against me and buried my nose into his dark, messy hair. His arms wrapped around my neck, hugging me close.

"All right. Tech and Blaze, I need you two to do what you can to find out about this ship's destination."

"There's a fuckload of ships that port all over the US," Tech said.

"I know," Country answered. "But I also know that you and Blaze will get this done."

"Shit." I sensed Tech standing and pulled my head up.

"Are you all right, mon amour?" Henri whispered.

I nodded.

"Henri, a woman connected to the Hawks MC has been abducted. She's on a boat to the US," Death explained.

But the real reason he would be telling Henri was for him to keep an eye on me. To calm me as he had and ground me if my thoughts went too dark.

"Saint, Gun, and Wreck, pick up Torch and get to the streets. I'm gonna reach out to our cop friend and see if he knows anything," Country said.

Saint, Gun, and Wreck nodded and left, while Tech approached me.

"You good to head downstairs?"

Henri wasn't due to work yet. I wanted to stay with him, but the need to search pounded into me.

"Go, mon amour. I'll hang about until my shift starts. I have many things to do for the business venture too."

"Stay inside."

He nodded. "I know you love me, and I know I come first in your life, but I want you to put your time into finding this woman. I promise I won't get too snippy."

Snorting, I wrapped a hand around the front of his neck and made him rise to his toes. I dipped to kiss him hard before I walked out of Country's office.

In the elevator, I leaned against the back wall and looked at Tech. "You texted Henri?"

"Yeah. You know I investigated you when you first showed. Know about your sister. Knew this would mess with you. I didn't overstep bringing Henri up, right?"

Shaking my head, I grumbled, "Thanks."

"Got your back, brother, like I know you'd have mine. Even when you aren't a patched-in member to the club."

Christ, that hit hard to my chest.

I'd always distanced myself from people due to the work I'd been in. Henri was the only one who I wanted in my orbit. It had been him who made me see it was important to have people in your life.

But I never realized how lonely I'd been for a brother-hood connection in the way the Diamond MC had. I wasn't a member, but they treated me like I was, and it felt fucking good.

More importantly, they'd accepted Henri into their fold too.

The door opened, and Tech glanced at me. "If you think you're being swallowed by darker thoughts, just let me know, and I'll get Henri to you right away."

Snorting, I nodded and realized Henri was my emotional support person.

"What?" Tech asked.

"Nothing. Just appreciate the help, Tech."

"Hell, I can't lose the only person who understands computers like I do."

I'd made a good call ending the shady shit I was into. My life with Henri was looking up, and I was in a position where I could help in situations like these, with people I wanted in my life by my side.

CHAPTER EIGHT

HENRI

With a yawn, I shut down the computer and stood. Since it was Tuesday, Polished closed at midnight. It was the same for Wednesdays and Thursdays. Friday to Monday the business stayed open for twenty-four hours a day.

Blaze was still in the computer room with Tech. They had been diligently working at finding any information they could against the culprits who were stealing people. He hadn't sat with me on our break time, either, his mind consumed with helping. But I did take him food and stole a kiss.

This would hit a lot of the men in the club but more so my poor amour due to what happened to his sister.

All I could do was to be there for him if the horrid memories took him under.

Once at their room, I knocked once before opening the door. Their fingers never stopped moving over the keys as I went closer.

Image after image of missing men and women popped up over their screens.

"There's over fifty, and they just keep coming," Tech said, tension clear in his tight tone.

"They cannot be all connected to this trafficking, correct?"

Blaze let out a frustrated sound and scooted his chair back. "There's a lot more people missing, but the ones we're concentrating on all have a few things in common. They're aged between eighteen to twenty-five, and they're all slim, short, and have naturally blonde, dark brown, or black hair. So, then we widened the search. It's not happening just in Australia. It's here and the UK too. Fuck," he bit out, scrubbing a hand over his face before he slammed a fist to the desk.

"Dude," Tech yelled. "Careful of our babies."

Blaze stilled.

Tech froze.

Mirth filled me. "Ah, is there something I should know? Mon amour, when did you sire some offspring? Actually, please tell me who birthed these babies?"

Tech groaned, and Blaze snorted, but at least I noted some of their tension had eased.

"I'm tired. Don't tell the brothers I said that, Henri," Tech demanded.

"I will try to keep my lips sealed. It's Blaze you should worry about. He's the biggest gossip I know." All lies, which Tech obviously knew too from his chuckle. "Mon amour, are we going home or do you plan to stay and work more?"

Blaze stepped in front of me. With his fingers in my hair, he pulled my head back and kissed my neck. "I've got a few hours left in me. Tech?"

"Yeah. Then I'll probably nap on one of the couches and get back to it."

I slid my hand up my beast's wide chest. "I can go home and bring back some clothes for you if you want to stay here for this."

"You're not leaving without me."

"Mon amour—"

"No, Henri. You're not out of my sight."

He was scared.

"Then what is it you wish for me to do? Sleep on the couch too? I will do it if you want me to, and we can go home in the morning to shower and change."

"Brother, go home 'til mornin'. I'll do what I can and then you take over for me tomorrow while I get some shut-eye," Tech suggested, but Blaze said nothing, just stared down at me. "Blaze, I don't have a partner to worry about."

"He doesn't need to worry about me. I know how important this is."

"I know you do, Henri, but your guy needs a clear head, and I think steppin' away for a while will be good for him. Hell, I'll even do the same thing now, and we can come back to it refreshed at seven?"

Blaze's brows pinched. He didn't want to leave, and I didn't want him to stress more than he was.

Reaching into my pocket, I quickly tipped up to kiss Blaze's chin and then moved around him. "Tech, be a chéri and stop into our place to grab some fresh clothes in the morning. We will stay here for the night."

"But—"

I shook my head. "It is what he needs, and I understand that more than anything."

"Henri, I don't want you to suffer because shit's spinning in my head." Blaze turned, jaw clenching. "Tech can drop you home." He stretched his neck out.

"Non, mon amour. I want to stay by your side."

"Henri—"

I slapped my hands to my hips and told him in French, "No, you don't get to tell me what I can and can't do. You worry about me, but I worry about you too, you big oaf, and I know you will not settle until you're at your computer working while I stay here in this room so you can make sure I'm safe. It is not difficult to ease your stress by sticking close, you big beast."

Tech whistled. "That sounded like a scolding."

Blaze shot him a glare, and Tech slid his pinched fingers across his lips, mimicking he was shutting up.

"Thank you, firecracker," Blaze said.

Relaxing, I smiled. "You are welcome, mon amour." I turned to Tech again. "Are you able to stop by our place for some items on your way back here?"

"I mean, I can stay too."

"Chéri, my man is still riled up. Before he starts working again, I'm going to suck his cock to drain—"

"Jesus fuck, man. I don't need to know." He took the keys from my hand. "But, yeah, ah, shit. Thanks for warning me, I guess. I'll be back in a few hours." He rushed to the door and out it, closing it after himself.

Cackling, I faced Blaze and stopped laughing. He stared at me hungrily.

"I know, mon amour. I love you too," I told him. Reaching out, I took his hand and guided him over to the couch. "Let me take care of you before you take on the world with your toys."

Blaze sat when I pushed at his chest, and I dropped to my knees.

"They aren't toys, firecracker."

I patted his thick thighs. "Oui, oui, mon amour." Sliding my hands up, I undid his button and zipper. I slipped a hand in and pulled out his already-hard cock. "Just relax, close your mind down for a moment, and feel me."

"Always do."

With a hum, I leaned down and licked from his base all the way up to his tip before sucking him into my mouth and tasting his salty goodness.

His scent drove me just as crazy as I knew mine did to him.

I smirked around his massive dick when he threaded his fingers into my hair and tugged. His other hand wound around the front of my neck and tightened.

Control.

My beast got off on it, and I liked to surrender my body to him in any way he wanted.

The only part of me I worked with was my mouth as he forced my head up and down, and I sucked and slid my tongue all around his length.

A growl rumbled out of his chest, almost like a pleased, rough sound. "Fuck, firecracker. You know just how to suck me. Love your mouth. I'd have it wrapped around my dick all damn day if I could. Have you on your knees under my desk so you could warm my cock whenever I want. I'd slip it back into your warm mouth and fuck you until you choked on my cum."

Moaning around him, I lifted a hand to grip my erection as my cock throbbed from his words.

"Yeah, of course you like the thought of that my little cock-warming slut."

Pure lust tingled down my spine as my balls drew up.

"Christ, that mouth. Your mouth, fuckin' perfect. Nearly as good as your ass. Shit, Henri, I'm gonna come, and you'll drink it down. Want to warm your belly with my seed. Mark your insides like—fuck—" He groaned low as he filled my mouth, and I swallowed every drop he gave me.

He released my neck and used my hair to lift me off his dick. I took a shuddering breath and blinked dazedly up at him, blissed out from the feeling of his control and love.

He suddenly lifted me up to straddle his waist, and a gasp dropped from my lips. "Stand," he ordered.

"On the couch?"

"Yeah." He pushed me up. I had to plant my feet on the couch at each side of him. "Knees here." He tugged me forward, and I landed with my knees digging into his shoulders, but he didn't seem fazed. No, my beast was too busy working to undo my button and zipper and swallowing my cock down as soon as he'd freed it.

"Mon amour," I cried out as he bobbed up and down quickly.

Since I was already highly aroused from sucking him off, the tingle of release started in my gut and shot down to my balls. Blaze hummed around me and swallowed around my tip.

"Baiser, Blaze. I'm going to fill your throat, mon amour."

With another hum and swallow, I crumbled and ejaculated deep, which he drank greedily.

His hands guided me back as I watched my dick slip from his red lips. I dropped to his lap and moaned into his mouth as we tasted each other on our tongues.

Blaze gripped the front of my throat to push me back as his warm gaze ran over my face. He smirked.

"Oui, mon amour, you fucked my face well." His fingers tickled over my neck. "Non, it doesn't hurt. Just a little sensitive." I grinned. "Nothing I can't handle, my beast."

He grunted. "Good."

Leaning against him, I rested my cheek to his shoulder. "You need to get back to work, but can you find a blanket for me?"

He stood with me in his arms before he turned and planted me on the couch. I bent to remove my shoes as Blaze explained, "We've got shit in the cupboard here in case we ever need to crash."

It was a good idea to have already prepared items since I was sure there'd be many more times when they wouldn't want to go far from their main computers.

I stood and removed my slacks as Blaze lay a blanket along the couch. He held another in his hands to place over me when I lay down, but I needed another cuddle first.

I squished my face into his chest and hugged him tightly.

"We're gonna find them," he said, his mind already back on the missing people. My man with such a big, beautiful heart—unless someone screwed him over or messed with me.

Looking up at him, I rested my chin between his pecs. "I know you will, mon amour. You're the smartest man there is. After all, you did claim me."

His lips twitched. "Exactly."

"But you know, if you need help switching your brain off for even a moment or if the dark thoughts get the best of you, I will be here to help."

He bent, kissing my brow, nose, and lips. "We're a team."

"The best kind. And I suppose I will allow Tech on the team since you had his babies."

Snorting, he shook his head. "Not a word to anyone."

"So, I can't put it in the group chat I have going with Dusty, Eve, Courtney, Raya, and Wrenley?"

"No."

"But—"

"Not even in the other chat with Lucas, Gun, and West."

Sighing, I rolled my eyes and went to my toes to kiss his jaw. "Fine, mon amour. You are lucky I love you."

"I know I am," he told me with a squeeze to my ass. "You get some sleep. You've got interviews to conduct tomorrow."

"Okay. Kiss me again."

"Greedy."

"Always with you."

He hummed low. "I know, and that's how I like it. I'll text Tech to grab the balm for your neck too."

"Pish posh, it won't be needed. Now kiss me."

He did just that and had me soon panting for more, but my man needed to get to work. He rested the blanket over me after I slipped onto the couch and then moved over to his computer.

Tucking my hands under my cheek, I watched him for a while. It didn't matter if I was tired for the interviews tomorrow, since they were the employees from Polished P & P so we already knew they would be perfect for a role at the Playhouse. We just needed to check if they wanted to work in both places or switch to the Playhouse fully. Also, we had to find out if they would offer private dances. Not only that, but we had to check if the wage was suitable, since the money on offer was less than what they earned here.

We wouldn't interview any outsiders until we knew we needed to. We wanted to see how many from Polished would work at the Playhouse first.

Blaze licked his lips before he took a sip of his soda. His fingers tapped and tapped away, his gaze moving from one screen to another and then another and back over again and again.

He was amazing at what he did.

Smart.

Stunning.

Grumbly.

Hot.

Protective

And very possessive.

He's my heart and soul.

I would do anything for him, which was why I was on this couch even when God knows what could have happened on this piece of furniture.

But for Blaze, I would do anything.

"Henri," he called.

"Yes, mon amour?"

"Sleep."

"Oui, captain."

"Firecracker," he warned.

"So bossy," I mumbled.

"You need a boss."

I did.

"All right, amour. I will sleep and let you work. Goodnight."

His grunt had me smiling as I drifted off.

CHAPTER NINE

*L*eaning forward, I looked around Gun and asked, "Can I ask what you are doing in here?"

"*Da.*"

I glanced to Gun. "What?" I knew what "da" meant, but saying yes wasn't an answer.

Gun shrugged.

"You may ask what I am doing here," Adrick said, like that explained it all.

"Then why?" I questioned. When he swung his hard gaze my way, I ducked back behind Gun, who chuckled. Adrick was scary. I wasn't sure what it was about the man, but he put the fear in me with one look.

"Why are you hiding? I did nothing."

Gun sighed. "Where's West?"

West was the sweetest man I had met. No wait, that was

Lucas. West was also sweet, but I often wondered about his sanity when it came to being married to an ex-mafia Russian man who could kill with a flick of his wrist.

Okay, and maybe my man could do that, too, but the Russian was scarier.

I hadn't been around at the time, but I'd heard the story of Adrick snapping West's father's neck for torturing Adrick lover. I was sure that if Adrick hadn't done it, someone in the brotherhood would have. Even I would have given it a go after West told me the full story, and I was more a lover than a fighter.

"He is working at Death's security place."

"And you left him alone?" Gun asked.

"You think me a fool? No. He is guarded, and they know to kill anyone who upsets West."

"Then tell us why you strolled in here and pulled up a seat."

"Country didn't inform you?" he asked, flicking lint off his slacks.

"Non."

There was a knock, and the door to Saint's office opened. Country stuck his head through. "You found them. Forgot to call, but Adrick is willing to advertise the Playhouse in all his casinos and clubs. He just wants to be involved in return for the *free* advertising." He waved with two fingers and shut the door again.

Merde.

That explained why the scary man was here.

"I am good at reading people and decorating. I will assist on the decor of the warehouse."

"You can *help*, but I have final say. Saint promised me this," I warned.

"Da. Good to see you have backbone."

"And they have to accept our offer first on the warehouse," I said. We had made our proposal earlier to the agent and were waiting on a call back.

Gun snorted. "They will. I saw the fear Blaze put in the agent with that look."

I smiled. "This is true."

"You fear me and yet you are married to a fierce yeti. I do not understand," Adrick commented.

"I don't fear you," I lied.

He leaned forward, and I quickly looked away while saying, "When will Saint get here?"

Gun chuckled. "Any second and then we can start the interviews."

Thankfully, the door opened, and Saint walked in. "It's crowded out there," he commented as he made his way over. He leaned down and kissed Gun before he took the spare seat beside his man. "Boo, you remember the time I interviewed you?"

"No," Gun shouted, jolting to sit straighter. "Zip it, Zion."

"Aww, but it was the best night of my life."

"I want to know," I said.

"They are talking about when Gun proved to Saint that he was a master at giving blow jobs to men."

I gasped, then cackled. "Really? Is that how you two started dating?"

Gun groaned and buried his face into his hands. "I'm going to kill West for tellin' you."

"You will not," Adrick warned.

"We didn't start datin' right away. I had to woo my man for a while." Saint leaned over and kissed Gun's flaming cheek.

"Let's get on with the interviews," Gun demanded.

"I would like to hear the whole story. It sounds thrilling." I smiled.

Gun stood and went to the door. Opening it, he called in our first interview.

Hours later, we had been through twenty applicants from Polished, who were interested in a position, and all seemed promising. With one more to go, it seemed not only would Polished need to take on new employees, but the Playhouse would too. We'd need as many as we could to make sure we had enough dancers for shift changes and such. Then there were employees just for waitressing.

Apparently Quake loved the idea of his next pub in a strip club, which was wonderful since he'd oversee that area, and we wouldn't have to worry about bar staff when opening.

"Carnal, tell Pixie to come in when you go out," Saint said.

"You got it, boss." Carnal wanted a position, but he also wished to stay working at Polished P & P.

Carnal exited, and moments later, Pixie walked in with a blush to his cheeks. He scuttled over to the seat opposite us and stared at the carpet. I loved that he was interested in working for us, but would it be in replacement of here or added on top of his hours like Carnal?

"Bonjour, Sawyer. Thank you for coming in today. You're interested in a position at Polished Playhouse?"

He nodded, clasping his hands together on his lap, knee bouncing. His nerves were high, but the timid boy lifted his gaze to meet mine. "Yes, please." He looked at no one else but me. I was happy to be his sole focus if it helped him.

"Very good. Are you wanting a full-time position or part-time and continue here too?"

When he opened his mouth to answer, Adrick's phone rang. He pulled it out and answered. "*Moya lyubov'*, is everything well?" Adrick paused and grinned when West said something that sounded loud and irritated. "Da, I told Dimitri to look after you. It is not my fault Rule got too close for Dimitri to tackle him to the ground." West yelled again. "Maybe Rule should not have given you a drink. It could have been poisoned.... I am not paranoid. I take care of what is mine, and you are mine, moya lyubov'." His jaw clenched and then he sighed. "Da, I will allow Dimitri to sit up the front of the building and not in the room with you. I'm sure Rule will now know not to get too close." He pulled the phone away and glared down at it. "He hung up on me."

Saint snorted.

Gun sighed.

And I grinned. West totally had Adrick under the thumb like I did Blaze.

Glancing over to Sawyer, I caught his small smile before

he bit the back of his finger. He seemed more relaxed now, which was good.

"Adrick, you've been around the club for years. Don't you think you can trust all the members around West now?" Gun asked.

"*Nyet*. West is very good-looking. Men pass him on the streets and want him. I see it in their eyes. Rule is single. I do not like single men or women working around West. I have told this to Death, but he does not listen."

Death was like most of the men in the club, who didn't like being told what to do by anyone other than their partner.

"Sawyer, sorry for the interruption." I smiled. "Are you looking for a full-time, part-time, or temp position?"

He shifted on his seat, looked up, away, and back to me. "I'd prefer a full-time position if possible."

"Do you have rhythm, Sawyer?" Saint asked.

He nodded, shrugged, and said, "I think so?"

It sounded more like a question. He had probably never even tried pole dancing or lap dancing before.

"That's fine. There'll be trainin'," Gun explained.

Sawyer nodded.

"We're still a way off yet. But for now, we need to work out who will be joining the Playhouse team and if Polished P & P will have to hire replacements," I told him. "We'll mark you down for a full-time spot and let you know when we're closer to opening the Playhouse. We will also inform you of the training coming up."

"Thank you."

"Just a word of warning, kid," Saint said, and I was sure

we all saw Sawyer tense. "If you don't pass the training, you won't be able to move over to the Playhouse."

His hands tightened together, but he nodded. "I understand."

The door abruptly opened, and Loyal slipped in, closing it after him. Adrick and Saint stood.

"What's wrong?" Saint asked.

Tensing, I bounced up to my feet, hands pressed to my chest. Blaze was downstairs.

"Theres a situation. A customer demanded someone. They want to take them with them."

My stomach bottomed out when Loyal flicked his gaze down to Sawyer and back up.

Unfortunately, Sawyer saw it too since he was looking up at Loyal with a blush to his cheeks. He scrambled up and backed away. "W-Who's down there?"

"Chéri, this will be handled. The brothers will deal with it quickly." I walked over to him and placed a hand on his shoulder while looking at Loyal. "That is why you're in here, oui? To make sure Sawyer stays in here until it's dealt with?"

"Yeah." His mouth pulled into a tight line. There was something else going on.

"Henri, stay in here with Sawyer and Adrick. We'll be back in a sec," Saint said, starting for the door with Gun.

When they left with Loyal, Adrick tried to reassure us. "I have men downstairs. They will assist too. There is nothing to worry about."

Panic and fear pushed at me to seek out Blaze, but I knew he would want me to be safe. I would be nothing but a distraction for him if I walked out there. And I also stayed put for Sawyer's sake. He wasn't faring well.

His shoulders rounded, gaze wide and wild as he shook his head and backed up another step. "Who's down there?"

"Some people want things they can't have," I tried to say, wincing when his bottom lip trembled. "I think—"

Two shots were fired. I jolted and cried out. Sawyer screamed, slapping his hands over his mouth.

"Both of you on the floor behind the desk," Adrick ordered. As he made his way to the door, he pulled a gun from his back holster.

I grabbed Sawyer's hand and dragged him behind the desk, then tugged him down to the carpet. I hugged him to me as he whimpered. "Everything will be all right, chéri."

Voices rose outside the door just before another shot went off. Adrick stayed by the entrance with his back to the wall. There was more shouting beyond, followed by another shot fired.

Sawyer and I clung to each other.

"I have to get out. I have to go home. I can't stay here. I need to go."

Loud footfalls sounded outside the room.

I rubbed up and down his arm and gripped his other hand. "You will. This will be over soon."

Please, please let it be over soon.

And I swore Blaze had better keep himself safe or I was going to beat his ass.

I peeked around the desk when the door opened. Adrick had his gun pressed up under Blaze's chin. In a swift move, Blaze knocked his arm away and had Adrick around the throat.

"Blaze," I yelled, getting to my feet hands out. "Mon amour, let him go. Adrick was helping us." I wiggled my fingers down at Sawyer. He grabbed my hand and stood. "Look, mon amour. No one got hurt."

My beautiful beast released Adrick, grunted at him, and stomped over to me. He tugged me into his arms and stuck his nose into my neck, inhaling.

Someone got close. Blaze let out a grumbly noise and moved me away from them.

"The guy had held the receptionist hostage," Saint explained.

No wonder my man was freaked out. He would have pictured me in that situation.

I hated to think if something did happen to me how Blaze would react. I worried for those around him and hoped they could get him to see reason and not run into any danger after me.

My stomach rolled at the thought, and I prayed we wouldn't be put in that situation.

Running my hands up and down Blaze's back, I told him, "I am here, mon amour. Relax for me, oui?"

He grunted into my skin.

"I'm just going to turn around in your arms. You can keep me tucked against you, safe."

When he grunted again, he lifted his head slightly as I turned to face the others. Blaze wrapped me up again and placed his nose in the crook of my neck, where it hit my shoulder.

Loyal stood near Sawyer, grounding him with a hand to the back of his neck. The boy's cheeks were on fire, and his body shook a little.

"What happened downstairs?" I asked Saint.

When Blaze's arms tightened around me, I reached one

hand behind me to palm his thigh and the other up to clasp his forearms that crossed my chest.

Saint's gaze flicked to Sawyer. "We shouldn't talk—"

"Please," Sawyer begged, hands pressed to his belly. "If it was about me, please tell me." His bottom lip trembled.

Saint's brows pinched, and his lips thinned.

"Tell him," Country ordered from the doorway.

Saint nodded, but his jaw clenched. They were pissed about something. "Our doorman decided to go to the bathroom as soon as this man entered Polished."

Merde. That explained why they were all still on edge. The guard mustn't have been a Diamond MC member; they wouldn't have been swayed by any offer to walk away.

"He'll be fuckin' dealt with," Country stated.

Saint drew in a deep breath through his nose before he carried on. "It was lucky the silent alarms went off after the body scan identified a weapon. We just watched the camera footage of the man walkin' right up to the front desk, wantin' to rebook an appointment with Sawyer. Elle was there, and she told him the only available time was in two weeks. Blaze, Tech, and other security members rushed the area. He panicked and reached around the counter to grab Elle, pulling her out by her hair. He demanded to see Sawyer." Saint met Sawyer's gaze. "He wanted to talk to you. Needed you to go with him."

"Why?" Sawyer whispered.

"That's what we're trying to figure out," Country said, moving into the room.

"Can't you ask him?" Sawyer suggested.

The room silenced for a moment.

Until Country started to say, "He shot two men—"

"My men," Adrick snarled, waving his phone around. Someone must have alerted him by text about who had been harmed.

Sawyer made a strangled noise. Loyal moved closer to him, his fingers tightening a little around Sawyer's neck while he glared at Adrick.

"We had to get control of the situation right away," Loyal said.

Blaze straightened. "I shot him. He won't answer anything because he's dead."

Quickly facing him, I placed my hands on his chest. "Mon amour—"

"I'd do it again too." He was serious; I could see it in his eyes.

I nodded, silently telling him I understood. He'd been scared, and I had little doubt he had pictured me in that situation.

My big, beautiful, protective beast.

BLAZE

Finally, I could fucking breathe again. My heart slowed, and the anger ebbed as soon as Henri nodded. He understood where my mind had gone. Why I did what I did.

"Sawyer, since we don't have answers, maybe you could help us out?" Country asked.

Henri tipped to his toes and kissed my jaw. "Love you, mon amour. Nothing will change that," he said softly.

Grunting, I tugged him in and tucked him under my arm. With a kiss to his temple, I nipped at his earlobe. "You're mine, firecracker. Always got my love."

Our attention shifted to the kid when he said, "The man's dead?"

"Da, that is what he said," Adrick said.

"Adrick," Saint warned. "How about you go see your injured men?"

"Why? They did their job. They will get paid well for it."

That man only had an inch of emotions inside him, and they went to his husband, West.

Saint sighed. "Fine. Then how about you keep any comments to yourself?"

The Russian glared at Saint but crossed his arms over his chest and gave him a look, as if to say "Well, keep going."

"What was his name?" Sawyer asked.

"Bernard Simpson," Country supplied.

Sawyer paled.

Shit. What the fuck had that motherfucker done?

The kid gulped.

"Sawyer, what is it?" Henri asked.

The kid shook his head.

"Sawyer, you gotta tell us," Country said softly.

"S-Sorry, I will.... I just didn't expect it to be him. He's been hinting for me to live with him. Telling me he can take care of me. Saying he doesn't want me with anyone else." Tears welled. "I-If I'd thought he was serious.... He never got angry with me. Never hurt me."

Henri shook his head as he tapped at my arms trapping him. I dropped them, and Henri moved over to Sawyer. "It matters not if he never hurt you or got angry, chéri." He curled an arm around Sawyer's shoulders, which meant Loyal had to drop his hand from the kid's neck. He didn't look happy about it but stayed silent as Henri went on, "Did you tell him you would like to live with him? That you wanted to be with him outside of Polished?" The kid was already shaking his head. "Exactly. You are not at fault for his actions. He wanted someone he could not have, and he didn't handle that well."

"I-I would have come to you if he was... if he was mean to me." He wrapped his arms around his waist. "I felt like I was being watched, but...." He shook his head again.

"You get attention like my West." Sawyer glanced over at the Russian. "You are used to people looking at you. You probably thought the feeling of being watched was just that, the attention you get. You wondered if you were overreacting," Adrick said.

Sawyer's gaze widened, but he nodded.

"Adrick, can I be the one to tell West you think Sawyer's good-looking?"

Adrick advanced on Loyal, but Saint stepped in front of Adrick with a laugh to hold him back, and Sawyer moved closer to Loyal.

Looked like the kid might have something for the biker.

Henri glanced over to me and widened his eyes, silently asking me if I saw that.

My lips twitched. He was the only reason I relaxed, and he made the anger dim enough to think straight.

"I will kill you," Adrick shouted.

"Man, it was a joke," Loyal said.

Country pinched the bridge of his nose. "Brother, we don't joke with the Russian. He has no sense of humor."

Adrick stopped trying to step around Saint and crossed his arms again. "I have humor."

Everyone stared at him.

"I only give it to West."

Henri smirked over at me, one brow cocked up.

Wait. Was my little firecracker trying to tell me I was like the Russian?

What the fuck? I wasn't cold or…. Fuck me. Maybe I was like Adrick since Henri was the only one who saw all sides of me, like West did with the Russian.

Not that I cared that we were similar. If anything, it made me understand Adrick more and his need to protect West in any way he could.

"Sawyer," Country intervened. "Loyal can give you a lift home if—"

"No!" He slapped a hand over his mouth and shook his head. Slowly, he dropped the hand, fisting both at his sides to hide them shaking. "I-I mean, I don't need a lift. Thank you, though. I should go." He nodded. "I need to go."

Yeah, that wasn't suspicious at all.

"Thank you—not that I'm thanking you for the—" He made a strangled sound and shook his head as he headed toward the door. He turned back and added, "Just that, I'm glad it's been dealt with." He groaned low, running a hand over his face. "Not that I wanted anyone dead." He flicked his gaze to me and back to Henri before he quickly said, "And not that I don't appreciate the issue being dealt with. He held her hostage. The outcome was inevitable." He was near panting now.

Henri moved over to him. "Relax, chéri. We understand. Are you sure you don't want to ride Loyal home? Loyal will be good with it."

Loyal dropped his head, eyes to the floor, hiding his expression.

Fuck me. Did Henri understand how that sounded?

Saint choked on his laugh.

"What?" Adrick asked.

Country snorted. "Henri, want to check how you said that?"

"Sorry, I am French. Sometimes I get things wrong."

Fuckin' bullshit. But God, I loved that man.

Sawyer blushed. "N-No? I... I'm not far. I should go." He reached out and patted Henri's arm awkwardly before he spun around and slipped out of the room.

Henri spun on Loyal. "Maybe you should check on him before he leaves?"

Loyal looked at Country, who nodded, which had Loyal moving out of the room quickly.

Saint let out a long whistle. "Everyone can see the sexual tension between those two, right?"

"We are not standin' around gossipin' when we have shit to do," Country stated.

Henri ignored Country and said to Saint, "They would be amazing together, but I fear little Sawyer is way too shy or there is something else holding him back." His brows drew together before he lifted his gaze to me.

"I've looked into the kid, but there's nothing that stands out as troublesome."

"Then again, we did not know about this client stalking him," Henri commented.

Goddamn, that was true.

"Not like we can track all employees outside of work," Saint said. "They need to come to us for help."

"But it is as I said," Adrick stated.

That Sawyer got a lot of attention.

"Henri, check in with Sawyer when he comes into work tomorrow," Country said. "For now, we'll have to table this and get Polished back open. The cleanup should be done by now." He turned to me. "I was heading to your office earlier. Any updates?"

"One. We hacked a satellite to check all boats in the ocean against their routes heading to the US. There are two that started from Australia who never logged their trip. Two we'll keep an eye on and see where their destination could be."

"We need that information before they even port so we can get onboard."

As if I didn't fucking know that. But instead of saying anything, I clenched my jaw and nodded.

"There is a month to follow their trail. Blaze and Tech will figure it all out, and we will help these people," Henri offered.

Country sighed. "I know, Henri."

"You are stressed. You should go see your Dusty and Seth."

His lips lifted in the corner, but I could still see the tension in his gaze. "Yeah, I'm headin' home as soon as Wreck arrives." He turned to me again. "Keep me updated."

With a grunt, I tipped my chin up.

Henri's phone rang when Country walked out of the room. He glanced at the screen and over to me then Saint. "The agent. Cross your fingers."

I didn't move, but Saint humored him by crossing them on both hands.

"Bonjour, Nathaniel." Henri looked down as he bit his bottom lip, listening, and then grinned, his gaze seeking mine. "Oui, that is fantastic news. We will be in touch to sign the papers tomorrow and get a wire transfer organized.

… Oui, see you then." He tucked his phone away and ran at me. He jumped, and I caught him in my arms. "We have the warehouse, mon amour."

"Good."

He kissed me hard and quick before dropping his feet and spinning to Saint. "The Playhouse is a go. We need to see the bank to open a new joint business account between us all managers and organize the money for the seller."

"Then let's take a trip to the bank," Saint said.

There were some daylight hours still left. I wasn't sure it'd get done that day since we'd have to register the new business, but it could be sorted soon.

Henri faced me. "Mon amour, are we staying here tonight too? If so, Tech failed to bring the right bathroom items. I will need a trip home. Saint could take me while we are out seeing the bank people."

For me, he was willing to sleep on the couch again.

But I could tell that he'd woken with a stiff neck. Not that he'd said anything.

"We'll go home." In fact, I wanted to go there now. "I'll drive us to the bank to meet Saint there and then take us home."

Henri's head cocked to the side.

Fuck.

He'd figure out what I didn't want to say since it'd just end in a fight.

"Mon amour?"

I crossed my arms over my chest.

His gaze widened. "You don't want me back here to work."

"How the fuck did you read that from his look?" Saint asked.

"Da, he always looks like this."

Henri's hands slapped to his waist. "He is willing to come with me when I know he wants to work on his computer. That told me he will take me home in hopes of never letting me out again."

"Henri—"

His hand cut through the air. "Non, Blaze. I understand where you are coming from. I know the fear you feel, but I won't allow this to put a stop on our life. Just think, mon amour, would I have allowed some stranger to grab me by my precious hair? Non. Only you get to tug on it. I am strong, mon amour. I can protect myself until you come along to save the day."

Saint snorted.

"But—"

"Non, buts, mon amour. I have not many days left working here since I will, no doubt, move over to the Playhouse full-time eventually. You won't stop me working there either. I will be up on the third floor in my own corner office where no nasties can get to me. I will have people we trust working in the other offices at each side. I won't be alone. Plus, there will be security on the same level watching the live feeds. I will be surrounded and safe, which means you do not upset your friend by moving all your toys again. I will only be next door, and we can make sure we work the same time so we're coming and going from work with each other. But for now, we will make sure the desk downstairs is more secure so no one can reach around."

"It'll be a brother on the door from now on, no

outsiders, so the customers will be searched before enterin' the buildin'," Saint added.

Henri waved a hand toward Saint. "See, mon amour. Things will be safer."

I ground my teeth together, eyeing the man I loved with every fucking fiber. Snapping my gaze to Saint, I demanded, "The desk had better be reinforced by the time he starts his shift."

Saint's lips twitched. Sensibly, he said nothing and just nodded.

Henri got close to slide his hands up my chest. "Thank you, mon amour."

Gripping the front of his neck, I pulled him even closer. "You'd better fuckin' stay safe at that desk."

His eyes sparkled. "I will."

"Saint will take you to the bank and back here for your shift. But we'll sleep at home tonight."

"I like that plan, mon amour." He rolled up to his toes and kissed my jaw. When he went to pull away, I dragged him back in and claimed his mouth. After breaking the kiss, I stared down at him. His damn eyes were still glittering, knowing he was getting what he wanted.

"Eyes on him at all times," I said.

"Saint, he is speaking to you," Henri informed him.

"Right, yep, got it. Don't stress, Blaze. It'll be me and Gun takin' him."

I drew in a deep breath and straightened, nodding.

"See you soon," Henri said.

When I grunted, he kissed my chest and walked out the door with Saint, asking, "How is Elle after all that?"

When I looked at the only person left in the room, Adrick smirked.

Fuck me.

"What?" I asked.

"You are like me."

Shit. Even he figured that out.

"So?"

He chuckled. "It is good to know I am not the only one who has to deal with a stubborn partner. If only they'd listen and do as they are asked."

"Would you change it if you could?"

He grinned. "Nyet. Never."

Yeah, me neither.

"They ground us in ways no other can. It is good, even when it drives us crazy."

Snorting, I nodded. We really were on the same damn page.

"Got shit to do."

"Da, I will leave you to it. West's shift has nearly finished, and I must speak with Rule."

Good luck to the brother.

CHAPTER ELEVEN

"What do you think of this?" I asked the people around me while we sat at a table in the Diamond MC compound. It had been two weeks since the drama at Polished, and things were settled. Usually, I would have hungered for more drama, but I was too busy with other things for the Playhouse to want any action happening.

The desk area had been changed where no one could reach around or over, and it had caught a few questions from clients. All we told them there was an incident that called for the change, and we weren't at liberty to discuss. No one pressed for more information, and really, I doubted they cared since gossip wasn't what they were there for.

"Da, that is a better choice," Adrick said.

"I like it," Eve said, Tech's sister and one of my friends.

"Why am I here again?" Gun asked.

"You are to be part owner. You need to have input on behalf of all other biker owners," I explained while looking down at the paint sample.

Adrick grunted as he picked up a color sample. "I think that color with this vivid white for skirtings. It will give a calm feeling."

I nodded. "Plus, with the offset of the black furniture, it will appear classy but homey." Smiling, I ran a hand through my dark hair, relaxing. "I think we have finally figured out the Playhouse colors."

Since we had cash, with an added extra big bonus, we were thrilled when we were able to rush through the purchasing process to have received the keys just yesterday. It always amazed me how money could get things moving unconventionally fast. What also helped was the connections the Diamond MC had, which assisted in speeding things along.

In levels one and two, on the outer edges where there were already offices, the rooms would now be used for private dancing, and each floor had a medium-sized room, which would be secured for functions. They were blocked off from the main area by walls.

Luckily, there were already three bathrooms on both bottom and second levels—two for guests and another for employees only. At the back of the building, there would be break and dressing rooms, and in front of those, where the wall separated those rooms, would be the long bars. Then, in the large middle area on each floor, there would be two stages with tables and chairs placed between each. Booths would line the walls, and on the other side of those were the halls that led to private rooms.

Upstairs, the third story would hold the offices, security, another break room, bathroom, and a VIP room, which was away from those downstairs.

All the preparations kept me nicely busy. I hadn't had time to grow bored, which Blaze loved since he was still occupied with searching for information on the trafficking.

I was sure any day now Blaze and Tech would figure out what area they needed to be in for when those ships docked, and then, the Diamond MC would be there waiting. They would deal out their own punishment. But Officer Jones would also be there to assist with the victims.

He was the club's inside man at the local police station. Though, Blaze did tell me the club was helping Jones, too, by keeping an eye on the chief of police and Detective Marco Brown, who had been associated in the trouble with Jones's old partner, Officer Plank. So far, all drug trade that they were putting on the streets had stopped. The club also believed trade had ceased because Plank was behind bars and the damage done to him had scared the other two enough to either take a break or stop completely.

I hoped it was the latter.

Still, they would be watched, and if they sneezed in the wrong direction, the Diamond MC would be all over them.

"Great," Gun said, bringing me from my thoughts. "I'm going to get some lunch. Surely Dusty's finished cooking by now."

Eve snorted. "You're brave. You remember the last time Quake went into the kitchen while Dusty was cooking and asked something?"

Gun smirked. "Yeah, but she loves me more, and Quake is always stealing food *as* she makes it. At least I wait until she's done."

"But what about your input here?" I asked. "We still must pick the rest of the furniture. The flooring. The lighting."

Gun stood, giving me a look I didn't understand, but his words made sense. "You've got more style and sense than me. I'm sure you'll do fine without me. We trust you, Henri."

My chest warmed. "This is true. I do have more style. Thank you, Gun."

He smirked, rolled his eyes, and moved off toward the kitchen doors.

"All right, what do you think of these black booths, which will"—I grabbed the layout of the club and pointed to a spot—"hug these walls on each floor? Then in the large space in the middle we can have tables and chairs."

Adrick grunted. "I believe Gun is correct. You have style, little French man."

I beamed at the scary man and glanced to Eve, who raised her hands. "Hey, I'm just here for moral support. This is all you. But I do love the idea and that both men and women are welcome there and not just as dancers but as patrons. Makes everyone feel welcome."

"Da, I have a feeling this club will be very busy."

My excitement shone through as I wiggled on the seat. "This makes me very happy."

"Not like I do," a gruff voice said from behind me before an arm wound around my waist and I was pulled up off the bench seat. Blaze's teeth latched onto my neck, making me close my eyes and sigh happily.

I loved his claiming.

"Fuck me, I need to get laid," Eve mumbled.

"At least you have Quake here. My West—"

Blaze lifted his head, and I opened my eyes like we both expected something to happen.

Eve didn't disappoint.

"You don't know what the fuck you're talking about!" Eve snapped, standing and resting her hands to the table. "There's nothing going on with me and Quake. Got it?" She stormed off toward the kitchen before Adrick said more.

"Was I supposed to pretend I know nothing about them when they are obvious about it?"

"Oui, Adrick," I said.

It was well known that Quake and Eve did the horizontal tango, but Eve would never be locked down into a relationship. She had commitment issues from past trauma. Though we could see that Quake adored her. He was a sweet man who would treat her right.

Adrick swore in Russian, then waved a hand as if to brush it off. "Does not matter. But maybe when West tells me things, he needs to warn me of these secrets too." His gaze narrowed. "Everyone knows about them, da?"

"Everyone but Eve's brother."

"She has brother?"

Blaze snorted at my back.

"I am joking. I know the technology man is her twin brother."

"Then don't say anything to Tech about Eve and Quake."

"It bothers me not. Can we get back to this?" He nodded down to the table.

Turning in Blaze's arms, I asked, "Do you have more things to do here, mon amour? Or are we headed home before work?"

He lowered down to nip at my bottom lip, which sent a tingle right to my balls.

"Home."

"What about this?" Adrick asked.

Turning, I started packing up, placing the papers in the bag I'd carried in with me. "Tomorrow, we can meet for a coffee at that cute little cafe down the street from Polished. Bring West if he is free. Saint should be available too."

Once I zipped the bag up, I caught Adrick's nod before Blaze took my hand and led me out of the compound.

We'd been so rushed that morning we hadn't had time to play, and it seemed my beast was in the mood to have some bedroom fun.

On the drive home, I asked how the investigation was going. When his hands tightened around the steering wheel, I knew it wasn't a good sign.

"I can't fuckin' stand the waiting game. Both boats are headed to North America. We think one will port in Los Angeles and the other Mexico. The satellites can only be used to show their routes. We can't see what's happening on the vessels. If we could, we'd know which boat to watch more closely. We'll have to split teams and be at both destinations. At least we have enough men to cover both areas. The brothers from Hawks wanted to be involved. Wanted to travel over, but Country has asked them to wait. With a lot of negotiations and promises, they finally agreed. For now. Besides, if we have more people flooding the area, it could alert the wrong people, and shit could turn bad." He drew in a breath. "This shit is still fucked, though. We don't even know their end destination after they make their stop."

"You will save them, mon amour. There is no need to worry about what could happen after they arrive here. You will stop them from moving on."

"We need to fuckin' find out who is behind all this."

"You will. And at least there will be people to question from the ships. Then, you and the club could talk to Officer Jones to see if he wants to be the one to deal with the people in charge. If he can't do anything within the force, then I am sure Country will know how much the club should be involved after learning who the mastermind is."

He reached over and took hold of my hand, drawing it up to his lips to kiss the back of it. "Thanks, firecracker. My head's been spinning, and you say the right things to help settle it down."

I brought his hand in mine over to hold it against my chest. "You would have thought of it as soon as the stress stopped messing with your mind."

"You gotta know I'm waiting on a call from someone who might know something about this shit."

I scrunched my brows, placing our joined hands to my lap. "Who, mon amour? And it better not be an ex of yours that I'll have to set straight?"

His lips twitched. "No, firecracker. You never asked, so I didn't say anything about who I sold my business to."

Oh.

No, I had never asked, because it was the part of Blaze that had kept him away from me, and I was being selfish by not wanting to know about that darker side.

It probably made me a bad person. Some would even say

I should want to know everything about my lover, but I couldn't bring myself to ask about trafficking body parts.

However, my beautiful beast understood my wishes, and he hadn't pushed for me to know anything I didn't want to.

"You think this person will know why these people are being trafficked?" I swallowed. "Is it because of organ selling?"

Please, don't let it be.

"We need to rule it out and this guy is the biggest dealer in this area. I doubt it's him. He's…. Hell, he isn't too bad, even when he deals in that shit. He doesn't traffic people, which is why I doubt it is him. But he might know something."

Blaze was saying this man wasn't bad, even though he sold body parts. I never understood how that made sense. But I didn't have to worry about it any longer, as my Blaze had given that up for me.

"Hopefully he has answers." I licked my lips. "You and he…." If they had some type of relationship, I would hate them speaking, but I wouldn't stop it if it eased Blaze's mind. He would just have to put up with me being salty for a while, knowing my man was speaking with someone he had his tongue and dick in.

Blaze looked over at me, saw I was glaring, and smirked. "I wouldn't do that to you, firecracker. Malice and I have never had anything like that."

I screwed my nose up. "Malice?"

"Yeah."

"No kissing?" I checked.

"None."

I relaxed and smiled. "I won't have to hurt you now."

He snorted. "You were going to?"

"Only if you were speaking with someone who knows intimate information about you." I wiggled my fingers his way. "That body is all mine. I do not like knowing others have had their taste of you."

His hand clamped down on my thigh and then slipped up and cupped me between my legs. My cock stiffened, and he smirked my way before he said, "Feel the same, firecracker. I'd go as far as hurting an ex if you wanted to talk with them."

"Oh, mon amour, that should not turn me on, but it does." We were different and yet the same when it came to those types of things. Which was why I had to be sure. "You promise there was no touching at all between you and Malice?' I spat out his name.

His hand ran up and down my length as he drove along. "Malice and I haven't done shit. Promise. And I'll only be talking to him if the fucker ever calls back."

"Do you think of him as a friend?"

"I trust him. In the past, we've hung out a few times. But he knows I want no part of that business. I don't even want to be around it, which is why I haven't talked to him since we got back together."

"All right, mon amour."

"I trust you more," he told me as we pulled onto our street.

"And I shall show you how much I appreciate that trust when we get home."

I'd let him worship me in all the ways I knew he liked.

CHAPTER TWELVE

BLAZE

It was a week later when my phone rang. I glanced from the computer down to the screen and quickly hit Accept, then placed it on speaker. "About damn time you got back to me."

"Hey, dickhead. Good to hear from you too. I can't drop everything just to have a chat."

Max Garcia, also known as Malice, was the only man outside of Henri and the club who I trusted. After all, he was the one I'd sold my business to. He also ran one of the biggest mafia organizations in North America who traded in not only organs but guns and drugs too.

The door to the office opened, and I glanced back to see Henri stroll in. I glanced at the time on my screen and silently cursed. His shift had ended.

"Need some information."

The smartass replied, "Usually, you play with me a little before jumping right to business."

Tech shot me a look.

I scowled at him as I heard Henri suck in a sharp breath.

"Haven't got time to play, Malice. This is important."

"Play?" Henri snarled. He stomped close, planted his hands on his hips, and glared at me. "What type of *playing* is this?" In French, he blasted, "You told me he was nothing to you. Did you lie, my love? I swear, if you lied to me, I will have your balls and not in a pleasant way. You will feel pain like none before, and I will withhold my body from you too. So please tell me, my beast, did you lie?"

A chuckle swept through the phone before Malice hummed low. "Sounds like you're getting a good scolding, Blaze. Would this happen to be the famous lover of yours?"

"That's him," I said, smirking at Henri, whose mouth had dropped open.

Malice snorted. "No wonder you gave up everything. He has the fire you need to keep you warm."

"Can you not talk about him?" I didn't like Malice knowing too much. I hadn't even given him Henri's name.

There was another deep chuckle. "I won't speak of him again. But I will tell you that if you need information from me, I want something from you."

Shit.

"He will not do anything for your business," Henri said, stepping closer.

Sighing, I pinched the bridge of my nose and glared at a smirking Tech.

Malice laughed again. "He is as protective as you are,

Blaze. That's good for you. Will your lover allow some computer advice?"

"What type of advice?" I asked.

"I need you to find a couple of people who are being difficult to locate."

Henri's hand slipped to the back of my neck. I knew exactly what he would be wondering. If the people Malice were after were good or bad. Usually, I wouldn't care, and I would do what I had to so I could have the information *I* needed. However, my life was different, and that was for the better. Which meant I didn't want to step back into any type of involvement in Malice's world. Still, if I refused, would I jeopardize the information I had to have?

What the hell did I do?

We needed to find out if Malice knew anything.

I suppose I could....

"What about if I find someone else to handle your thing?"

There was silence on the other end.

"Malice?" I called.

"You really want nothing to do with this world?"

"Nothing."

"Will this person be willing to work with me on more than one occasion?"

"She could for the right price."

"She? Call me intrigued. Ask her if she will do what you won't, and if she agrees, only then will I help you."

"And you call me greedy," Henri snarkily commented.

Fuck.

"He didn't mean that, Malice," I said quickly.

"I only allow so much, Blaze. It's fine to scold your man,

Blaze's lover, but *I* won't be talked to like that. Especially not when it's your man who called me for a favor in the first fucking place."

Fear and fury filled me. I knew what Malice was capable of. I'd been there when he'd shot his own brother in the shoulder at the fucking dinner table for not respecting their mother. But I also wouldn't let anyone talk to Henri like that. "Malice—"

"Non, mon amour." He squeezed my neck before running his hand over my shoulders. "Mr. Malice, I must apologize for how I spoke. I will keep my fire for my lover only," Henri offered.

"Fucking hell, no wonder you got Blaze wrapped around your finger with that sugar-sweet tone. Bet it gets you outta a lot of shit."

I glanced up at Henri, who smirked. "I am but an innocent angel."

Malice guffawed. "Fuck off you are. Blaze, get back to me, and this time, I'll take your call." He hung up, and I swung my chair around to Henri.

Tech, with horror in his tone, said, "That was Malice. As in the North America mafia boss?"

"That's him."

Tech cursed and scrubbed a hand over his face.

Henri slid his ass on to my knee and hugged me close. "Sorry, mon amour. My mouth gets away from me sometimes."

"Lucky I love your mouth," I told him.

He leaned against me and kissed my chin. "It is very lucky."

"Can we stop with that type of talkin' and go back to how you know Malice? Shit, I should tell Country, right?"

"Your prez already knows I know him," I told Tech, curling an arm around Henri's waist. "Malice is the one I sold my business to."

Tech opened his mouth, closed it, and nodded. He sighed. "Makes sense."

Picking up my phone, I dialed in a number. "This won't take long," I told them.

It rang a few times before she answered, "Why, if it isn't my sweet sugar daddy. What are you doing calling me this late? I'm surprised with your age, you're not tucked up in bed. I can join you if you're lonely."

While Tech choked and quickly moved away to cover his laugh, Henri stood, faced me, and waved a hand at the phone with a glare.

"Gwen, please say I'm not actually your sugar daddy and that you call everyone a pet name before I get killed." Like Malice was the only guy I trusted, Gwendolyn McKenna was the only woman I was sure of and could count on. We'd never met outside of online, but we'd gotten close back in the day when I'd gone to her to teach me more about computers. I already had some skills, but the rest I learned from her. Even still, I knew Tech and I could never measure up to what she knew.

"But, *Daddy*, I only use those names for you."

"Gwen," I warned.

There was a tinkle of laughter. "Hello, Henri, it's a pleasure to *see* you, you handsome man."

My gaze snapped to the monitors. "You fuckin' hacked us. What have I said about that shit?"

"Relax, Daddy. I'll slip out at the end, and you won't have even felt me."

I palmed my face as Tech jumped back into his seat, his fingers at the board as he tried to work out how she got in.

"Naughty, naughty, cutie. You won't find me."

"She's right, Tech. She's the only one who can manage this shit. She taught me everything I know."

"I am but the best. Henri, sweetie, I promise your big horndog is *just* a friend. I only like to mess with the big grump."

Henri smiled and waved at the screen. "Well, I suppose I can forgive you since it is fun to mess with my Blaze."

"Oh, my little dandelion. Blaze told me you sounded like heaven, but I didn't believe him."

While I cursed, Henri gasped and quickly sat on my lap again. "He's spoken to you about me?"

Gwen squealed a little, and her voice seemed closer to the receiver than before when she said, "Oh boy has he. Daddy Blaze is like a big huffing dragon, and you're his treasure. He's only threatened me like a million times to not look you up. Not unless I wanted my fingers and toes removed. You're the light in his life. The one—"

"He knows all this," I clipped. "Can we get back to business?"

Henri rested against my chest, patting my other thigh. "Oui, mon amour. But I would like Gwen's number. Chéri, we will be talking more."

"Yes! Oh, please do. I would love that." She took a breath. "Okay, sugar daddy, what do you need?"

"I need information from Malice, but he wants me to

find some people. I won't work with him, Gwen. Hoping you will so I can get my information."

"Is this about the missing men and women you're investigating?"

"Stop looking through our system," I warned. "But yeah."

"Fuck that," Tech muttered, and he went faster at finding her to cut off her connection.

"Tell your friend to stop, Daddy."

"Tech—"

"No. This is the club's system. We've got private shit on here. I don't know this bird, so I don't trust her."

"I do," I simply said, eyeing him.

Tech's jaw clenched. "Fuck," he bit out before he sat back.

"Aww, you do love me, Daddy. Thank you. Out of respect to your biker friend, I'm backing out and just connected to your camera. Whatever I found will stay with me. And, Blaze, if the information you want is for the missing people, then tell Malice I'll do it, but he'll be paying top dollar. And you give him my rules. If he can't follow them, then I can't do it."

"Understood. I'll text you his details after I've spoken to him."

"You got it. Later, guys. Henri, speak soon."

"Au revoir, chéri." Henri hit the End button.

"How much do you trust her?" Tech asked.

"All the way, brother."

Tech's jaw clenched before he took a deep breath and stood. "She better be worth your trust, brother. I'm goin' to get some food. Call your *mafia* friend back and let me know what he says."

"You got it."

When Tech left, Henri asked, "Do you think he will tell Country about Gwen?"

"He's loyal to the club, so yeah, he will. But I know he'll also let Country know I trust Gwen, and that should be enough for the both of them."

"Look at you growing with your friends."

I gripped the front of his neck. "Shut up."

He cackled. I curled my arms around him and picked up my phone again. When I hit Malice's number, Henri slid from my lap to the floor between my legs.

My gaze flared. He fucking wouldn't. Not while I was on the damn phone with Malice, of all people.

His fingers went to my button and zipper, and I rested my hand over them and shook my head just as Malice answered. "How'd it go?"

Henri giggled silently and got to his feet to straddle my legs and rest against me.

I should have known he was teasing. Henri wouldn't do that when he knew this call was important.

"She's willing to work with you. She charges two thousand an hour. But you have to follow her rules and let her work remotely. You don't get anyone else to find her. She does the job, and all contact stops. I've known her for years and have never seen her face-to-face. She taught me what I know, so believe me when I say she'll get what you need."

"Fair."

"I'll give her your number, and she'll be in touch."

"Does she know who I am?"

"She knows fuckin' everything."

"All right. What's the information you need?"

After I explained about what was happening, I asked, "Do you know anything about what's going on?"

"I've heard rumors."

"I need to know about the rumors you've heard."

"Men and women are being picked up and shipped to Ireland. The Murphy gang has branched out from prostitution to auctioning off their merchandise. I heard they make a lot of money because their product is imported from all over the world."

The Murphy gang was run by the Irish brothers Finn and Cian. They were ruthless with their businesses, and anyone who stepped in their way was quickly dealt with in the ugliest ways.

"Fuck," I snarled.

"Did they take someone you know?"

"Someone that's connected to a motorcycle club."

Malice snorted. "They'll be taught a lesson then. Good."

"We have two ships heading this way. Do you know where they'll port?"

"That I don't know. But I'm sure you'll figure it out. Now, what's the name of this woman?"

"Gwen. Be nice to her, Malice."

"I'll try," he said before hanging up.

"Mon amour, do you need to speak with the others?"

I ran my hands up his back. "Yeah, firecracker. Sorry, but bed won't be for a little while."

He sat up and stretched. "This is important. I can wait." He kissed my jaw and stood. "You might have to carry me to the car, though." He walked to the couch and lay down. "Wake me if you need anything."

Standing, I went to him and crouched at the side, tucking some wild hair behind his ear and tracing a finger over the outer edge. "I won't be long."

"Take as long as you need, mon amour."

"Fuck, I love you."

He smiled. "Love you always." He puckered his lips at me. I bent, kissing them before walking out, while texting Gwen, to go find Tech and drag him along to see Country in his office.

At least we knew who was behind this shit.

CHAPTER THIRTEEN

HENRI

For once, Blaze and I were at home in the kitchen cooking together before we headed into Polished. Actually, Blaze was doing all the work while I admired him.

"Do you remember the first time you cooked for me?" I asked, moving over to pull myself up onto the counter to sit beside him.

His lips twitched. "You thought I was a burglar and raced into the kitchen holding an umbrella."

Rolling my eyes, I kicked out at him. "It was all I had close by."

"At least when I looked over, you were holding it like a baseball bat ready to swing."

"It was your fault I was scared to begin with. Who breaks into someone's house to cook for them?"

"I do."

Yes, he did.

"We were still testing the waters between us."

He scoffed. "We were set in stone."

"It had only been a week."

"A week where I'd spent every night at your place fucking you."

"Well, yes, but you can't honestly say you knew I was the one for you within a week."

"I did."

I shoved at his arm when he just kept chopping. "Blaze."

He sighed and finally quit cutting to look at me. "Are you telling me you never believed me all those times I said I fell for you instantly?"

Eyes widening, I opened my mouth and closed it. He couldn't be for real. I had definitely been taken with him, but I didn't love him straightaway.

"You are messing with me," I said.

He placed the knife down and slipped between my legs, hands cupping my hips. "Guess you've never believed me when I've told you this many times before, but I'll reiterate again that I fell the day you found me in that alleyway. You didn't know me, and I was a large, injured man. Yet, you were willing to help me. To annoy me back to health." I slapped his chest before he went on. "Then, besides some family members—" His jaw clenched, and I knew he was thinking of his sister and how the rest of the no-good people who fell apart after she was murdered acted like Blaze wasn't there and alive. He kissed my nose. "I've never had a lover show me that type of care. There was just something about you in that moment. My dark heart connected to yours. Why do you think I kept coming back every night?"

"But...." He picked his business over me. When I overheard his call about how he could get his customer a healthy kidney, I had given him the choice. Work or me. He walked away that night and broke my heart, even though I saw it caused him pain to do so.

His jaw clenched before he nodded. "Yeah, I'll forever live with regret for leaving the only man I've ever loved. I told you it was one of the stupidest moments in my life, where I thought you were trying to control me, and I... fucked if I know. I felt like I needed to prove to myself that I didn't love you as much as I did. Prove that you weren't my heart and soul. So, I rebelled in the worst way by losing you. It didn't take me long to realize you were just telling me that what I did wasn't something you could live with. You gave me a choice, and I picked wrong."

I slid my hands up his chest. "Mon amour, I know how much you regret that. We're not talking about that. You have shown me in many ways that I am your world. I just couldn't believe that you loved me in that first moment."

"Well, I did, and you don't have to believe it. I just know in myself that you had my heart in the palm of your hand the moment I saw you in that alleyway. I hate that we missed so much time together. That I watched you from afar and didn't force myself back into your life like I should have. But I was scared that you wouldn't have me, that you couldn't possibly love me like I did you."

"My beautiful beast, you are my air. I need you to live. I need you every day, all day, and nothing will change that. It may sound cheesy, mon amour, but we do complete each other."

He hid his grin against my neck where he then kissed. "Very cheesy."

I lightheartedly shoved his shoulder before I wrapped my arms around his neck. "I love you."

His hands squeezed at my hips, and my cock took notice, thickening. "You've got all my love, firecracker. Even when you're a pain."

I bit his shoulder. "I am never a pain."

He straightened, so I shifted my hands to his waist, clutching his tee. His brow cocked. "Remember when I had to pick you up and carry you out of that shop?"

I gaped, then huffed. "That woman wouldn't stop ogling you. I had to give her a piece of my mind. I did it for all other couples in the world who do not wish for their partner to be eye fucked while trying to find clothes." I huffed and then smirked. "What about the time we were in the bedding department, and you nearly suffocated me with a pillowcase?"

"You're too good-looking. I either had to cover your face or remove the guy's eyes."

Snorting, I smirked. "We are as bad as each other."

"Because we don't like sharing or people staring at what belongs to us?"

"Oui, that, mon amour."

He cupped my jaw, tipping my head back as his gaze ran over my face. His thumb slipped up and into my mouth where I sucked around it.

His gaze locked onto my mouth. "You could've been with anyone."

My teeth dug into the base of his thumb before I gripped his wrist and drew it out to hold it between my hands. "I saw no one but you."

"You should have your head checked."

Laughing, I squeezed his hips between my legs. "My mind is perfectly normal." Blaze raised a brow, and I scowled. "It is."

He stayed silent, watching me, annoying me.

"Fine. I'm not exactly normal, but no one is."

His lips twitched as he nodded once. "No one is."

"You're lucky I love you. No one else would put up with this."

He chuckled, fingers threading into my hair before he yanked me close. He claimed my mouth roughly, thrusting his tongue between my lips to slide and play with my own. I hooked my legs around the back of his and clawed at his tee, wishing to tear it from his stunning body.

For the rest of my life, I would love every kiss, every touch.

His fingers worked at my jeans until he got them undone. He pulled back to watch his hand dip in to drag my cock free.

A moan fell from me when he dribbled saliva down over the head of my prick. I loved when he did that. Blaze wound his palm around my dick, spreading his spit while jacking me off.

"Mon amour," I breathed, leaning my back to the wall and flicking my gaze from his face to his hand around me, over and over.

"What, firecracker?"

"I am not spilling over your hand...."

He smirked. "Then what does my greedy man need?" He trickled more spittle out and down, rubbing it into my skin.

"Non, I mean... I am not spilling over your hand unless you are buried in my ass first."

He chuckled. The beast. "We can make that happen." I lost his hand around my cock because both went to the waist of my pants. I lifted and he tugged them down my legs, pulling them all the way off with my underwear and throwing them to the kitchen floor.

"What about the food?"

He snorted. "I'll be eating in a minute."

Laughing, I shook my head, but then gasped when he palmed my cock again. "Not what I meant, mon amour."

"I can clean and fix dinner later. My firecracker wants my attention. I've got to give it."

Nodding, I panted and spread my legs more when he teased my balls in his big palm. A finger rubbed at my taint, teasing toward my hole, all while he jacked me off.

"Fuck me," I demanded.

I lost his hands and glowered up at him.

"Who's in charge?"

"Fuck you, you big ogre." His brow rose. "Mon amour," I whined.

He turned away and went to the kitchen table.

"Please, ma bête. I'll be good. You can just use my hole however you like."

He picked up a chair and brought it back to place it against the counter. He went for another and did the same. One for each foot.

"Stand and face the wall. Offer me your ass because I'm hungry."

My groan was strained, almost painful with the desire rushing through me. My legs shook a little, but I managed to stand, turn, and bend over, hands to the counter, cheek to the wall.

I presented my ass to my controlling ogre.

Since he was tall, like the beast he was, my hole was at mouth level. He didn't waste time, diving right in. His hands parted my cheeks, tongue licking over my puckered hole.

I started to reach for my cock as he ate at my hole, but he slapped my hand away.

"Not yours to touch," he clipped, nipping at my ass cheek. I squirmed and cursed at him in French, but he chuckled into my crack while licking and tonguing.

My cock ached, wanting attention.

I glanced down and saw he was just as hard under his jeans.

That beautiful cock would soon be buried in my ass. I whimpered and groaned, slamming my eyes closed when his grip on my hips tightened. He'd shoved his mouth and nose right in there.

Devouring me like he loved to.

This man was made for me. He was relentless with the attention he spent on my ass. Totally focused like he had all the time in the world. My legs trembled, toes curled, and I bit down on a gasp so hard, my teeth ached.

"Mon amour, please, I need you. Please, ma bête."

He took one long swipe over my hole, before pulling back. "Stay still." He undid his jeans and got rid of his tee before he pulled a lube packet out of his pocket. He tore it open and poured half over my ring and the rest over his cock. He threw the packet to the floor and ordered, "Come here."

My stomach fluttered as I turned and jumped. He caught me easily, like I weighed nothing, with his hands pawing at my ass. "Lock those legs."

I wound them around his waist, linking my feet.

"Use me. Fuck my hole and mark it as yours. Do what you want with me, mon amour. I am yours," I told him, peppering kisses over his face and neck.

His growl was harsh and low. When I leaned back, holding onto his neck, he pressed my ass down, using his fingers to push his cock into place so he could enter me.

I bore down and still it stung from his girth, but I loved the pain mixed with pleasure each and every time.

"Christ," he clipped before his jaw clenched.

My ass squeezed around his dick snugly as he pushed all the way in.

Biting my lip, I ran my gaze over his body. Muscles straining in ways that were such a turn-on that I shivered.

"Goddamn, firecracker, you feel fuckin' good."

Nodding, I gasped when he pulled me off his cock and thrust back in, hitting my prostate. "Yes, mon amour. Just there. Just like that." My cock leaked between us, all over his stomach and my groin.

His fingers dug into my flesh, and he fucked me faster up and down his cock, using my hole to pleasure himself.

"Who do you belong to?"

"You," I panted.

"Who owns you?"

"Always you."

"Mine to use, to fuck however I want. Christ, you were

made for my cock. To keep it warm and wet, like the little slut you are."

"Amour," I cried out, coming apart on his cock. My cum splashed down over us both.

"Jesus," he drew out. "Fuck, that's it. Milk my cock." He groaned, slamming in and out of me, and as he finished emptying inside me, I curled against his chest.

Lazily, I kissed his shoulder blade. My ass gripped him nicely as he slowly withdrew from me. I felt some of his seed drip to the floor.

"Bath or shower?" he asked.

My stomach rumbled.

He chuckled. The laugh was quick but enough to warm me all over. "Quick clean, then I'll feed you before we take a bath."

My sweet beast, wanting to take care of me. I would never tire of his attention.

"We don't have to linger for a bath, mon amour. I know you want to get to the office as soon as possible." I kissed his chest again. "Thank you for this time together."

"Fuck, firecracker, don't thank me. You deserve more. Tech has shit sorted for now, so we're taking a bath after we eat. Let me take care of you."

I sighed happily, brushing my cheek against his big, wide chest. "You know I won't say no, but as long as you're sure."

He grunted and released my ass. I dropped my feet to the floor, my legs wobbling a little. They always did after a good, hard fucking.

Blaze stroked his hand up and down my back, waiting until I was steady. He went to my jeans and pulled out my boxers. When he handed them to me, he told me to wait before I put them on. He disappeared for a moment only to reappear with a warm cloth.

"Turn," he ordered.

When I did, placing my hands on the chair at the counter, he swiped the cloth over my sensitive hole, making me hum. I would still leak, but it would do for now. Besides, sometimes I liked feeling his cum slicken me up.

He threw the material to the floor toward the laundry room and kissed my shoulder before wrapping me up in his arms. I liked basking in the aftercare my beautiful beast gave me. He made me all warm and fuzzy on the inside, and he'd admitted he got that same feeling too when he took care of me.

See, we really were made for each other.

CHAPTER FOURTEEN

HENRI

 couple of days later, Blaze and I walked into the compound hand in hand. We went straight into the common room where I was meeting some friends to go over the outfits for the Playhouse.

As soon as I saw Raya with her sister Wrenley, and Courtney, I turned into Blaze and lifted to my toes kissing his jaw.

"You have fun, mon amour."

He snorted, kissed me quickly on the lips, and made his way over to the other table that was occupied by Torch, Death, and Quake.

The only reason Blaze was with me and not glued to a screen at Polished was because Tech had warned him off or he was going to blow up all their babies. He was totally full of shit, but he could see Blaze needed some extra time away before they were glued to their computers as the boats drew close.

"Bonjour, ladies, I appreciate you joining me." I opened the folder and handed out the papers I'd printed. "What are your thoughts on these?"

"I'm not sure about the doctor and nurse outfits. They're not very sexy," Wrenley said with a wince, like I wouldn't want to hear that suggestion.

"Thank you, chéri. That is the advice I am after."

"You can't go wrong with a cowboy and cowgirl." Courtney passed that sheet over to Raya, who rubbed her bulging belly while she looked at it.

"What are the waitstaff going to be dressed in?" Wrenley asked.

"For both men and women, I would like cropped, white, short-sleeve shirts. On the bottom, black shorts that stop just below the bottom, and combat boots since they'll be on their feet day and night."

"I love that," Raya said.

Courtney nodded. "Yeah, running shoes wouldn't match the outfit, but you can get away with boots. So much better than heels."

"Oui, we need them to be as comfortable as we can." I glanced up at Torch as he stopped behind Wrenley. He tipped his chin up but didn't say anything, just wound Wrenley's hair around his hand. She smiled softly, leaning back.

"School wear would also be a good one," Raya suggested.

I spread the papers out. "I thought I had some printed,

but I must have forgotten them. What about this one?" I pushed the paper into the middle of the table.

Torch snorted but stayed quiet. Raya, Wrenley, and Courtney grinned.

"Do it," Courtney said

"Hey, whores," Eve called before she made her way over to us. Quake watched her walk before Death asked him something.

"Sorry I'm late." She glanced down, and her eyes widened. "Yes. Do that. It's wicked." She pointed at the biker and biker babe outfits.

Smiling, I pulled my phone out for notes. "Perfect. I'll write down these ones as a definite. Any other suggestions?"

"What about fantasy?" Wrenley asked. "Vampires, prince and princess. Elves."

I gasped and pointed at her. "Oui, I love that idea." As I went to add it to my notes, my phone rang, but the screen lit up with a number I didn't recognize.

Brows furrowed, I answered, "Bonjour?"

"H-hi, um, Henri." The soft tone had me straightening.

"Sawyer, is everything all right?"

"Blaze," I heard Torch call.

Sawyer made a noise. "Sorry. I'm really sorry to call."

"Chéri, I told you to reach out to me at any time. What can I help with?" A large hand pressed down on my shoulder, my beautiful beast showing me his support.

"I... I don't know anyone else." He made a frustrated sound. "My neighbor, Miss Cora, she usually looks after my brother when I work, but she's sick with the flu."

"Can't you take the night off, chéri?"

"No! I mean, no, sorry, I can't." He needed the money.

He made a good wage, so where was it all going if he was desperate to work?

"What do you need from me, Sawyer?"

He sighed. "Do you think they would let me bring him into work?"

"How old is he?"

"Eleven. He's really quiet and polite and good but shy with new people."

"Chéri, I doubt they will allow a boy his age into the building. What about one of the old ladies from the club? I am sure one of them can help." Courtney was already nodding and at least she had two children herself. Younger than the brother, but that didn't matter.

"I-I don't know them."

He knew me. He trusted me. He wanted *me* to look after his brother, but he was worried to ask, knowing I worked his hours too.

My chest warmed. I wanted to help him. After all, he had come to me, even when he probably hadn't wanted to reach out.

"Sawyer, give me one moment please."

"Um, okay?"

I took my phone away and muted the call. "Mon amour, I would like to help Sawyer by babysitting his brother for him tonight, but I need someone to cover my shift."

Blaze grunted and pulled his phone out. He stepped away while he made a call.

"Torch, since Sawyer said his brother was shy, I think the compound would overwhelm him. Do you think Death could add my house to his schedule tonight and have the security firm do drive-bys? I know, even with the cameras inside my house, Blaze would be more at ease if that could happen while he's at work."

"I'll talk to Death," Torch said. He kissed Wrenley's temple before he too moved over to the table where Death was still with Quake.

Lifting the phone, I unmuted the call and rested it to my ear. "I am back. We are waiting to hear if I can be replaced tonight and then I will take care of your little brother."

"Henri—"

"Non, chéri. It is not set yet, but please do not argue with me over my offering. I would very much like the night off and to spend it in the company of your brother. Let me help if I am able. Please."

Silence met me on the other end.

"Henri," Blaze called.

"I will be back, Sawyer." I muted the call again and shifted on the seat to face Blaze.

"State has someone to fill in. We'll go pick Sawyer up, and I'll stay—"

"Non, mon amour." I glanced to Torch when he walked back. He nodded. I smiled. "You do not need to stay with us at the house. We will be safe. You have the cameras you can watch from your toys at Polished. Plus, Torch has organized the security office to put our place on rotation for tonight." I smiled. "All sorted."

His jaw clenched. He didn't like it, but I would be safe.

"Take this panic button for home," Death said from behind me, making me jolt. He handed me a small device. "Just press there, and the cavalry will come."

"Thank you, chéri." After pocketing it, I reached out and took Blaze's hand. "See, we will be safe."

When my lover nodded, I kissed his hand before dropping it and hitting the Unmute button before placing the phone to my ear. "It is organized, Sawyer. Blaze and I can drop over to pick up your brother—"

"Wait, um, no, thanks. I can drop him at your place before I go to work. Is that okay?"

He wished for us to not see his residence. Why?

"That will work, sweet Sawyer." I gave him our address, and we ended the call. Standing, I got all the scattered papers together. "Sorry to cut this short, ladies. But I have a babysitting duty.... Wait, what do eleven-year-olds like to do? We have those gaming systems you love, mon amour. Do they color? What do they eat? What time do they go to bed?" I dropped to the seat again as my body twisted with nerves. "I should not have agreed. I know nothing about eleven-year-olds."

"Relax, Henri. You'll do fine. You were a little boy back in the day," Raya said.

"Kids like pizza, ice cream, and cookies," Courtney suggested.

"You can call any of us if you're stressing out. Or reach out to Lucas's parents. You're not alone," Eve told me. I nodded.

Blaze's hand clamped around the back of my neck. "There's nothing you can't do."

I tipped my head back and stared up at him. "Thank you, mon amour." I stood again. "And many thanks to you all. I will reach out if needed."

"Good luck," Wrenley said.

I blew her a kiss, and we said our farewells. I wanted to

make sure the house was tidy and we didn't have any sex toys lying about.

Blowing out a breath, I clasped my sweaty hands together and looked to the clock on the wall again. They should be here any moment, which would leave Sawyer enough time to get to work. Turning to Blaze, who sat on the couch watching me with a slight smile on his lips, I suggested, "You and Sawyer should drive to work together."

His brows rose.

"It would save taking two cars and then I know you'll come home at a decent hour to get some sleep if you have to drop Sawyer back."

"You want me to talk to him?"

"Well, yes. If he will talk to you."

"What happens if he's too scared to get in a car with me?"

I scoffed. "Please, you are not scary, mon amour."

"Others think differently."

"You are big, but you are not the only one. Quake is ginormous too."

He stood, crossing his arms over his chest. "Ginormous?"

I snickered. "You are large, mon amour, and if you cut out the resting bitch face, I am sure Sawyer would be happy to travel with you. Tell him it's for safety."

"How about we see what he's like when he rocks up?"

"Fine." I rolled my eyes. "But—" I heard something outside and headed toward the window. Sawyer climbed out of a small, beat-up car. "They're here," I informed Blaze, rushing up to kiss him and then running to the front door.

I watched their approach through the peephole. Sawyer's brother looked like him a lot. Both had blond hair, slim builds, and were on the smaller side in height. I suspected their eye color matched too. Sawyer had an amazing light blue.

When they grew close, I opened the door and smiled. "Bonjour, Sawyer and brother."

Sawyer gave me a hesitant smile in return. "Hi, Henri. This is Arlo. Arlo, Henri."

The boy glanced up and waved before he looked down again while his other hand tightly held the backpack strap over his shoulder.

"Come in. Make yourself comfortable, Arlo." I stepped aside, and they walked by. After closing the door, I went into the living room where Blaze still stood. "Mon amour, fix your face before you scare them," I warned.

Blaze rolled his eyes but kept looking grumpy like he always did. Just the way I loved him.

"Sawyer, you know my grump. But Arlo, this man is mine, and his name is Blaze."

"Hi, Blaze," Sawyer offered shyly.

Blaze grunted, and when Arlo looked up and up and up, his gaze widened as Blaze tipped his chin, and said, "Hey, kid."

"You're big," Arlo blurted.

"Arlo," Sawyer snapped with a wince. "Sorry."

I laughed. "No need. Blaze is big, Arlo."

Arlo nodded, still watching Blaze.

"Thank you for doing this, Henri."

"It's no problem, chéri. Arlo and I will find some fun. We have all the streaming channels. Well, most I think, and Blaze has some of those video games. Plus, I haven't had pizza in a long time, so I was going to order us some."

"Arlo would like that. Right?" He nudged his brother in the shoulder.

"Yeah. Thanks." He finally looked away from Blaze and down to the floor again.

"He's got some homework to do too," Sawyer said, which made Arlo grumble under his breath.

"I will make sure it gets done." I hoped I knew what Arlo was learning. What grade was he even in? "Sawyer, Blaze thought it would be a good idea—"

"Henri," Blaze bit out, tone scolding.

I sighed. "*I* was thinking it would be easier to go from here to work together since you have to come back to the same destination. It will also help me get mon amour away from those computers at a better hour."

Poor Sawyer looked like a deer caught in headlights.

"Don't have to, kid. No stress."

"No, I, um, I don't mind. It'll save gas." He blushed, probably not meaning to admit that. "Thank you."

But why did he need to save on gas?

From what Blaze said, Sawyer lived in a relatively nice area in a three-bedroom house. His wages could easily cover repayments, if there were any, and all the expenses on top.

There was something we weren't seeing. I glanced to Blaze, and he caught my stare and nodded. Yes, he was suspicious too.

"We'd better go," Blaze announced.

I clapped. "Do not fear, Sawyer. I will take care of your little brother."

Sawyer nodded before he clasped Arlo's shoulder and turned him around. "Be good. I'll be back just after midnight."

"I will," Arlo said softly. Sawyer pulled him into a quick hug and went to stand near the doorway.

Blaze stopped in front of me. He pinched my chin and stared down at me before he ordered, "Be good."

I was no child.

"Mon amour—"

His brow cocked.

Glaring, I snapped, "I am always good when you are not about."

He snorted. "That I believe." He kissed me hard, fingers gripping my hair. When he lifted away, with a final peck, he looked to Arlo and tipped his head my way. "Keep an eye on him."

Since Arlo was already watching wide-eyed, an abrupt laugh escaped him when I harrumphed, and Arlo quickly covered his mouth.

"You are not funny, mon amour."

He smirked. "The kid thinks so."

"He is only being nice." I looked at Sawyer. "Bye, Sawyer."

He smiled with shining eyes. He'd been watching too. "Bye. Thanks again."

A hand clamped to the back of my neck and squeezed before Blaze walked off with a grunt.

Facing Arlo after they left, I grinned. "I will order pizza. What type do you like?"

He shrugged. "Um, ham and cheese?"

"Perfect, I will get that and some garlic bread. You will share with me, oui?"

His head jerked back. "Wee?"

"Sorry, I am French. Oui means yes in my language. Please let me know if I say something you don't understand."

He nodded, looking away and back to me. "Ah, yes to garlic bread, please. And it's cool. The, ah, accent."

"Thank you, sweet boy. We will work out what we're going to do after I order. I won't be long." I quickly slipped out of the room toward the kitchen. I wanted to give him a little time alone to look around without me hovering.

I really hoped this night went well. I already liked Arlo's company.

CHAPTER FIFTEEN

*T*ech snorted beside me at the desk, so I told him, "Fuck off." I already knew what he'd be on my case about.

"Brother, just go home. There ain't much we can do here besides watching the boat's path."

With a grunt, I shook my head and tore my gaze away from the surveillance cameras at home. "We can keep trying to hack the Murphy headquarters again." I already told Tech I wouldn't get Gwen involved with those fuckers. If they ever caught her, I couldn't imagine what they'd do to her. At least Tech and I had the club at our back.

Tech groaned, dropping his head back on his office chair. "Brother, we've tried fifty times already. They're locked up tight. Hell, it's probably for the best to leave it right now. We

"

don't want to get on their radar since we'll be fuckin' with their shipment."

We already had plans set for when we needed to make a move on the ships. The closer the vessels got to land, the better chance Tech and I had at gaining access to their computers, which would confirm their porting destination.

The plan was that we'd head off a few days beforehand to scope out the areas. There'd be two teams. One for each ship since we needed to look at both.

"Brother, we'll get them one way or another," Tech said.

Grunting, I looked back to the monitors. Henri sat on the couch with Arlo. They were talking while watching a movie. I thought Henri was complaining about something, which was making Arlo laugh.

They already got along well. Arlo didn't say much—not that I had audio on the camera—but I hadn't seen his lips move as much as Henri's did. Then again, I did tend to watch Henri more closely than Arlo.

Still, the kid seemed to enjoy everything Henri said; his smile told me that. It really hadn't taken Henri long for Arlo to warm up to him. I think he started hanging off everything Henri said, while beaming, after they'd finished eating. It didn't surprise me. The man was too damn charming. It was just lucky that this time it wouldn't get Henri in trouble, and I wouldn't have to warn anyone away from him.

They were fun to watch, though. Tech knew my attention wasn't on work while I had my own show happening at home.

Hell, I could watch Henri all day, every day.

I only missed listening to all the things he was telling

Arlo. I had to fix that problem. Especially if this was going to happen again with Henri at home and me here.

"Blaze, can I ask you somethin'?" When I grunted, Tech went on, "Would you be pissed with a brother if he was seein' your sister behind your back?"

Shit.

Slowly, I turned to him and raised my brow.

He nodded. "They think I'm fuckin' stupid. But it's goddamn obvious Quake and Eve have somethin' goin' on. I see their looks. It fuckin' pisses me off. He was supposed to be a brother and look out for my sister, not do shit with her." He cringed. "I don't want to know what the fuck they get up to, but I know it's somethin' they're hidin' from me. So, would you be pissed at them?"

Christ. I didn't want to get involved, but Henri did tell me shit, and I didn't want to hold it back from the one man in the club I'd call a close friend. Not that I'd admit it.

Fuck me.

I was going to have to share and talk.

Sighing, I glanced to the monitors, wishing I could go back to watching Henri with Arlo, but I'd be a dick if I ignored Tech.

He groaned, palming his face. "Sorry. I shouldn't've even said anythin'. I guess I just wanted to rant. Don't worry about it."

Grunting, I scratched at my thigh. "Say whatever you want. I listen more than talk."

He chuckled. "Yeah, I can tell."

"Henri talks. A lot."

He smirked. "I've heard."

"He's told me some shit, and I'll share as long as it

doesn't bite me on the ass with Henri." Not that I thought it would, since it wasn't bad. But if Henri found out I talked to Tech about this, he'd relentlessly tease me about gossiping.

And I wasn't.

I just wanted to help the guy out, since he'd never been a dick to me.

"Brother, I won't say shit to anyone," he said.

I nodded once.

All right. Here the fuck I went.

"Henri's mentioned that the only reason they haven't said shit to you is because Eve refuses to call what she and Quake have a relationship. She gets pissy when anyone suggests she's dating Quake. Eve's probably threatened Quake to keep his mouth shut or else whatever they have will end."

Tech's jaw clenched as he stared down at the floor.

With a sigh, I continued, "I get why you'd be cut that Quake didn't say anything, but in a way, he's doing what Eve wants. If you've seen them look at each other, you'd have noticed how damn taken Quake is with Eve. He wants her as his old lady, so he'd do just about anything she asks him to, and that'd include him not saying anything to you. Maybe your sister has commitment issues, which is why she won't say anything to you too."

His gaze was wide when I finished speaking. Probably because I never talked that much.

Still, the guy had to get the fuck over the shock and process what I said.

I could tell he did when his expression smoothed out and then he clipped, "Fuck." He scrubbed a hand down his face. "Eve and me had a shit home life. She thinks if she sticks with one person, they'll eventually grow bored and cheat. Both parents did it to each other. Both showed the hate they held for each other and us in their actions and words. They shared all the twisted shit they did to each other with us. Our rotten mother tried to get Eve into drugs to pimp her out. We were starved, beaten, and...." His jaw clenched again. "Yeah, it wasn't healthy, so that shit is gonna fuck us up somehow. I thought since we got away from them when we were sixteen, we'd heal. But livin' on the streets was a whole new level of fucked-up shit to get through." He shook his head. "Fuck me, you don't need to hear this shit. Anyway, thanks for tellin' me. At least I ain't so pissed with them anymore."

Jesus Christ. I knew they'd had family issues. I just didn't know how bad it had been.

Tech's occasional flinch if he was in the zone on the computer and I moved too quickly made more sense.

"Brother," I said, his gaze shot to me, and once again, it was wider than it'd been. "I—"

He explained the look he'd given me with "You never call me brother."

Hell. He'd noticed. "I ain't a part of the club. You probably shouldn't call me brother either."

"Fuck that. You're club. You just don't wear the patch." He turned back to the computer. "Didn't know me sharing my sob story would get you to call me brother." He smirked over at me.

"Fuck off. I was just respecting the club."

"Appreciate it and you listenin' to me."

"Anytime. And I think Eve will wake up eventually. You can either say something now or wait until they come to you about their history and tell them you already know. Imagine their faces."

Tech grinned. "Yeah, I think I'll do that. But Quake also gets my fist to the face for datin' my sister. Fuckin' prick knows she should've been off-limits."

Snorting, I turned back to the monitors.

"Seriously, brother. Get the fuck home."

"Will do as soon as Sawyer finishes work."

"Shit, that's right. I forgot you brought him in. How was the drive?"

"Silent. The kid fidgeted and looked like he'd be sick if I tried to start a conversation with him."

Tech winced. "Damn. Good luck for the drive home."

Yeah, I reckon it'll go about the same way.

But I also did a little more digging on Sawyer and his brother. Learned they weren't living in the address that was on file. I wasn't sure if me bringing it up on the car ride home would be good or bad. Probably bad, though. I could scare him away from the security he had within Polished. But there could be a chance he might open up to me.

Unless I left it up to Henri. He was the charming one.

I THINNED my lips as I drove down the road. Sawyer looked exhausted. More so than usual. Why was the kid doing this to himself? What was he hiding?

Clearing my throat, I caught him tensing.

Fuck.

I wasn't that scary, right?

"I won't hurt you," I offered.

"I know," he said quickly, wrapping his arms around his stomach.

Fuck it. Guess I'd do a little more opening up for the night since I hated that the kid felt uncomfortable around me. Also, I had a feeling Henri was going to get attached to him and Arlo, which meant I had to at least try to put him at ease.

"First time I met Henri was when I was bleeding out in an alleyway after being shot and beaten."

He gasped, turning to me, but pushing himself into the passenger side door. Likely wasn't the best thing to start with.

I shrugged. "My French firecracker cursed at me and called me a fool when I refused to let him call for help. He could have walked away. But it wasn't in him. He likes to help anyone he can. His heart is big and beautiful. He deserves the fuckin' world, and it's my job to make sure he has everything he wants."

"Why are you telling me this?"

"He took me to his house, patched me up, and looked after me. That was when I fell in love with him. But I fucked up and picked my business over him. When he gifted me with his time again, I made sure I'd do nothing to fuck that up again. I'd do anything he asks of me."

"Blaze—"

"He's worried about you."

Sawyer groaned, as if my words pained him. "He doesn't need to be."

"Don't cut him off from your life. He likes you. Likes Arlo. I can tell already from what I've seen on the cameras."

"Why would I cut him from my life?" he asked softly.

Christ. I hoped I didn't fuck this up. "Henri would do anything for you. Means I would too."

"Why do you think I'll cut him from our life?" he pressed, voice tight with anxiety.

"You're hiding something. I know you don't live where you said. I don't know what you're going through, but Henri and I will do what we can to help. You just gotta reach out to him. Us. I fuckin' hope I didn't screw this up and you run because Henri will make my life hell if I did."

I chanced a glance at him to see he'd dropped his head and tears were dripping onto his lap.

Fuck.

"I ain't saying you have to come to us and spill all the beans now, kid. Just, fuck, please reach out if you need us. We'll do anything to help. Henri's already proved that by having your back."

Sawyer sniffed, swiping at his nose with the back of his hand.

"Did I fuck up, kid?"

He sniffed again and shook his head.

What did I do now?

Henri was gonna kick my ass for making him cry, and I doubted Sawyer would let me go inside on my own to send Arlo out so Henri didn't see how upset the kid was.

I was screwed since I just turned down our street.

"I... just need a little more time. If my plan doesn't work out, I'll talk to Henri."

"You won't up and disappear because I said anything? I

really gotta know so I can keep an eye out for the traps Henri sets, or he'll just straight up kill me in my sleep."

Sawyer snorted but cut it off. "He isn't that bad."

"Kid, you haven't seen Henri on a warpath."

Sawyer's bottom lip trembled, but he bit down on it as he drew in a deep breath through his nose. "We won't disappear," he whispered.

Grunting, I nodded. "Good. You just saved my ass."

I caught him rolling his eyes as I pulled the car into the driveway. He didn't believe me, but it was the truth. Henri would be a terror to me if Sawyer up and left because of something I said. Especially since Henri had been worried about saying something to Sawyer. He hadn't wanted to risk anything.

When we got out of the car, I heard the front door open. Sawyer and I walked around the corner to see a smiling Henri.

His smile dropped, and his brows pinched.

Jesus.

He looked from me to Sawyer to me and back to the kid before scowling at me.

"What did you do?" he demanded viciously.

Sawyer shot wide eyes at me before Henri pulled Sawyer close and tucked him under his arm, walking him into the house.

"Chéri, you tell me what my beast said to you, and I will make sure he regrets upsetting you."

Sawyer's bottom lip trembled again, which Henri caught.

My little firecracker sucked in a breath and turned on me.

In French, he snapped, "I swear if you have done something to make him vanish on me, I will hold back my body for the rest of our lives. No, I will... I don't know right now because I am so angry, but it'll be something drastic and mean."

I snorted. He didn't have a mean bone in his body, and he was only lashing out now because he saw Sawyer upset and wanted to protect him. Even from me. Even when he knew I wouldn't have done anything on purpose. Henri was just overwhelmed with worry and said shit he didn't think about.

"Firecracker, take a breath."

His gaze glowed with fury. "Take a breath, mon amour? Take a breath? I will take your balls—" He quickly cut himself off and turned to Sawyer, but Arlo was also there peeking around the corner. "Come, my children. It's time for bed."

Huh?

His children?

Bed?

"Sawyer, Henri said we could have a sleepover because he knew you'd be tired. We have to share a bed, but that's okay. We do it at home anyway."

"I can drive," Sawyer said quickly, as if he was trying to get his brother to stop talking. His cheeks flushed a little.

"Non, you will sleep here, and it will save Arlo going out into the cold night air. Then, in the morning, no matter what time everyone wakes, we will make pancakes and waffles." He curled his arm around Sawyer's shoulders and started to move them toward the spare room.

"Henri," I clipped.

He paused, sighed, and quickly rushed over to give me a kiss. "Welcome home, mon amour."

I cupped the back of his neck but asked Sawyer, "Kid, let Henri know how I made you cry."

"From being nice. I... I'm not used to people wanting to help. But I'm okay now," he said and then added softly, "We won't disappear."

Henri's gaze ran over my face as his own eyes misted. "I suppose I was hasty in my actions."

"Like always, but I wouldn't want you any other way."

He grinned. "I am glad, mon amour, because you are stuck with me."

"Now maybe ask Sawyer if he actually wants to stay."

Henri nodded and spun around to face the boys. "Sawyer, if you agree, I would very much like for you and Arlo to sleep in the spare room. I have a towel and some of my spare clothes in the bathroom already for you. However, I understand if you wish to go home."

Sawyer smiled and glanced to his brother who said, "Please, Sawyer. Waffles *and* pancakes."

The kid didn't have a chance. Henri had already won Arlo over, and Sawyer had already warmed to Henri when he'd started at Polished.

He wouldn't want to disappoint Henri.

Which was why he said, "Okay. Just tonight."

Arlo and Henri cheered, and they rushed off while Sawyer looked back to me. "Thanks for saying something, and... I haven't seen Arlo this happy in a long time. I've tried my best but...."

I stepped up to him and gripped his shoulder. "Kid, I'm sure you're doing the best you can in whatever circumstance you have. Just remember, you have other people who want to be in your life and help."

He nodded, gaze dropping to the floor, and I heard him sniff again. "It's hard to rely on people."

"Yeah, I can understand that."

Suddenly, he offered me a small smile before he said, "I better not cry anymore, or I worry Henri will kill you."

Chuckling, I nodded. "Now you're getting it."

CHAPTER SIXTEEN

I walked into the café and waved to West, Lucas, and Adrick. Gun followed me since we had come together from my place. Blaze had the poor man staying with me while he was away, staking out the port in Los Angeles. He'd left a couple of days ago with Torch, Wreck, Quake, State, Saint, Loyal, and a few other club members. Country had gone to the Mexico port about a week ago with Tech, Death, Rule, Boss, Chaos, Boomer and their team.

As we weaved through the tables to our friends, I pushed my worry for Blaze down. He could take care of himself. All the brothers who were there were capable too. They would also have one another's backs. But knowing it didn't stop my rising concern and make my stomach stop twisting anxiously.

Still, I would keep praying that everything would go

smoothly, and they could save the kidnapped people without anyone getting hurt.

So, I plastered a smile on my face and called, "Bonjour."

West and Lucas beamed over at Gun and me, but Adrick only tipped his chin up, which was exactly what Blaze would have done. It had my smile turning real.

"Who would be a gem and grab me a coffee and treat?" I asked, taking a seat with a sigh. "I am exhausted."

Gun snorted. "I'll get it. What do you want?"

"The biggest cookie there is, any flavor, and a black coffee with two sugars." I went to hand him my card, but he waved me off. "Thank you, chéri," I called as he walked away.

"I will get you something, West," Adrick said before leaving.

Lucas let out a frustrated noise. "I can't pick what I want. I'll make up my mind at the last second." Lucas stood and moved toward the line at the registers.

That left West and me. He cocked his head to the side. "How're you holding up?"

I gave him a tight-lipped smile and a shrug. "I'll be fine as soon as he's home. As soon as all of them are." But mostly the man I couldn't live without.

Fear clogged my throat. I quickly looked away and swallowed thickly.

West's hand closed over mine on the table. "He'll be okay."

Tears welled, but I blew out a breath and swiped at my face, then waved a hand around. "I know he will or else he has me to deal with."

He promised me he would take care of himself.

"I'm sure he wouldn't want your wrath."

"Very true, sweet West."

"I'm going to slip to the bathroom quickly. Be back." He caught Adrick's attention when he stood, knowing he would need to tell his husband where he was going, so he pointed toward the back of the café. Adrick tipped his chin up, and since there was still a line to the register, he watched West move all the way to the bathroom.

Drawing in a deep breath, I shifted my gaze out the window.

The day was overcast, the darker day matching my mood. I had thought this catch-up to talk about the Playhouse would take my mind off things, but I doubted it would. Not when Blaze was a constant thought.

It was then a person caught my attention, and I snapped my spine straight. "Sawyer," I muttered.

I noticed Sawyer frantically looking around from where he stood across the road. I rushed to the front door and out it.

Besides at work, Blaze and I had seen Sawyer and Arlo one other time when I organized another sleepover.

When they weren't around, I missed their company and had told Blaze we should have them over more often. They were such sweet boys, who seemed to like our company too.

Of course, Blaze agreed since he'd never go against my wishes, but I also had a feeling my big, beautiful beast had a soft spot for them as well. It was why he had pushed Sawyer the first night they drove home together. I was grateful it had worked. Sawyer hadn't shared his secrets, but he was becoming comfortable around us.

"Sawyer," I called.

His gaze swung my way. I saw his mouth move over my name and the clear panic in his wide eyes.

I put my hand up, pressing down on the air, and mouthed, "Wait there." Looking both ways, I raced across the busy road when it was clear. Thankfully, Sawyer had stayed where he was.

When I grew close, he grabbed my wrist. "Henri, I-I don't know what's going on."

"Talk to me, chéri." I looked back to the cafe and saw Gun and Adrick coming out the door, eyes on us.

"I went to Polished since I forgot my wallet and... I don't know. I'm getting a feeling of being watched again. I only stopped here to test it out and so they didn't follow me home. That's *if* I'm even being followed." Agitated, he growled under his breath.

"It's okay, chéri." I curled an arm around his waist and moved us to the edge of the footpath to cross the road again. "I have friends across the street. They can help. We will figure this out."

He nodded and drew in a deep breath.

There was a screech just as a van stopped in front of us and the side door opened. "Take the blond one," someone shouted.

"Non!" I screamed, my voice cracking with fear, as three masked figures exploded from the van and closed in on us.

Shouts rang out—Gun. Adrick.

One of the masked men yanked Sawyer from my arms. "No! Let him go." I clawed, punched, kicked, doing anything—everything—to stop him. My fists hit fabric and bone; I didn't care what. The man dragged Sawyer toward the van, and I threw myself at him, wild and desperate.

"Grab him too. We gotta go!"

Then strong arms grabbed me and lifted me. I thrashed and screamed, but I was slammed into the back like a sack of nothing. The door clanged shut behind us, and the van lurched into motion.

Heart pounding like a drumbeat in my throat, I scrambled across the freezing metal floor to where Sawyer lay trembling. I pulled him up and into my arms, curling around his small, shaking body, shielding him the only way I could.

He whimpered, the sound soft and broken. I bit down on a sob and clenched my jaw, fury and terror tangling in my chest.

"What do you want?" I demanded, tipping my chin up in defiance.

"Shut up," one snarled. He looked toward the front to the driver. "At least the extra guy has an accent. Even though he isn't in the age bracket, I reckon someone will buy him." The other two in the back snickered.

"Good. At least we didn't fuck up grabbing him too, then," the driver replied.

Obviously, they were the ones watching Sawyer. They were there to kidnap him.

My body froze.

Were these men involved with the people in charge of those ships? What was going to become of Sawyer and me?

"Do you know who our friends are? You need to let us go" I warned. He lunged at me, slapping me across the face, and I cried out. The sharp sting had me gasping, but only made my fury burn brighter.

"Shut up," he snarled.

Fucking fool. They didn't know who our people were,

but they would, and I looked forward to Blaze getting his hands on them.

Blaze.

God, was it crazy of me to wish these men were actually involved with those ships and they were taking us to the port where Blaze and the others would be?

"Henri," Sawyer whispered, touching my cheek. The music coming from the front of the van would hopefully keep our soft words from prying ears.

I took his hand in mine, ignoring the sting to my flesh, and smiled at him. "I am fine, chéri."

"I'm sorry they took you—"

Shaking my head, I hugged him tighter to me. "Non, I am glad I am here with you." I leaned closer to his ear. "I was with Gun. He will follow. We will get help. We just have to hold on."

He nodded.

"Besides, you know my Blaze. He will tear the world apart to get me back."

GUN

"FUCK," I yelled. Grabbing Adrick's arm, I shoved him toward the café and ordered, "Go get Lucas and West. I want us in my car in seconds, hear?"

"Da." He disappeared as I watched what way the van went.

As soon as I heard the others, I raced toward my car, cursing at my leg for the ache.

I got in behind the wheel, started the car, and held out my phone to Adrick. "Call him."

"Nyet," he said, and pushed the phone back at me.

I threw it to his lap and pulled out. "I'm drivin', dickhead. Call Blaze."

He sighed as I weaved out of the cars, trying to gain the time back. I was sure I could see the white van up ahead. At least I damn well prayed it was the right one.

"Nyet, this is Adrick. Your French man was ripped off the streets and kidnapped. They—"

"What the fuck?" was roared through the line.

"Exactly what I said,' Adrick said.

Fuckin' hell.

"Adrick," West snapped.

Someone reached between me and Adrick and took the phone. "Blaze, this is Lucas. Henri left the cafe when he saw Sawyer. The kid looked scared about something. Before we could get to them, a white van pulled up and loaded them in. We're currently following the vehicle."

Lucas cried out when I made a rough turn and again when I hit the brakes.

The van had vanished.

Fuck no.

No, no, no.

"Christ," I clipped before I moved slowly along the quiet street, looking down every alleyway.

"What? Oh, hey, honey. No, Gun wouldn't take me into

danger." There was a pause, and Lucas tapped me on the shoulder. "Wade wants to talk to you."

Lucas was married to Wreck, a brother in the club, and any other time I'd let him give me what for but not now.

"Where is van?" Adrick asked.

I grabbed the phone and put it on speaker. "Eyes on everythin', guys," I ordered. "Wreck—"

"What the fuck're you thinkin'—"

"Listen, I don't have time for your tantrum. Lucas is safe. Henri and Sawyer aren't. I lost the fuckin' van, Wreck."

When the line went silent, I knew he'd figured Blaze was gonna lose his shit even more.

"Did you get anythin' on the van?"

"Number plate."

"Call Tech. He's on a plane right now, but he should answer. Mexico ship arrived early. It was just guns, no people, so they're headed to us. Get Tech to run the number. But if you can't reach him, call Jones. He's around this place somewhere. The cop won't be able to look it up, but he might know someone who can help."

Run to a brother first before someone outside the club, got it.

"Will do," I answered.

"This ain't on you, brother."

I shook my head. "I shoulda been faster."

"It ain't on you."

"Let's fuckin' pray these are the same guys as the ones the club's hittin' today and this van is travelin' your and Blaze's way, and it ain't just some coincidence."

Wreck grunted. "If they are comin', means it'll take them four hours to get here."

"Your ship still lookin' to port sometime today?" I asked.

"Yeah, probably around the same time the van gets here. Could mean a quick port to load up more people and then go again."

"Fuck. I've got everythin' crossed we're right and they're connected." That was the best-case scenario, because if these cunts in the van were just randoms, and I'd lost them.... My gut twisted painfully at the possibility.

"Same, brother. Keep us posted if you get anythin'. I'll tell Blaze.... Hell, I don't know.... Torch is talking him down at the moment, but I ain't sure how long that'll last."

"Good luck," I said and hung up, before throwing the phone to the center console. "Anyone see anything?"

"Nyet."

"No," West said.

"Nothing," Lucas added.

"Right." I parked the car. "Adrick, you're drivin' while I make some calls." I got out and swapped with the Russian. When I was belted up, I told him, "Start headin' toward Los Angeles."

And let's fuckin' beg all the gods above that we're on the right track.

CHAPTER SEVENTEEN

HENRI

I considered checking to see if the door we leaned against was unlocked since we were so close. But if it was, the fall could kill us at the speed they were going. So instead, I stayed still and silent, watching the men staring at us. Even with the gaps in the masks at their eyes and mouth, I could tell two had indifferent, almost bored expressions, but the one who had slapped me scowled at Sawyer and me.

He may as well have a big red sign above his head that flashed homophobic. Unless he was one of those who pretended to despise us but really wanted to fuck us.

Either way, I could see the hate clear in his gaze. He wanted to hit me again.

Sawyer shifted against me. "What will they do?" he whispered.

Rubbing up and down his back, I told him softly, "I do not know, chéri."

I wished I had answers I could share to help ease him, but I didn't. Not when we weren't allowed to ask questions.

"Do you see the car anywhere?" the driver asked.

The passenger replied, "No. I think we lost them."

My heart sank along with my stomach. The only car that would follow would be Adrick or Gun or both.

"Henri," Sawyer muttered, fear tightening his tone.

Louder, I told him, "It's all right, chéri." I wanted to see if they would give any information away, and one fell right into my trap.

Evil Eyes snorted. "No, it won't be. Not where you two will be going."

"Greg, shut up," the driver clipped.

Greg reached through the gap and smacked the driver upside the head. "Don't use names, fuckface."

One of the others in the back laughed. "Not like they've got anyone to tell. We'll dump them off like the last ones and won't see them again."

"Maybe we should have some fun with them first." Greg's suggestion had my skin crawling. Sawyer tucked in on himself next to me.

"We don't touch," the driver said.

"Come on. Not like they're not used already. One's a hooker, and I bet the French fucker has been taking shit up his ass for decades."

"No," the driver snarled.

"You're not the boss of me," Greg bit back.

"Both of you quit it," the passenger barked. "Greg, you've never wanted to touch one before, so why now? The pretty boys getting the best of you? You wanna screw them in the ass like some fag?"

Greg dove for the passenger, but the other two pulled him back.

"Enough," the driver roared. "If I crash this car from all this shit going on, and that kid doesn't get on that fucking ship, his buyer will come after us. Any of you want that?"

"Let's hope the kid's buyer will pick up the other one too. Even though he's a bit older and wasn't on the website."

So, the person wanting Sawyer had found him on the Polished website.

Wait....

Ship.

The guy said ship.

Oh my God. We really were headed in the direction of my beast.

No, wait, we could be taken to the other port in Mexico. Which way were we traveling? I couldn't see anything. There were no windows except up the front, but that didn't give me any clues.

No matter, Sawyer and I had people we trusted at both destinations.

My heart galloped with hope. We would be safe eventually.

"What the fuck are you smiling for?" Greg snapped at me.

I quickly wiped my grin off and shook my head.

When the asshole started talking with one of the others, I rested my cheek to Sawyer's head to tell him with confidence, "Everything *will* be okay."

He tipped his head back, and I nodded.

"Okay, Henri," he whispered, leaning back into me.

In a way, it was probably best if we were headed to Mexico and away from Blaze because I knew from the sting to my cheek, I would be marked. If Blaze saw that, God help anyone who got in his way.

I wanted him safe like he wanted me. But I feared he would put himself in danger to retaliate against the man who marred my skin.

So yes, Mexico would be better.

Still, for now, we just had to keep still and quiet. I really didn't trust the look in Greg's eyes since it'd shifted from hate to hunger, which was now directed at Sawyer.

If Greg ignored the driver's warning and tried anything, I would go full papa bear on that bastard to make sure Sawyer stayed protected.

"How long we got?" someone asked.

"Roughly three hours still."

Three hours.

Three hours meant our destination would be the port in LA.

Where my beast was.

My pulse raced in worry and excitement.

Mon amour will know what to do.

Blaze would take care of everything. And I would take care of him.

Blowing out a quiet breath, I leaned my head back and closed my eyes.

Please let this end smoothly. Please watch over Sawyer and Blaze.

I needed my beast in my life and at our home, not locked up in jail.

Sawyer shifted against me. I wound my arms around him and held on tight. This poor boy. He already had enough done to him. My blood boiled that there were people who wished to capture him because of his looks. People wanted to use him, own him, and none of it was in a good way like my beast did me.

They wanted to ruin him.

He needed protection. He needed security in the form of people who cared for him and his well-being. He held the weight of the world on his eighteen-year-old shoulders, and it wasn't fair.

No one at his age should be working the hours he did. Should be the sole carer for their brother. He shouldn't have to be the adult and live a life where he wasn't able to go out to have fun and enjoy his prime age.

"Henri," he whispered.

"Oui, chéri?" I brushed over his hair with my hand.

"Our parents died when I turned eighteen. I have full custody of Arlo. They had debt up to their ears but also loan sharks wanting payments. I sold the house to pay off what I could and moved us into a terrible area, but we have a good neighbor. Miss Cora helps me with Arlo when I'm working. Still, there's people always wanting money. It's never-ending...." He swallowed thickly and sniffed. "I-If I don't get back to Arlo, they'll take him. They'll hurt our neighbor. The only reason they've left us alone is because I give them most of my wages. But if I'm not there...."

"Shh, chéri, we will get you home to Arlo. By nightfall, you will be with him, I promise."

I really did have that much faith in Blaze and the Diamond MC brothers.

Only what Sawyer didn't know was that our help wouldn't stop at this situation. Somehow Blaze and I were going to get him and Arlo out of this debt.

"How can you promise that?"

I ducked close to his ear and whispered, "Because I believe in my Blaze. He will save us, chéri."

He gasped, lifted his head to look at me. "Really?"

"Oui."

The music cut off as Sawyer cried out when he was suddenly yanked away and dragged by his ankle down toward Greg. "What the fuck are you two whispering about?"

Sawyer struggled, but Greg climbed over him, holding Sawyer to the filthy, cold floor.

I launched myself that way, pushing at his shoulders. "Get off, get off. Leave him alone. Stop touching him." I punched and pushed at him.

Greg backhanded me hard enough I dropped to my side. Black spots danced in front of me. Ignoring the pain, I got up and pushed at Greg again. "Move."

"Greg, get the fuck off him," the driver yelled.

The other two in the back drew close. One said, "Come on, man. I don't want to have to deal with his buyer."

Greg shoved off Sawyer and moved toward the front while Sawyer scrambled my way. I pulled him to the back until we were pressed into the corner of the van.

Sawyer near buried himself inside me, and I held him tightly.

"It's okay. You're all right, chéri."

He nodded against my chest as he shook against me.

"I have you, Sawyer. I have you."

We would get through this.

"You got hit again," he uttered.

"Shh, don't worry about it. We will get out of this. We just have to be good and wait."

I hated violence, but I understood it. I knew some people only responded to violence.

And then there were the people who deserved it. Greg was one of those people. He would get what was coming to him.

We only had to deal with him for a few more hours and then he would see what it was like to fear someone.

I doubted he had ever had to worry about another person in his life. He would have been the bully. But Blaze would make sure he feared him.

My beast was coming for him, and I could not have been happier to know this man would get what was deserved.

Maybe that made me a bad person. But seriously, some people needed to be punched. Like right now, he glared down at us—watching and waiting for us to act up so he could touch Sawyer again.

The man's fists clenched and unclenched as he stared while ignoring the other men trying to talk to him about something.

I wanted to smile again. I wanted to crow in delight knowing Blaze would make him pay. And I wasn't even sure if I wanted to stop my beast from going too far.

That look in Greg's eyes, the sneer on his lips, had me thinking that if he was allowed to touch Sawyer, it would cause nothing but pain.

All of them in this van were bad people. After all, they kidnapped people for monsters who were willing to buy humans.

But at least this time they wouldn't get away with it.

CHAPTER EIGHTEEN

rubbed at my chest again as I paced behind a fucking shipping container at the port. The ache wouldn't quit. My heart was going to explode.

Henri had been taken.

Sawyer too.

He was just a kid, and Henri was my damn world.

Sawyer meant something to Henri, so of fucking course he'd go with him. He'd probably jumped into the van right after the kid. Didn't want Sawyer to deal with anything on his own.

I couldn't blame him for doing it. I would have done the same. We were both protectors.

But goddamn motherfucking hell, this terror coating my insides was gonna end me. I was gonna lose myself, and the only way to stop that was to have Henri in my arms. To have his scent clogging my senses. To have his words calming me.

But he'd been taken.

And since Sawyer meant something to Henri, he did to me too.

Both had been snatched.

Fuck me.

Fuckin' hell.

I wanted to spew.

No one knew where they were. They'd lost the goddamn van. How the hell did they lose it?

Crouching, I dropped my head and inhaled deeply through my nose.

Henri's smiling face flashed through my mind.

Another flash, but worse, and it was of Henri with blood coating him.

"Brother."

I stood, pulling my upper lip back and snarling over my shoulder. "Fuck off."

Torch moved into my space anyway. "I know what you're feelin'." Yeah, but when Wrenley got taken, at least he'd been with her. "You wanna leave, I'll back you all the fuckin' way and come with you. But, like I said, Tech reckons the cunts that took them are headed here. To the boat we're waitin' on."

"Tech's not certain," I bit out. I needed him to be sure, because if I stood around wasting time where I could have been looking for Henri, then I'd lose my shit in a worse kind of way.

"Brother, Tech wouldn't fuck around when Henri's at stake. He knows Henri means everythin' to you. Just wait a bit longer. The boat will port in the next few."

Fuck.

Christ!

Wait. Wait. Wait.

My gaze landed on Quake talking with Loyal, who was glaring at the ground and gripping the top of his head. Maybe he was feeling like I was since Sawyer had been taken and Loyal had a thing for the kid.

I would've talked with him, but I couldn't fucking offer anything when I was a jittery and stressed-out mess myself. Thank fuck, he at least had Quake.

I stared back at Torch. "Henri better be fuckin' coming this way," I warned and started pacing again.

"Yo" I heard from down the other end of the container. Country and the other brothers had arrived. Just in time.

Maybe I could slip away, get to a computer, and—

"Blaze," Tech called as he approached, waving his iPad around. "The van with the same plate just got pinged on a camera close by. They've got to be comin' here."

Stopping, I demanded, "You're certain?"

"Yeah." He nodded. "I reckon they're gonna try and get Henri and Sawyer on the boat."

Country approached. "You cool?"

"You fuckin' asking that for real?"

His jaw clenched. "I know you ain't, but I gotta know if you're gonna run off on your own and ruin this whole fuckin' thing. All I'm askin' is for you to try to keep your head on straight. We'll get these cunts. They'll pay for even thinkin' of touchin' Henri."

I nodded stiffly before Country walked off again.

Really, I'd try to keep my damn cool. For Henri.

"Any footage from the ship?" Torch asked Tech.

"Just shows masked men gettin' around on board. No sign of the taken, but there's a shipping container of interest. One where the men keep disappearing into with water and food."

"We aim for that container then," I said.

Tech nodded, gazing down at his iPad. "That's what Country said. But we'll have to get through at least three dozen men first."

"We'll do it." Torch grinned.

I ground my teeth together, wishing I had something to punch now. "Are you keeping an eye on the van?"

He showed me his screen. It was split with multiple traffic cameras. "I'll have them as soon as they're close. There's a camera at the front entrance to this docking yard. I'm connected to that too. You'll be the first to know about their approach."

"But," Torch started, "we're gonna keep in control until we can get Henri and Sawyer away safely."

Glaring, I snarled, "Like I'd fuckin' risk their lives."

"State and Saint are down the front too. They're questionin' some people who run this joint. Obvious there've been some payoffs for a boat that size to travel undetected from Australia to here," Tech said. He was probably just talking to take my mind off things, but there was nothing stopping me from thinking about Henri and Sawyer stuck in a fucking van with the people who nabbed them off the streets.

What were they doing to them?

It was bad enough they touched them to get them in the

van. That action alone signed their death warrants. But would they do something else to them?

"I'd say there were a lot of people paid off to look the other way," Torch added. I could feel his gaze burning into me. Studying me.

My goddamn insides felt like they were being flayed open. Bile rose, but I swallowed that shit down. I couldn't crack. I couldn't let my body get the better of me.

I had to lock it all the fuck down. Henri needed me.

I had to have a clear head and let the anguish burn into fury.

They would fucking pay for touching him.

For touching Sawyer.

My hands itched to start breaking bones. And I wanted every damn finger on their hands snapped. Hopefully I'd have time to do it slowly. I wanted to see the pain in their eyes, hear the fear in their cries.

But if I didn't have time, I'd make sure they couldn't breathe the same air as Henri again.

Tech hummed. "Yeah, true. Look at this place. Usually, I'd say it'd be busy with workers, but it's like everyone's got the day off."

"Even if that's the case," Torch said, "where's Murphy's people at? Why aren't they here guardin' the area for their shipment?"

"Maybe they really are here for a quick pickup and won't even step foot off the boat," Tech thought aloud. "As long as they've paid the employees and harbor control, this is an easy stop for them."

"Fuckin' Murphys. People are too scared to go against them."

Tech snorted. "But we're not."

I didn't give a fuck what they were saying or anything about the Murphys. I wanted Henri here. I wanted the van to pull in so I could start destroying those motherfuckers.

"Saint and State will get answers from the employees at least," Tech said.

A sharp whistle sounded. We all looked down to the other end of the shipping container. Country waved us their way. Tech quickly looked at his screen and said, "Ship's docking. We gotta move. It's pulling in five containers down," Tech said.

I stretched my neck, cracking the tension.

Torch pulled a knife free and smiled at the ground. He tapped his knuckles against his temple. His switch had been flipped, and he was ready to take lives to protect the unfortunate and the brotherhood around him.

In a lot of ways, I was like Torch, only my switch was always on.

Stealthily, we crept down between the containers. I was behind Tech, Torch at my back. It wasn't hard to guess that Country or Death had ordered Torch to keep on me. He was the only crazy one who'd go against me like I had him when he lost it.

Christ, Henri had ripped me a new one after I'd fought with Torch.

Henri.

Fuck.

My throat thickened.

Tech suddenly stopped and turned to me, gaze wide.

"What?" I demanded.

"The van just arrived."

My heart hammered and blood raced.

Country moved close with a phone to his ear. "Yeah, watch them. Make sure they don't signal the drivers in any way. Text when the van passes through checkpoint. Shit's about to get real." He hung up. "That was State. The owners were paid off with an excessive amount of money to get rid of their employees for the day while they manned the entrance and looked the other fuckin' way when they got a delivery of people. Saint and State will stay with them." His hard gaze locked with mine. "We stay hidden and quiet until we know we can get Henri and Sawyer without anyone gettin' hurt. Even if we have to wait until they're on the boat and safely locked into one of those containers before we take control. Hear?"

"I fuckin' hear," I clipped.

Country sighed. "Know how you're feelin', brother. But know we're right here with you."

I swallowed hard and nodded. I'd think about why he was suddenly calling me brother later.

Country turned, and the brothers parted for him to get close to the edge. I stayed behind him. I needed the perfect view of the van arriving.

I had to see Henri. Had to make sure he and Sawyer were all right.

Henri had better fucking be okay.

Torch was close at my back. Almost breathing down my neck if he were a bit taller.

"Loyal. If Torch's attention switches, you're on Blaze duty," Country said.

Fucking hell. Another babysitter.

I could feel the gazes of other brothers on me. Like I was

a rabid animal ready to attack anyone. Quake and Wreck, the biggest out of the brothers, got close to my side. They were ready to take me to the ground if I tried anything stupid.

Let us just pray that no one had harmed Henri or Sawyer.

My heart lodged in my throat when I heard the van's approach.

Everyone stayed silent.

We wouldn't see them drive by since we had to peek around the damn corner of the shipping container to see what was happening. But we all listened to the brakes screech when they pulled to a stop.

Country glanced over as he thumbed at him and me and then around the heaping metal. He knew I'd be looking no matter what he said. Any of the guys there would be the same when it came to the one they loved in trouble.

I needed my eyes on him.

Country crouched and peeked around. I hovered over him and looked.

My jaw clenched when the back of the van opened. Two masked men climbed out while the passenger and driver up front got out, slamming their doors shut after them.

"Get the fuck out," one of the dead men ordered.

Sawyer appeared first. A guy roughly grabbed his arms and yanked him from the back. Sawyer cringed, tugging his arm away from the guy's grip before moving closer to the van door again.

He reached out, and a slim hand slipped into Sawyer's.

Henri.

He jolted forward and yelped when someone in the van behind him kicked at his back.

Fury washed over me. Hands landed on my shoulders, holding me in place.

His cheek was marked. Someone had touched him. Hurt him.

The man climbed out. "Stupid fucks."

Guns were drawn by two of them and pointed at my firecracker and Sawyer.

One waved the gun to the side. "Move to the ship and don't try to escape, or we'll shoot."

I wanted to run out there and shoot them all, but it was a risk I wouldn't take.

CHAPTER NINETEEN

Blaze was hiding somewhere around here. That was all that ran through my mind as we boarded the large cargo ship. More armed masked men greeted the ones with us when we stepped onto the deck. While the driver stayed back to talk, one of the boat's men joined our group as Greg shoved Sawyer and me forward.

"Move," Greg snapped.

I clutched Sawyer's hand tightly in mine as we made our way through the passageways the cargo containers made on the ship. The containers towered over us with two high, and there were so many of them, intimidatingly so.

Blaze was here. He'd save us.

We wouldn't be on here for long.

Everything would be all right.

Just breathe.

Mon amour will be growling at me in no time.

God, how I wished it was now.

He was going to be huffing and puffing at me like a dragon for being taken in the first place, but I would allow it because his words would be out of fear. He could spew fire all over me as long as he stayed safe in return, and that included staying out of jail.

"Left. Hurry up," Greg snarled, shoving at my back again. I stumbled forward, and if it wasn't for Sawyer, I would have fallen.

I clenched my teeth, glaring over my shoulder at him. He smirked.

We stepped into an open square area with containers surrounding it, except where we had walked through. It was like a little courtyard. My stomach dropped when I saw two other armed masked men standing near one of the cargo doors.

"Stop," Greg ordered.

The boat crew watched us as their friend stepped forward with keys to unlock the large red door. He pulled both sides open for Greg to push Sawyer and me in.

I turned to see Greg grinning. "Enjoy your life, faggots." He turned and walked away with the men he'd come with, leaving only the boat crew behind. Three of them, and they were going to lock us in.

The door started to close, but someone from deep within the container called out with an Australian accent, "Hey, hi, hello. Can I use the toilet, pretty please? I really need to go, and I don't want to pee in here." A young woman approached. I moved Sawyer out of the way. He pressed up against the inside wall, and I stood in front of him. The woman looked grimy with long, matted dark hair, big eyes, yet she was still smiling.

"Stop. No break," one guy barked, pointing a gun at her. "Stay back."

Another woman and man stepped out of the shadows from within, coming up behind her.

The woman who spoke thumbed over her shoulder to the others. "I know it's early for a toilet break, but we really gotta go. We'll be good."

Before he could respond, she was in motion.

In one fluid move, her arm shot out, grabbing his wrist. With a twist of her body, she spun him around, using his momentum against him. Her foot slammed into his back, sending him stumbling straight into the man and woman behind her.

They were ready.

In a blur, they disarmed him—one wrenching the weapon from his hands, the other tackling him to the ground. He didn't even have time to shout before he was pinned.

The small woman—faster than anyone had a right to be—was already moving. Like a streak of lightning, she charged the two remaining guards.

"Stop! I'll shoot," one of them shouted, panic edging his voice.

She didn't break stride. She sprang at him, climbing his body like a jungle gym—one foot on his thigh, the other on his chest. Then her leg snapped around his neck, and with a powerful arch of her back, she flipped him off his feet and drove him into the metal floor. He hit the ground hard, choking and flailing as her leg cinched tighter around his throat like a vise.

The last man took a step forward, gun trembling.

She looked up at him, expression unreadable. "I don't want to shoot you," she said, breath calm, voice steady. "Drop your weapon."

"Get off him! Stand down!" he barked back, his finger tightening on the trigger.

The man trapped beneath her thrashed wildly—clawing, slapping at her thigh, his face reddening. She didn't flinch. Didn't so much as blink.

"I said drop it," she repeated, her voice colder now.

She let out a soft, almost regretful sigh. Then, without a word, she pressed her palm against her own leg, tightening the chokehold. The man beneath her bucked once... then went still.

Unconscious or worse.

In the same motion, she reached down and retrieved his blade, yanking it free from the sheath at his hip. With barely a flick of her wrist, the knife spun through the air and sank into the final man's hand.

He screamed, the gun dropping from his grip as he clutched his bleeding palm.

"Stay still, please," she said, rising fluidly to her feet with the unconscious man's gun in her hand trained on the only threat left. "Cal, take his weapon and watch him."

The man nodded and moved quickly, stepping over the fallen guard as he obeyed.

BANG. BANG. BANG.

Over and over, shots were fired, and screams started from deeper within the container.

The badass woman's face pinched with panic. "We need to leave. Cal, Jenny, round everyone up."

"Wait," I called. Taking Sawyer's hand, I rushed to her. "That will be my family. My man, he was here hiding with the Diamond MC and—"

"Get the fuck outta here. The Diamond MC? I've heard of them. I overheard my dad talking about our club doing a favor for yours."

I gaped. "Romania?"

She smiled. "Rommy for short. Oh wow, oh wow, is that why you guys are here? Did Dad call in a favor to help me? Aww, that's the sweetest thing."

"Oui, chéri. Our family was already here to help everyone when Sawyer and I, Henri"—I touched my chest—"were taken."

"I like your accent. French, right? I've always wanted to learn it." She smacked her palm to her forehead. "But now's not the time to talk about it. Will your guys be easy to notice?"

"Oui, they won't wear masks and will have the biker vests on. Except my man, Blaze, he's a really big man and probably the one going crazy on the kidnappers."

She laughed. "Cool, cool. I'm gonna go see how things are traveling. See if they need help." She checked the gun for bullets. "How about you all stay here and watch these idiots?" She kicked out at the guard on the ground. "He's still out. Good. I'll bring your guy back?"

She was like an energetic puppy.

"Oh, oui. Thank you."

"You got it." She turned to the other two, who were now armed and standing over the ship crew and smiled. "We're getting out of here. Yay!" After that, she took off running. At least Blaze and the brothers already knew what she looked like from the photo her family sent. I hadn't seen it because I didn't think I would be here in this situation.

Facing Sawyer, I cupped his cheeks. "Are you all right?"

He threw his arms around me and hugged me. "T-Thank you, Henri."

"Anything for you, chéri."

When I heard the hostages from within move closer, I turned us to face about fifty others. I gasped. Sawyer pulled his face out of my chest to see.

He breathed, "Oh my God."

I looked at the man, Cal, who had helped Rommy. "Will Rommy be all right?" She could obviously handle herself, but there were a lot more people out there.

He smirked from where he stood with a gun pointed down at the enemy. "Yeah. She'll be fine. She's been waiting for this day to come. Kept training in the small quarters here to stay strong."

Thank God.

Then I called, "Is anyone hurt?"

Another attractive, small woman stepped forward. "Physically... maybe dehydrated, hungry, and dirty, but mentally...." She shrugged. "It'll take a while."

Someone else moved closer, and in another Australian accent, they asked, "Is it really your family out there fighting to save us?"

I curled Sawyer under my arm and into my side. "Oui. They will make sure we are all safe before coming to get us."

Murmurs started, some began crying, and there were many looks of relief.

We all waited and listened, and finally, the noise beyond stopped. I shifted Sawyer and I around to watch the gap between the containers.

A few moments later, I heard, "Don't worry, big man, he's just down here. Once you see he's fine, you can settle down."

"Hot damn, you're just as big as Blaze, aren't you?" She cackled and skipped through first. She turned back and waved her hand our way. "See, all safe."

A scowling Blaze, who was covered in blood, stomped through. Thankfully none of the splatters seemed to be coming from within his body. Behind him was a scowling Loyal and a concerned Quake, and both were just as messy. But Rommy didn't have a drop on her.

Blaze stopped. His gaze ran over every inch of me, pausing on my cheek. His jaw clenched.

"So," Rommy drew out. "Is this standoff normal?"

Quake snorted. "Give them a moment."

"Mon amour?"

His jaw clenched again, but he unlocked it to order, "Here. Now."

My heart stumbled, but I grinned and took off running. He needed me to calm him down and didn't want to get close to the victims in case they were scared of him. He wouldn't say that, but I knew how my beast thought.

When I jumped, he caught me and wrapped me up in his big arms, burying his face into the crook of my neck and inhaling deeply.

I pressed my lips to his temple and closed my eyes as I rubbed at his shoulders and back. "I'm here, mon amour.

I'm fine. Promise. You can yell all you like later. Just know I am okay because you saved me."

He shuddered, squeezing tighter for a moment before letting off the pressure to draw in another breath of me.

"Aww, they're so cute together. Don't you think?"

Quake coughed and hesitantly said, "Ah, yeah."

She laughed. "You're cute too," she added.

Opening my eyes, I saw Quake blushing before he turned around and said, "I'm goin' to check on the brothers."

Rommy watched him go with a big grin and interest in her gaze. Until she blinked, clapped, and placed all her attention on the others. "Right, who wants to get out of here? I really gotta call my dad soon before he shits kittens. The tech guy said they messaged him I was found and safe, but he'll want to hear my voice." She waved her hand again toward the exit. "Let's go, people. Time's wasting. We need food and water and definitely showers. Huh, maybe that's why that guy ran off quickly." She lifted her arm and smelled under her armpit, then screwed up her nose. "Yeah, that's rank." She moved up behind Blaze. "Hey, big man. Just gonna put my hands on your waist and help you step to the side so people can get past. You just keep breathing in your man and calming down." She glanced up at me, as if checking for approval. When I nodded, she did as she said.

People filed by while I cooed some more at my man.

"Kid, you coming?" Rommy called.

She was talking to Sawyer, who stood by the containers watching Blaze and me. Loyal hovered close behind Sawyer with his hand gripping the back of Sawyer's neck. Sawyer had his arms wrapped around his waist while Loyal said something quiet that made Sawyer nod.

Only he didn't move.

"Well, let's go, mate. I've got a phone call to make."

With a kiss to Blaze's temple, I threaded my fingers into his hair and tugged his face out of my shoulder. When I had his eyes, I told him, "We need to move, mon amour. You can keep holding me, but I want to get Sawyer home to his brother."

He grunted, then barked, "Kid." I felt one of his hands move off my ass, and I glanced down to see he held it out to Sawyer.

My heart swelled.

My big, beautiful beast.

"Go on," Loyal said, dropping his hold.

Sawyer rushed over and took Blaze's hand, and together, we followed Rommy out as she talked about wanting to eat a hamburger and chips. "Wait, you guys call them fries, right? I can't believe I'm in America. You know, I've never been, but I've always wanted to."

The woman was something else. She wormed her way into your heart instantly, and I already wanted to know more about her.

But first, I needed to place all my attention on my man.

CHAPTER TWENTY

BLAZE

MOMENTS BEFORE

The men from the van walked off the ship and headed to their car. My body fucking hummed with adrenaline. I was ready to see their lives drain from their eyes.

They'd taken Henri.

They'd harmed him.

They would pay.

"Country," I clipped.

He nodded. "Now," he snarled. We rushed forward but didn't start shooting until one saw us and yelled to the others.

Drones flew over our heads that Tech manned. They

soared toward the ship, and I heard them fire off their own shots from the gun we'd connected.

I beelined for the van. The men were trying to rush to get in it. Torch threw a blade, and it landed in the leg of one of them. The guy's gun skidded away when he dropped it to hold his leg.

Fuckin' fool.

Aiming, I shot one of them in the arm, who'd been about to take out Death. Then I placed all my attention on the man I'd originally been headed for since he was the motherfucker who'd kicked at Henri.

He fumbled for his gun, but it was too late. Once I was close, I picked him up and threw him against the side of the van. I pressed my forearm to his throat and gun to his forehead.

"Was it you who marked Henri?"

He gargled, turning red.

"Brother, he can't answer if you crush his throat," Loyal said with an impatient edge to his voice.

"Go help the others," I bit out.

"Torch has that handled. He's gone loco. So, I'm good here. But you might wanna let him breathe if you want answers. And make it fast so we can get to Henri and Sawyer."

Fuckin' hell.

"Henri and Sawyer are waitin'," Loyal added.

I let the cunt breathe, crowding him with just the gun to his forehead.

"Did you punch Henri?"

He coughed. "Who's that?"

"The French man," Loyal supplied.

The guy's upper lip rose. "That faggot deserved—"

BANG.

I blew the cunt's brains out and let him drop to the ground.

Loyal grinned. "Let's fuckin' go." He turned and shot a guy in the back of the head as he tried to crawl away.

Moving on, Loyal and I dealt with the traffickers who were trying to escape as we climbed aboard to where the brothers were.

No one would be left alive to tell the Murphy brothers anything.

Close by, Torch let out a hoot when he saw a flamethrower.

"No. Shit will blow up," I warned.

The guy pouted and then grinned when another crew member got too close, eager to deal with him. But all that ran through my mind was Henri's whereabouts.

I need to get to him.

Quake caught my attention when he yelled in the face of his opponent and wrapped his hands around the guy's neck. He took him to the ground, choking the hell out of him. But his back was free, and another guy was creeping up on him.

I stalked forward, bringing my gun up.

But stopped.

My eyes shot wide when a little slip of a thing flung herself at this guy and took him to the ground. She hit him in the side of the head with her gun, knocking him unconscious.

When she bounced up, I wasn't the only one staring at her.

The ship had gone quiet. There was no one else rushing forward or trying to escape.

The woman waved. "Hey, hi, hello, hot biker guys. I'm Romania. But call me Rommy. You might be here to save me? I have the others who were kidnapped in the back." She shot finger guns at Quake. "Dude, you need to remember to watch your back." Then she pointed at me as I slipped my gun into the waistband of my jeans. "You've got to be Henri's beau. Come on. I can tell you need to see him." She tipped her head back. "This way. Wait, does my dad know I'm okay?"

Tech stepped forward. "I've just messaged them. They know we've got the ship under control."

"Thanks heaps." She waved me over. "Come on. You're barely hanging on. Your Henri is this way."

Quietly, I followed her, hands clenching and unclenching at my sides. I didn't hear anything she said after that. There was nothing but a ringing in my ears.

I had to get my eyes on him. I had to make sure he was okay.

Him and the kid.

When I stepped into the area, I drank him in.

Head, shoulders, chest, waist, hips, legs, feet, and then back up. I paused on his cheek, where that cunt had hit him. I wanted to take that guy's life over again but slowly.

"Here. Now," I ordered.

He smiled and raced toward me. As soon as I had him in my arms, I drew him in.

This was where he was supposed to be. He was mine and mine alone to touch.

Christ, his scent was like a drug, and I needed to fill my lungs full of him.

His words seeped in and warmed me in the only way his could.

The cold evaporated.

I had him in my arms.

He was here.

He was safe.

When he pulled my head back using my hair, I allowed it, needing to drink in the sight of his face but only to have the anger surface when I saw the bruise forming.

He wanted us home and Sawyer back with his brother. I'd do anything for him. When I looked to the kid, he was frozen on the spot even while his body shook.

Holding out my hand, I grunted. "Kid." My chest warmed even more when he rushed over to take my hand.

I'd get them home.

The woman rambled on and on about something as we followed her. And after we hung about while she said goodbye to the friends she'd made in that container, she ended up climbing into the same car as me, Henri, Sawyer. Up front was her and Country, who handed her a phone.

Some brothers stayed back to make sure things got clean and sorted. Officer Jones was taking care of the other victims, but Country had promised Dodge that we'd look after Romania until they landed in America. They were set to fly out in the morning.

Henri curled into me, and I kissed the top of his head. Sawyer sat on my other side with his hand still clasped in mine. It was my silent offer of support, which I could tell he needed.

A car drove toward us and skidded to a stop. Gun and Adrick stared at us through the windshield.

"Do we need to worry about these people?" Rommy asked, tensing.

A curly head of hair jumped out of the back.

"What the fuck?" we heard roared, and then Wreck was stomping his way toward his husband.

"Oh, they came." Henri kissed my jaw. "Mon amour, I will be back in a second." He was out of the car before I could say or do anything. I was going to have to strap my firecracker to me from now on.

He went over and hugged Lucas before Wreck got there. Then he hugged West and Gun and patted Adrick on the arm.

"Henri," I barked out the window.

"Everyone reminds me of home. There's so much love and caring going on it makes me teary. Shit, I better call Dad."

Henri waved goodbye and ran back to the car. When he climbed in, I let go of Sawyer's hand to reach around Henri to do his belt up.

"Stay here," I clipped, staring down at him.

He cupped my cheek and kissed me. "Sorry, I will. I'm right here, mon amour."

Grunting, I sat back and took Sawyer's hand again. I could feel the kid's gaze on me, but I didn't look at him. Though, Henri leaned forward to see Sawyer and smiled.

"I told you we would have you home today, chéri. It just may be a little later than we thought. Will Arlo be okay?"

Sawyer nodded. "Yeah, um. If I don't show at his school, he knows to walk home and go to our neighbor's."

"Very good." He reached over and patted Sawyer's leg. "We will get things sorted."

Sawyer nodded, and just as Rommy put the phone to her ear, the kid slowly rested his head against my shoulder.

I had a feeling Henri had gotten through to him somehow.

"Dad!" Rommy yelled as Country started driving. "I'm okay. I promise. ... They didn't hurt me. I swear. ... All right, I could use something to drink, some food, and a shower. I'm gonna stink everyone out in the car. ... No, I'm telling the complete truth. I'm fine, Dad. They had to keep us well for the buyers. ... Relax, it's not happening now is it. ... I know. I love you too. ... Yes, I'll make sure they take care of me. They seem really nice, Dad. ... Of course I kicked ass. I wasn't gonna sit back and let everyone else have fun. ... Okay, I won't call kicking ass fun. ... Yeah, I know you worry. ... Hey, Mum. How's Dad really been? ... I know you can hear me, old man, but Mum won't sugar-coat it. ... Yes, Mum. I promise I'm okay. ... I'll make sure they feed me right away. ... Love you too, and I'll see you tomorrow." She hung up and sat back, suddenly looking tired.

"You good, kid?" Country asked.

"Yeah. Can we please grab some tucker on the way?"

"Tucker?"

She rolled her head his way and grinned. "Sorry, I mean food. Hey, I like all your tattoos. There's so many. Are they all over?"

"Pretty much, and yeah, we'll hit a drive-through. Dusty, my old lady, will have more food at the compound too."

She moaned. "Sounds good."

"Where did you learn to fight like that?" Country asked. He pulled to the other lane when he spotted a burger joint.

"That was only a little of what I know. Dad made sure I was trained in all types of martial arts. With weapons and hand-to-hand. Good thing really." She straightened. "My mouth is already watering. I'll eat anything, so you just order for me."

I glanced down to Henri, who was leaning into me with his head back, mouth slightly open and breathing heavily. Sound asleep. At my other side, Sawyer was the same—both tired and drained from what they'd been through. I was just glad even Sawyer was relaxed enough to sleep around us.

When Country asked me if I wanted anything, I shook my head. I wouldn't risk waking them, and if they wanted something later, I'd make sure they got it.

CHAPTER TWENTY-ONE

HENRI

At the compound, Country and Rommy climbed out after I promised we would be back to see Rommy. While they headed inside, Blaze and I got into the front of the car, and my lover drove us to the address Sawyer gave.

I shifted on the seat to look back at Sawyer. He gazed out the window, biting his bottom lip as his leg bounced up and down.

"Chéri, are you all right?"

He glanced to me and then back out the window. Releasing a heavy breath, he softly said, "It's not a nice area I live in."

"We do not judge, Sawyer. You don't need to worry about what we think. All we wish to do is help you, and if you will allow us, we would like to take a look around."

He nibbled on his thumbnail and looked at Blaze before his eyes landed on me. "They could be there," he whispered. "Tomorrow is usually the night they collect the money, but sometimes they come early and before I finish work to threaten Miss Cora and Arlo. My wallet's in my car back down the street where you saw me. I didn't want to carry it with me in case...." His bottom lip trembled.

In case he hadn't been imagining being watched and was attacked or taken.

"Henri?" Blaze wanted to know what we were talking about.

Sawyer leaned over, moaning like he was in pain.

"Can I tell him, chéri?" When the boy nodded, I rested back in my seat and spoke to Blaze about Sawyer's past and how there could be loan sharks waiting at the apartment.

Blaze grunted, glancing at the rearview mirror and back to the road. "It'll get sorted."

"I don't want my trouble to—"

"Kid," Blaze called, stopping Sawyer. "You're one of us. We take care of our own in all fuckin' situations. This'll be nothing I can't handle, so don't even worry about me dealing with this."

"I can't ask—"

"You ain't asking, Sawyer. If they're there, I'll have a nice friendly chat with them while Henri gets you and Arlo out. Hell, we'll take the old lady neighbor too if we have to. We'll make sure everyone in your life is safe. You've done a fuckin' good job at dealing with all this shit on your own, kid. But no more. We're here to help."

A strangled sound escaped Sawyer right before he started sobbing. Covering his face, he curled into himself.

"Fuck, did I say something wrong?" Blaze asked, worry clear in his tone.

"Non, mon amour. It was perfect," I told him before I kissed his cheek, undid my belt, and climbed through to the back where I pulled Sawyer into my arms. "Oh, sweet boy, we have your back from now on. You and Arlo are no longer alone. I promise, chéri. We are here." I looked at Blaze. "And I am sure that if they are there and see Blaze covered in blood, they will know what fear is."

Blaze grunted, studying his clothes for a moment.

Sawyer snorted, then sniffed, wiping at his face. "I hope you're right. But... they're scary, too, Henri."

I brushed hair from his face and cupped his cheek, swiping the tears away with my thumb. "No matter who they are, I know my Blaze will be able to sort this out quickly. Besides, they may not even be there. Either way, we will resolve the issue. You believe in us, oui?"

He whimpered, but he also nodded.

"I am glad." I hugged him tightly against me again. "You are not used to having people care about you, are you, chéri?"

Another sob caught in his throat as his hands tightened on my arm that was wrapped around him. I felt him shake his head against my neck.

"You will now have to get used to it for me. You and Arlo are stuck with Blaze and me. And I am sure we won't be the only ones caring about you. Supporting and helping you. We want to be there, chéri. Will you let us?"

For a moment, he said nothing, just kept sniffing and wiping at his face, but his tears wouldn't stop. My heart lodged in my throat, anxious he would tell us to just leave him alone.

But then, finally, the sweet boy nodded. "Okay," he whispered.

This poor child had been through so much already in his short life.

"Kid, we're pulling up now," Blaze said as he slowed the car and stopped at the curb out front of a building that had seen better days. The paint was peeling off, boards were falling apart, and the garden was unkept.

Sawyer drew in an unsteady breath and straightened. He once again scrubbed at his face.

"You can stay here. You just need to tell us where—"

"No, please. Let me come."

"Okay, chéri." We all exited the car and the noise from the building amped up; music, loud voices, and to go with it all was a strong scent of weed.

Blaze's gaze shot to a vehicle pulling to a stop behind ours.

When the lights turned off, I saw who was behind the wheel. The door opened, and Loyal climbed out with a thinned-lip frown as he looked around.

"What's he doing here?" Sawyer whispered harshly. He took a step away, shaking his head. "No. He can't be here. Not him. No."

Loyal paused upon seeing Sawyer's reaction.

Blaze stepped forward and in front of Sawyer as the boy tried to catch his breath. I moved beside Sawyer, rubbing his back.

"Did Loyal do something to upset you, chéri?"

"What? No!"

"Then why do you not want him here? He could help Blaze if there is trouble. You and I both know we aren't the strongest tools in the shed. The smartest, oui, but not the strongest. I can throat punch a bully, but I would also hurt my hand in the process. I do not want that. You do not want that, and Blaze especially does not want that because I am the worst patient. However, if you wish Loyal to leave...."

He shook his head quickly, heat hitting his cheeks. He shifted closer and whispered, "I didn't want him to see where I lived." He gave me eyes that wished I understood more than he was saying, and I believed I read him right. Sawyer had a big fat crush on Loyal and wanted to hide the life he had been dealing with.

Unfortunately, he didn't understand that Loyal was also smitten and was ready to take care of what was his. However, sweet Sawyer was not ready to deal with Loyal's emotions just yet.

I smiled and nodded. "He will not care, chéri. This I promise. Loyal wishes you and Arlo safe like Blaze and I do."

He drew in a breath and let it out slowly. "Okay."

"Loyal," Blaze called, tipping his chin up the brother's way.

"Yo," he called as he approached. "What's happenin'?"

"How come you were tailing us?" Blaze asked, crossing his arms over his chest.

"Saw you guys leavin' the compound. Just wanted to make sure you got home all right."

That was very sweet.

"We're just getting Sawyer home. Check the place and see how his brother, Arlo, is," Blaze explained.

"Cool." He tried to look at Sawyer, but the kid stayed

behind Blaze with his head down. "You think I can meet Arlo, Sawyer?"

The boy's eyes shot to mine, wide and worried. I shrugged.

He opened his mouth and closed it, then took a breath. "I... all right."

"Let's go," Blaze said.

At the entrance, Blaze shifted to the side and looked to Sawyer.

Sawyer stared back. Then he looked at me, Loyal, and Blaze again. "What?"

"The code for the door, chéri."

His cheeks flushed as he stepped forward and pushed the door open.

Blaze wasn't the only one whose expression had darkened, but it was he who asked, "Who's the fuckin' landlord of this place?"

To my surprise, Sawyer jutted his chin out and up. "He's an old man who can't afford to fix everything, but it's a roof over our heads at a cheaper rate because of those repairs needed. You leave him alone."

We all stared at him.

My lips twitched, but I covered it with my hand. Loyal had to look away, and I knew he thought Sawyer snapping at Blaze was cute too. But I also loved seeing it; his actions showed how he didn't fear my big beast. He was accepting us and confronting us.

It was beautiful to see.

Blaze reached out and ruffled Sawyer's hair before he stepped into the building. "What floor?"

"The top." Blaze and Loyal made their way to the elevator, until Sawyer cleared his throat. They turned, and Sawyer shook his head. "That hasn't worked since I've been here."

Their jaws clenched in unison.

"How many stories are in here?"

Sawyer winced. "Four."

These boys had been climbing up and down four flights of stairs every day and night.

"What about your elderly neighbor?"

"The top floor too. She can do it. She's fit for sixty-five, but I also help her out by getting her things from down the street because she doesn't have a car."

Blaze's nostrils flared. "Wait," he ordered and then he took Loyal's arm and pulled him off to the side, whispering things.

"What's he saying?" Sawyer asked me quietly.

"He's probably warning Loyal about what could be happening up on the top floor." Since it was so far away, it was hard to hear through the other noises coming from within apartments.

Sawyer dropped his gaze, curling his shoulders in. "Okay." He disliked Loyal knowing what had happened in his life and was likely worried Loyal would think him weak. But he was not. He was the strongest boy I knew at his age. His parents passed away, and he stepped up to take care of everything. I was sure Sawyer wouldn't be the only one who would do the same in this situation, but there were also many who wouldn't.

Arlo was lucky to have Sawyer as his brother.

"Let's go," Blaze announced before he started for the stairs. Sawyer and I followed while Loyal took up the rear.

There were a few things we had to step over, like trash, but we ignored them all and kept moving.

On the third set of stairs, I was huffing and puffing.

Loyal snorted. "You need more cardio, Henri."

"Fuck off, chéri. I get my workout in when Blaze screws my brains out."

"Yeah, but I do all the work," Blaze announced. He stopped, looked at Sawyer, and was that a hint of a blush showing under these dim lights? "Sorry, kid."

Sawyer blinked and started laughing. He looked at me. "He does realize I'm a sex worker, right?"

I grinned. "But in our eyes, you are but a little boy who shouldn't hear those types of conversations come from us. Sorry, I should not—"

Sawyer groaned. "Please don't. I work at an escort agency run by bikers. I've heard worse things. Maybe don't talk about it in front of Arlo, but I'm not a child. I'm only a few years younger than Loyal."

"Six years," Loyal said. Like he had done the math many times already.

It was my turn to groan. I shoved at Blaze to keep moving. "You both make me feel so old. How are you faring, mon amour?"

"Fine since I'm not the one panting like I've done a marathon."

"Shut up, you big ogre, or I will—"

A loud bang sounded above, and someone yelled, "Open the fucking door, you old bitch."

Sawyer gasped, pressing a hand to his stomach. Blaze tore off, bounding up the stairs, his heavy feet slapping hard to the ground to reach the fourth floor. Sawyer and I rushed behind him, and Loyal was close to our backs. Once out the stairwell door, we rounded a corner to see two men down on their knees trying to pick the lock on the door and five others standing around.

"That's them," Sawyer whispered.

"Back the fuck off," Blaze snarled, starting for the group.

There were many of them and only two of us who could actually fight.

Loyal shifted Sawyer and me off to the side. "Wait there," he ordered.

"It's Sawyer," one guy called. "And he's brought some muscle with him."

Another laughed. "Fat lot that'll do."

The first one shifted more our way since Blaze was nearly on them. "Hold the fuck on, big guy. Your little pussy owes us money. You don't want to get in the middle of this."

Blaze pulled his arm back, and it flew forward as he said, "I really do."

One punch and the guy hit the ground with a thud. Another launched at him, but Blaze just picked him up and threw him on the dirty carpet while Loyal slipped in to break some fingers while disarming the ones who tried to use a weapon against Blaze.

They whimpered and cried out, slipping to sit on their asses in the hallway. No one landed a single blow on Blaze or Loyal. They moved in sync and took them all out in one way or another.

"Wow," Sawyer breathed.

"Oh yes. Wow indeed." I nodded.

I was going to suck Blaze's brains out through his dick

for making me all hot and needy from watching his gorgeous body move while making people pay.

When the fighting stopped, the only noises in the hallway were of the loan sharks who were still conscious and moaning, holding their hands to their chest.

Blaze stomped back to the first guy and picked him up, shaking him. "Quit fuckin' faking."

The guy's eyes went wide. He struggled and tried to kick Blaze, but Loyal drew a gun and pressed it to the guy's temple.

"We're gonna have a nice conversation," Blaze said.

The snort escaped me, and I quickly slapped a hand over my mouth.

"You two, inside with Arlo," Blaze ordered. "No one touches them," he warned.

I took Sawyer's hand, and we made our way toward Miss Cora's place, stepping over bodies and watching the others who were awake but too scared to move.

At the door, I reached up and knocked. "Bonjour, Miss Cora. It is safe out here now. I have Sawyer with me, and we would like to see Arlo."

"Child, no," I heard Cora say.

"It's okay. That's Henri," Arlo told her.

"I'm here too, Miss Cora. It's safe," Sawyer called.

There was some unlocking before the door swung open to reveal a happy Arlo and a concerned Miss Cora.

Arlo cried, "Henri." He ran forward and hugged me around the waist, clogging my throat with warm emotions.

I cupped the back of his head to me. "Sweet Arlo, it is good to see you."

He tipped his head back and smiled up at me, but then

something caught his attention, and he shifted away to take in the hallway. His mouth and eyes went wide.

"Inside," Blaze ordered.

Arlo's gaze snapped to Blaze, and he waved. Blaze tipped his chin up, lips twitching.

Sawyer took hold of Arlo's shoulders and moved him back around and into the apartment. I quickly followed, leaving my lover to do what he had to, to make sure no one bothered these people again.

CHAPTER TWENTY-TWO

BLAZE

As soon as the door closed, I shook the guy by his tee, banging his head into the wall. "You need to listen to what I say—"

"I have more people—"

Loyal clicked the safety off. "Listen, fucker."

The guy shut his mouth and glared out of his good eye. The other one was already swelling shut.

I pressed him against the wall, holding him there with a hand to the chest. "Whatever debt Sawyer's parents had ends today. The boy owes you and your cronies nothing. If you come for him or the old lady, you'll have me and the Diamond MC to deal with again." I moved in close. "And believe me, you don't want to see us again."

"You don't even know who I work for."

"Yeah? Who?"

"He'll kill you all."

"Give us a name," Loyal demanded, digging his gun into the guy's temple more.

"Adrick Hail. He owns half of Vegas with all his clubs and casinos. It's his money that fucker's parents—Christ," he barked when Loyal hit him on the top of his head with the back of the gun.

"Adrick Hail?" I asked, sharing an amused look with Loyal.

"Yeah."

I pulled my phone out and scrolled through my contacts, found the one I needed, and placed the cell to my ear. It rang three times before the Russian voice clipped through the phone. "Why would you be calling me? West and I were about to climb into bed."

"Adrick, I have a guy here saying he's collecting money from Sawyer because of what his deceased parents owe you."

The guy paled.

"Say again?"

"Loyal and I took out a group of guys that've been collecting Sawyer's wage off him for months because his parents owed you money. Sawyer had to sell the family home because of their parents' debt. He's living in the wrong part of town in a beat-up apartment building where nothing fuckin' works."

Shit. I didn't need to tell him all that, but the burning anger got the best of me for a second.

"*You* know the men who work for me, and *I* know the debt owed to me. Whoever you have is lying. What is his name?"

"Name," I ordered.

He shook his head.

"Give me your fuckin' name before I break your fingers," Loyal snarled.

"Stop," Adrick said, hearing Loyal.

"Wait," I told Loyal.

"Tell me where you are. I will send my men. They will deal with these people. You have all been through enough. Let me finish this."

"Agreed."

"Wait for my men. They will not be long. But my advice, in case these people are bigger fools than they have been, take Sawyer and his brother away from there while I get this sorted."

"Done," I said, and the call ended. "Adrick's sending his men."

Loyal chuckled. "You really should start shittin' yourself." His gaze landed on me. "You go in and sit with them. I'll watch these fuckers and knock when it's clear."

"You sure?"

"Yeah, brother."

With a nod, I released the soon-to-be dead man and went for the door to the apartment. "Thanks, brother," I said. Fuck me, that sounded weird coming from my mouth, but I couldn't deny the connection Henri and I had to the club. And since I'd started working for them, that link had grown, and they'd become important in our lives.

We were a damn family.

But Henri would always come first, and since I knew my French firecracker, our smaller household had just grown to add Sawyer and Arlo.

We were gonna need a bigger house.

I knocked once before I opened the door and entered straight into the living room where they were all seated drinking tea.

"Miss Cora, this is my other half, Blaze."

"Well, slap me silly and call me Mary, he's a giant."

Jesus.

"Miss Cora," Sawyer muttered.

"Arlo said he was big, but I didn't realize how big he'd be."

Arlo jumped up and ran over, taking my hand. "Come and sit down. Have some tea." He tugged me over.

"Mon amour, do we have time?"

I nodded as I sat in a chair, and Arlo took his seat next to Henri on the couch. Sawyer sat on Henri's other side while Miss Cora was in her own chair at the other end of the coffee table to me.

"I missed seeing you in the hallway, and now I wished I'd seen you in action against those pimple-dick assholes."

Sawyer sighed. "Miss Cora."

"What? You think Arlo hasn't heard swear words at school? I bet he has. The boy knows he can't use them until he's old enough or I'll wash his mouth out with soap. But I'm an adult. I can swear all I like in my own home."

"Okay, Miss Cora."

"I won't swear. I promise," Arlo added as he poured me a mug of tea and handed it to me.

I didn't drink tea, but the kid was looking at me expectantly.

"Arlo made that tea himself. He's been practicing," Miss Cora said.

Shit. Now all the attention was on me, and I was gonna have to try it.

Henri smirked over at me while I glowered back. "Yes, try the tea, mon amour."

His ass was gonna get an extra spank for that.

I lifted the cup to my lips and took a small sip.

Straight face. Straight fuckin' face.

But the stuff was bitter. I hummed and nodded. "Good."

Arlo beamed.

Hell, did I do the right thing by lying?

Henri snickered silently behind his hand, and Sawyer looked away to hide his mirth while Miss Cora grinned like a maniac.

She nodded. "Yeah, you'll do." Her gaze dipped to my clothes. "You want some clean stuff? My dear late husband, God rest his pain-in-the-ass soul, wasn't as big as you, but I'm sure I can find something."

I shook my head. "We'll head off soon." I looked at Henri and Sawyer. "We're just waiting in here until Adrick's men come to... tidy up."

"Why are they coming?" Henri asked.

I glanced down at Arlo.

Miss Cora noticed. "Arlo, come into the kitchen, and we'll find some cookies."

"But—"

"Come, child." She stood with a groan and made her way out of the room with a pouting Arlo following.

"What is it?" Sawyer asked.

"The guy lied about who his boss is when he used Adrick's name." Their gazes went wide. I nodded. "Adrick doesn't know who these thugs are. So, I think they used Adrick's name to try and instill fear in me and Loyal because their own names wouldn't be a deterrent to stop us. Obviously, they've heard of how Adrick runs things and thought it'd be good to drop his name." I shrugged. "We'll have answers in the end, but I'm guessing your parents did owe these guys money, and they saw how far you'd go to protect your brother, so they used that to get what they want. But it'll stop from now on."

Tears filled his eyes. "Really?"

I nodded. "Still...." I started, already hoping Sawyer wasn't put out by this.

"What?" he asked softly.

There was a knock before Loyal stepped in. He waited by the door and said, "All cleared. Dimitri will be in touch."

Dimitri was Adrick's right-hand man. He'd definitely get the answers we needed.

I tipped my chin his way just as Sawyer asked, "Blaze, what were you going to say?"

"I think it's best if you and Arlo come stay at our place for a while, and we'll need to get Miss Cora somewhere too in case these guys are stupid or have other idiot friends that'll come here."

"We... we need to leave?"

"Chéri, Blaze and I would love to have you and Arlo with us. You'll only have to share the room at our place for a little while until we get a bigger house where we'll all fit."

Knew I'd guessed right.

Sawyer jerked his head back and sat straighter. "You're asking us to move in with you guys?"

"Oui. It'll be cramped for a little while, but between all

of us, we can work around everyone's schedule to make sure someone is home with Arlo all the time."

Loyal cleared his throat. "While you guys find a bigger place, I have room at mine. I even have a self-contained unit out the back that the old lady could use. My house has two living rooms and three bedrooms, so the brothers don't have to share."

Sawyer stared up at him, mouth gaping, eyes wide. "N-No—"

"I think it's a wonderful idea," Miss Cora announced as she walked back in. "Thank you, young man. The kids and I will move in until Henri and Blaze have a bigger house for the boys to go to. Then once things are settled, I'll come back here."

"Don't feel you have to," Loyal said. "The unit is yours to use for however long. Used to be my dad's, but he passed away a couple of years ago."

Sawyer let out a strangled sound. "Miss Cora—"

"Hush, child. These are good people. They want to help, and we're going to let them. Too many nights I lose sleep worrying about you and Arlo. I know you'll be safe with them. These apartments are too easy to break into."

Tears filled Sawyer's eyes, but he wiped at them and sniffed. "Okay, Miss Cora." He looked at Henri, Loyal, and me. "Thank you."

Henri clapped and cheered, reaching out to hug Sawyer. "This will be wonderful, chéri. Come, let us go pack a few bags. Blaze and Loyal can assist Miss Cora." He stood, dragging Sawyer up with him. "Arlo, come with us," he called. Arlo zoomed in, stopping at Henri's side. "Arlo, that is Loyal. He's a friend of ours. Someone you can trust. You,

Sawyer, and Miss Cora will be staying with him until Blaze and I find a bigger house, and then"—he cupped the boy's cheeks—"you'll move in with me and Blaze."

The kid's face screwed up before a sob tore out of him. He pushed into Henri, who tipped back to sit on the couch, and Arlo followed him, sinking to his knees, hugging Henri tightly.

"Chéri, what is it? Why are you upset?"

Sawyer whimpered as he watched his brother. I stood and went over to him. As soon as I was close, he turned to me and dropped his face to my chest. I cupped the back of his head, holding him to me.

"My sweet boy, please tell me what is wrong. Do you not want to move? Blaze, we will buy this building and live in it, making it secure for Arlo if he wishes to stay."

The kid let out another wail, clinging harder to Henri.

When I nodded, I heard a sniff close by and saw a teary Miss Cora.

Hell.

What the fuck was going on?

I ground my teeth together.

"Arlo, chéri," Henri cooed, rubbing at the boy's back and hair. "Talk to me, please."

Loyal moved closer and sat on the chair I'd been on. "Kid, you're feelin' a lot at the moment, right?" Arlo managed a nod against Henri. "Yeah, I would be to. And I bet you appreciate everything Sawyer has done for you, but you've been worried about him as much as he has for you."

Arlo pulled back. "H-He does so much for me. There've been so many horrible people around us, except for Miss Cora, and no one wants to help. Not even my teachers. They think my brother is no good. But he is. He's the best brother there is in the world. I just want him safe and to have people who care about us." He stared up at a misty-eyed Henri. "You care, right?"

Sawyer's hold on my tee tightened as he whimpered.

"I absolutely care, sweet boy. Blaze and I care so much about you and Sawyer. Loyal cares about you all too. We are here in your lives from now on, Arlo. This I promise you. Your brother is safe, and so are you and Miss Cora."

He hiccupped through a sob and hugged Henri again.

My French firecracker stared up at me. The love he had for these boys was clear in his gaze. He was ready to go above and beyond for them, which meant I'd better start looking for a damn big house.

CHAPTER TWENTY-THREE

HENRI

I pretended to be asleep so Blaze would carry me inside. My beast wanted to dote on me as well as yell at me for getting into trouble in the first place. Of course I would let him.

I heard my door open and felt his large arms lift me from the car. I curled my head against his warm chest. "Mon amour," I muttered.

"Shower, then bed," he said, kissing my forehead.

I hummed under my breath, keeping my eyes closed.

When he flicked a light on, I blinked at the brightness and noticed we were already in our en suite. Blaze placed me on my feet, cupping my cheeks so I looked up at him.

"You're not a very good actor."

I glared. "I am so."

He smirked, but it faded when his gaze slid to my bruised cheek.

"Are you going to yell at me now, mon amour?"

His jaw clenched, fingers slightly grazing over my sore cheek. "I should," he grumped.

"I will let you."

"Let me?"

"Oui. I will allow it because I know how scared you would have been. I would be the same if it had been you." I had been the same when he was in Los Angeles, ready to take on the bad people.

His thumb brushed over my sore cheek. "They had their hands on you. They fuckin' hurt you."

"I know, mon amour."

"No one touches you but me."

Pouting, I said, "Can I at least hug the boys? They need our love, my beast."

He grunted. "I know."

"They hardly had anything in the apartment to pack."

He nodded.

"I want to take them shopping. They'll need other things at Loyal's, and we must get everything for them."

"We will."

"You are not angry I have invited them to live—"

"No," he clipped. "Fuckin' never. You have a big heart, Henri, and you should share it with those boys. They need your type of loving."

"And yours. You'll make them feel safe."

Another grunt.

"Do you think Sawyer will be okay at Loyal's?"

"He's shy with the brother, but for Arlo, he'll get by. I'll start looking for places close to Arlo's school and the Play-house. We'll find something and put a rush on the sale, offer them more money. They'll be with us soon and then they can start living like they're supposed to."

Lifting to my toes, I wrapped my arms around his neck and kissed him. His mouth opened under mine, and the kiss deepened. His teeth teased over my bottom lip before he sucked on it. My cock thickened under my pants.

This man made me fall in love with him every day.

He made me giddily happy, like I was flying.

He kissed down to my chin where he nipped. "Shower," he ordered before stepping away from me to remove his clothes. As I watched him, I took my own off and waited until he had the temperature perfect.

He held his hand out to me, and together, we stepped into the shower. He was the first to reach for the bodywash, so he assisted me and then I him. We made quick work of our hair and then shut off the water, moving out to get dry.

As I ran the towel over my hair, I admired my man bending and stretching as he finished. When he caught me staring, his brow rose.

"Bed, firecracker."

"Mon amour—"

"You're tired. You need to rest and then your ass will be mine in the morning."

"Promise?"

"Damn right."

I sighed and hung my towel up. "Fine, but you are warming my side of the bed first."

He snorted and walked naked toward his side. Still, I knew he'd turn back around, like he was doing, and moved to my side. Once he got in, I lay over him, our cocks brushing and noticing each other as they twitched, but we really were too wrung out. Blaze pulled the blankets up over us, his hands brushing over my back and ass under the covers.

Kissing his chest, I rested my cheek there next. "I love you, my beast."

His arms tightened. "Love you, firecracker."

I WOKE WITH A WARM, wet cock and opened my eyes to see Blaze between my legs, worshiping my erection.

Humming, I stretched. "I like this wake-up call, mon amour."

He kissed and tongued at my slit. "Good, you're awake." He sat back and moved from between my legs to sit on the side of the bed.

"Mon amour!" I cried out when he grabbed me and shifted my body around to lay over his knees. "You cannot be serious!"

WHACK.

I gasped when his palm connected with my ass cheek and then snapped, "Blaze."

He rubbed over the sting, tracing two fingers up and down my crack. My cock was already hard from being in his mouth, but it now ached. I shouldn't like this so much, but I did.

WHACK.

"That's for running into danger."

Another gasp tore out of me. I bit down on the back of my finger, but I still moaned around it.

WHACK.

I cried out at the sting burning me. "I swear—"

"And that's for fuckin' terrifying me."

For a second, I stilled at the raw emotion darkening Blaze's tone. I looked over my shoulder and saw him working his jaw, clenching it over and over.

I scrambled up, sat astride his lap, and hugged him to me. "I am sorry, mon amour. I hate that you were worried. But I'm here. I'm safe." Pulling back, I cupped his cheeks —his jaw was still going crazy. "Blaze. I know the fear you felt. I do. Because I have that same twisted-up feeling inside me when you go into danger. But we cannot predict what will happen. We still have to try and help, though, right? You would still assist the brothers. I may not walk into danger on purpose, but for those boys, I would. For you I would."

He nodded, nostrils flaring. "I'll just have to make sure you lot stay fuckin' safe and keep myself from trouble, so you don't worry."

Smiling, I cupped the back of his neck. "Oui, that sounds like a good plan. But if things do arise, we can talk about it and see how much we will involve ourselves. We have kids to think of now. Not just you and me."

He blinked. "We have kids."

"Oui. You don't regret—"

"Never," he said instantly.

Leaning in, I pressed my lips to his. "I am glad, mon amour." I kissed his neck, his shoulder. "We must find a big enough house where our room can be at the other end, so they won't hear us."

He grunted, stuffing his nose against my neck and inhaling.

I licked and sucked and kissed at his skin. "We should make love and eat and then go see the boys to take them shopping. It is late enough, oui?"

His hand slid up between us and gripped the front of my neck, pushing me back. His eyes locked with mine. "Yeah. After, I'll text Loyal to bring them and the old lady to the compound so you can see Rommy before we take the boys out. But now, firecracker, we ain't making love. I'm gonna fuck you like I own you."

A shiver raced down my spine. "Prove it."

Blaze's chest rumbled when he stood with me in his arms and turned, placing me on the sheets. Luckily, we were already naked, so Blaze crawled back between my legs. He picked them up and threw them over his shoulders, diving his face between my ass cheeks, which he spread with his hands.

"Mon amour," I cried, shifting my legs wider.

He groaned under his breath, and as he ate, I heard him take a deep inhale.

This man was truly fascinated by my scent, and I loved it.

My cock leaked and throbbed, wanting attention, but I didn't give it any because I knew my possessive ogre would want to be the one in control.

Like always.

And I would give over my control each and every time

since he treated my body so well. He worshiped every inch and made me come alive with all his attention.

"Yes, mon amour. Eat me. *Devour* me."

"Mine," he growled against my hole before stuffing me full of his tongue. He wiggled his tongue deep, nibbling at my hole with his teeth.

"Merde, ma bête. You make me feel so good."

His hands squeezed my ass cheeks, fingers kneading into my flesh. He was punishing me and pleasuring me at the same time.

"Please, Blaze. *Please.*"

He licked to my balls, gently drawing them back down and sucking on them softly.

"What do you want?" he asked, his voice raw, rough, and hot.

"You."

"I'm gonna fuck you hard," he bit out. Blaze went to his knees and leaned back, stroking over his cock. "I'll show you who you belong to. Show you who owns you." He climbed over me, drawing my legs up over his hips and stuffing a pillow under my ass. "And show you how pissed I am that someone harmed you."

"Yes, my beast. Punish my ass. Make me feel you for the rest of the day."

"You will," he clipped.

Reaching over, he yanked the drawer open with such strength that the bedside table nearly fell forward. He grabbed a tube of lube, flicked the lid, and squirted some between my legs. Once done, he threw the tube to the bed, gripped his cock, and rubbed it in the lube against my ass and between my cheeks.

I reached back, holding under the headboard, knowing what was coming.

He glowered down at me. I loved his angry fucks.

"Come, mon amour, let me have it."

His hands dropped down to the bed, and I felt the tip of his cock before he thrust in. Pain and pleasure mixed, drawing a cry out of me.

"More?" he asked.

"You know it," I taunted.

He pulled back, one hand to the mattress, the other holding my hip tightly, and he fucked forward, slamming into me. I held on as he drilled in and out of me with his hard cock.

"Yes, my beast."

"You're mine."

"I know. I feel it."

"Fuckin' mine."

"Yes."

His hand slid from my hip to up over my stomach and chest, down over my cock, jacking it a couple of times before lifting his hand to wrap around my throat.

Leaning down, he screwed into me, hips pumping forward and back, hitting his cock in the perfect spot. He made me moan and groan and mewl like the best porn star there was.

My body tingled, my belly fluttered, and heart raced. This man. My beast. He fucked like a god.

"Mon amour, close," I warned.

He nipped and licked and sucked at my skin, marking me in his ownership.

"Yes. Yes, mon amour," I cried, my cock jerking up and

down on its own as my cum splashed out and emptied onto my stomach.

"Fuck. Christ," he clipped. "You're mine. Henri. Mine," he roared, his dick thickening and releasing inside me. Filling me. Warming me. Marking my insides.

A beat later, he pulled out gently and slumped to the bed, bringing me with him to sprawl over his chest.

After a while, as I caught my breath, I asked, "What time is it?"

"Eleven," Blaze answered, tracing his hand up and down my back.

I stretched, my ass stinging a little. Yes, I would definitely feel him all day. "How long have you been awake?"

He grunted, massaging my ass cheek. "A while."

"Have you heard about anything?"

"As far as we know, the Murphy brothers have no clue what happened. The owners of the port area have disappeared with all their money, and we left no survivors. We'll keep an eye on the ones kidnapped. Make sure it doesn't happen again. And Jones has a few friends in the force in Ireland he trusts. They're making a case against the Murphy brothers."

"Let us hope they are dealt with soon."

Another grunt. "Found some houses to look at."

My belly fluttered. He was such a big softy. "Show me later."

"You wanna get going to see the boys?"

"Oui, please."

"You shower first. I'll text Loyal to let him know the plans."

Lifting off his chest, I demanded, "Kiss me first."

He smirked. "My greedy firecracker."

"Always."

CHAPTER TWENTY-FOUR

Once again, Henri and I walked into the compound common room hand in hand. Only we didn't stay that way since, as soon as we entered through the door, our names were shouted, and an eleven-year-old ran at us. Arlo wrapped his arms around my waist and Henri's, squishing us together. I patted his back a couple of times.

Laughing, Henri cupped the back of his head. "Good afternoon, Arlo."

He pulled back. "Hi."

"Did you sleep well?" Henri asked.

"Better than I have in a long time. So did Sawyer, I heard him snoring."

"I was not," Sawyer said as he approached. Henri held out his arms, and Sawyer moved in to hug him.

Reaching out, I messed with his hair. "Hey, kid."

He quickly brushed his fingers through his hair, fixing it, and smiled. "Hi. You know we don't have to go shopping. We don't—"

"Please, chéri. I need this time with you both after everything. I like spending money. It makes me happy, and I want you both along for the trip."

"You'll probably have to carry bags," I told them.

"I'm good at it," Arlo announced.

Henri smiled. "Perfect, chéri. Are Miss Cora and Loyal coming?"

Sawyer glanced over to Loyal, who was talking with Country, but Loyal's gaze was already on the boy.

Sawyer blushed and faced us, shaking his head. "Miss Cora stayed at the unit, which she thinks is amazing, and Loyal has some things to do around here."

Henri curled an arm around Sawyer's waist. "This is good. it will mean more room for bags." The kid chuckled. "But first, I promised Rommy I would see her today. Have you noticed her around here?"

Before he could answer, the kitchen doors flew open, and Rommy walked out with Saint. "I'm telling you, if you just tried doing it the way I said, your baby will run smoother."

"I ain't no mechanic. You got time to show me what you mean?"

"Hell yes. I'd be glad to get my hands on her." She noticed us and smiled brightly. "Hey, hi, hello." She grabbed Saint's arm and shook it, announcing, "It's Henri and his big man," as if Saint hadn't already seen us. She skipped over as everyone watched her. Hugging Henri, she said, "It's so good to see you. My family should be arriving later. Will you be here to meet them?" She moved over to me, and I stiff-ened when she embraced me. I caught Tech and Country snickering. Even Henri was grinning at me. She pulled back and added, "Sorry, I'm a big hugger. I think I scared Eve earlier from it. But I'll get her to warm to me. Anyway, I'm gonna try to get my parents to stay around for a while. Like a little family holiday. It'll be so cool. You'll love my family; they're the best. I wish you could meet everyone, though."

This woman needed to breathe more.

"So do I, chéri. And we may not be here later, but if they do stick around, I will have the pleasure of meeting them another day. Blaze and I are taking the boys shopping."

"These your boys? I remember you on the ship." She quickly hugged Sawyer and then said to Henri, "But I didn't pick up that he's your son. And who are you, little man?"

Arlo wasn't looking at her. He stared up at Henri and me. "Are we?" he asked.

"Arlo, you can't—" Sawyer started to say until Henri placed his hand on his arm, stopping him.

Henri stepped closer to Arlo. "What are you asking, Arlo?"

His jaw clenched. The kid was fighting his emotions as he briefly glanced around at everyone while a blush rose.

"Kid, don't look at them." I moved to his other side, blocking him from the people in the common room. "Just talk to us. We're always gonna listen no matter where we are or who's around. If you've got something to say and want to, you just say it. Yeah?"

He bit down on his bottom lip and sniffed but nodded. In a whisper, he asked, "Are we your boys? You and Blaze?"

Christ.

In that moment, I fucking knew I would move fucking hell if I had to for them.

Henri's eyes welled, and before he could say anything, I did. "Yes. Fuck yes," I told him and then looked to Sawyer. "Know it's fresh and new, but we already know that if you and Arlo would have us, we'd like to be the ones to help you through life. I've already looked at some houses this morning. They're close to Arlo's school and the Playhouse, so once we check them out, and if you both agree, this shit is happening. It's real. You belong with us, and we're a fuckin' family."

"Mon amour," Henri uttered, tears running down his cheeks. Sawyer and Arlo also sported wet and red cheeks.

"Do you agree?" I asked, and all right, it did come off a bit snappish, but I was fucking pissed at what these boys had been through. Obviously, their parents were crap ones to begin with, if they left the boys to deal with that much debt. And I doubted their parents showed them an ounce of care in their lives.

"Yes," Sawyer whispered.

"Please," Arlo cried before he pushed his face into my gut and hugged me.

I patted his head. "Good."

Rommy nervously shifted on her feet near us. "Sorry if I said something wrong."

"You didn't," I told her. "We're just working things out."

She smiled. "I can see that, and I think it's amazing."

With a grunt, I looked at Loyal. "Text me your address. We'll drop them there later."

He tipped his chin up. "You got it, brother."

I glanced to Country, who met my gaze. "No work for the next week for you and Henri, brother."

There it was again.

Brother.

That word, along with his intense stare, told me the past was forgiven, and I *was* club. *We* were a part of the family he'd built. And Christ, that shit hit me right in the gut in the best kinda way.

I nodded, jaw clenching, and he grinned before walking over to his woman, who was misty-eyed from watching us.

Henri pulled Sawyer with him as he cried out, "Family hug." He and Sawyer stood at Arlo's and my side and wrapped their arms around us. Sawyer let out a watery laugh, resting his chin down on his brother's head.

Henri puckered his lips at me. I dipped and kissed him.

"Shopping is calling me, boys," Henri announced.

IN THE MALL, Sawyer moved closer to me in the store and asked softly, "Is there any way I can get Henri to stop buying us things?"

Snorting, I shook my head.

Sawyer sighed.

"Does it really bother you?" I asked. If it did, I would put a stop to it. But Henri was having the time of his life finding things for Arlo and Sawyer.

Sawyer scraped his top teeth over his bottom lip as he

thought about it. "I guess... I just never want you two to think we're taking advantage."

"We never would, kid."

"I'm nearly nineteen, Blaze, and I work full-time. And now I won't have people breathing down my neck, so I can afford stuff for us."

"That's good you can. You buy whatever you want, but we'll still want to get you two things, and it doesn't matter how old you are, Sawyer. You'll be a kid to us even at twenty-fuckin'-five. But the difference is, now that you've accepted us, you'll be our kid. You and Arlo."

His gaze dropped to the carpet in the store. He stayed like that for a while. Henri glanced over, brows drawn.

I tipped my chin, telling him I had this situation, and my firecracker went back to showing Arlo things.

"You know," Sawyer whispered, sniffing a bit, "I've heard people talk. Usually, you're the quiet one, who doesn't like to talk."

Chuckling, I rested a hand on his shoulder. "I *don't* talk much, kid. I *am* better at listening. But I'm finding that I like speaking to you and Arlo. But don't fuckin' tell anyone I said that. Everyone will try to have a chat with me."

Sawyer grinned up at me, even with misty eyes. "Your secret is safe with me."

I grunted. "Good. But serious, there could be days when I don't have anything to say. Just don't think you or your brother have annoyed me in some way, because it'll never be that. Some days I just need to watch and listen."

"Okay, Blaze. I'll tell Arlo too."

"Appreciate it."

"Mon amour," Henri called. He and Arlo were walking

our way from the register with the boy holding another new bag. I already had three. "We have decided we need food." Arlo stood beside him nodding.

"You're done with shopping?"

Henri grinned. "For now."

"Guess it's lucky this mall is open late. I'll message Loyal that we're having dinner here."

"Can I have a burger and fries?" Arlo asked.

Henri rubbed a hand over his hair. "You can have anything you like."

The boy's eyes rounded. "Anything?"

"Oui."

"Can I add an ice cream too?"

Before Henri could readily agree, I said, "How about we see how full you are after your meal?"

"Deal," Arlo said, then at Sawyer, he said, "Look at this." He stopped and pulled out the winter jacket.

Henri sidled up and leaned against me while the brothers talked. "I love you, my beast."

I stared down at him, gaze flicking over his face and stopping on the bruise. He'd already received a few looks for it, but he always did get attention everywhere we went anyway.

"You're my heart, firecracker. Now kiss me so we can go eat."

He grinned and rocked up to his toes, kissing me.

After, Henri pecked at my jaw before we turned to the boys, who were watching, both softly smiling.

"Ready?" I asked.

"Yep," Arlo replied, and together, we walked toward the closest burger restaurant in the mall.

I pulled the door open and waited for everyone to enter. At the front counter, the waitress asked, "Table for four?"

"Oui, please."

"That means yes," Arlo said with a big grin.

The waitress smiled politely and nodded before she took us to a booth. Arlo and Sawyer slid in on one side, and Henri moved in first before I did. I tucked the bags under the table and picked up the menu.

Only I didn't look at it. Instead, I watched the others as my chest warmed.

This felt good.

Made my throat thicken at the realization of always wanting this with Henri. We hadn't talked about kids, which was probably for the best since I didn't think babies would be our thing. I doubted Henri could handle all the shit and spew.

However, it did seem that older kids were for us.

They were ours even when they weren't staying under our roof yet. We'd claimed them, and they'd accepted. There were no take backs, and even if they tried to walk away now, I wouldn't let them.

I already had a perfect partner and a fucking good life with him that held so much goddamn love. But I believed that our life would be richer with them in it.

"Mon amour, what are you having?"

I unlocked my jaw and swallowed thickly. "Whatever Arlo is."

Arlo beamed over at me. "Really?"

"Yeah, kid."

"Awesome. We're gonna have the deluxe burger and medium fries."

I nodded. "Sounds good. What about you, Sawyer?"

"Um." His eyes traveled over the menu. "Maybe a salad."

"He never eats much because of work," Arlo said.

"Arlo," Sawyer snapped.

"Hey," I said, tipping my chin at Sawyer. "It's okay. We're all working things out between the four of us on what to share and what not to share."

Sawyer nodded.

"Chéri, you can have more. You should ask for some time off—"

"I don't need time off. I need the money."

"Do you?" Henri asked softly. "Blaze and I wanted to talk to you about work anyway." Sawyer looked away, glaring. "Chéri. Eyes please." The kid drew in a deep breath but didn't shift his gaze from out in the restaurant.

"Sawyer," Arlo said, slightly panicked.

Was the kid worried we'd get upset with Sawyer?

"Arlo, it's cool. Sawyer can take his time. And even if he doesn't want to talk about this now and here, that's okay too. He's just gotta tell us what he wants."

Arlo nodded, looking from one person to another.

"Chéri, Blaze is correct. You won't have to talk now or at all." Henri lifted the menu. "I think I'll have the grilled chicken sandwich."

"I'm sorry, Henri," Sawyer said softly. "What did you want to know?"

Henri placed the menu down. "I would like for you to think if you enjoy your job and want to continue there until the Playhouse is opened or if you wish to have a break from Polished. If you want that break, chéri, Blaze and I will support you."

His jaw clenched over and over.

The waitress suddenly appeared and asked, "Are you ready to order? I can take your drinks first."

"Two Dr. Peppers," I said. "Kids?"

"Can I have an orange soda?" Arlo asked.

"Sure can," the waitress replied, noting it down on her iPad.

"I'll have a cola," Sawyer said.

"For food, Blaze and I are gonna have the deluxe burgers with medium fries, please," Arlo informed her cheerily.

Henri ordered his meal, and Sawyer looked down at the menu quickly and then up. "I'll have the cheeseburger and large fries, thanks."

"No problem. They won't be long."

When she walked away, Sawyer looked at Henri and me. "I would like to quit Polished and only work at the Playhouse."

Reaching over, I knocked my knuckles against the top of his hand. "You got it."

Henri smiled softly. "Thank you for telling us. You don't worry about anything, okay? You have Blaze and me. Just come to us when you need something."

Henri and I had talked about it earlier that we thought Sawyer wasn't happy at Polished. He just always had to work. Now he had us, so he didn't need to. Made me proud that he was confident enough to tell us.

Henri gasped. "Imagine all the things we can do together. You can help me get the Playhouse up and running."

Sawyer grinned, even with a tremble to his bottom lip. "I'd like that."

EPILOGUE

HENRI

MONTHS LATER

"Arlo, are you getting ready?" I asked, tapping on his door. I didn't want to be too loud since his brother was still asleep in the next room. Sawyer had worked until three in the morning at the Playhouse; he needed more hours of rest. But Arlo was another story. "I'm coming in," I said as I twisted the handle and pushed it wide.

Only there was no sign or Arlo.

My heart jumped up into my throat. I turned and fled, running downstairs, I passed the living area, the kitchen, and down the back hallway, where our bedroom and bathroom were, then to the stairs that led to the large basement below.

I threw the door open and called frantically, "Mon

amour!" His music always played loudly while he worked out, so he probably didn't hear me, which was why he didn't answer. I quickly stepped down the stairs and stopped.

Arlo sat on the weight bench with a small dumbbells in each hand, curling them up to his chest with intense concentration on his face.

The sight made me all melty on the inside, even as I tried to catch my breath.

"This right?" he asked, loud enough to be heard, looking up at Blaze.

Blaze hit a button on his phone, and the music quietened. "You got it, kid. A couple more and then you'd better go get ready for school."

Quietly, I snuck back up the stairs and into the kitchen where I started cooking some eggs and bacon. Surely, I couldn't mess those up. Blaze had been teaching me a few things, and Sawyer, but I was thinking of taking a cooking class to learn more.

Maybe one day I would have some spare time to do so. But for now, the Playhouse had only been opened for a couple of weeks, and we were still working some kinks out. But I wasn't alone in managing the strip club, thankfully, so I had plenty of time to spend with Blaze and the kids.

Plus, there were still some boxes up in the attic that needed to be unpacked.

"Morning," Arlo called as he raced by. "I'm going to get changed."

"Keep the noise down. Your brother is sleeping."

His loud footsteps lessened their noise when I felt an arm sliding around my waist. Lips touched to my neck.

"Did you have fun spying?"

"You saw me?"

He scraped his teeth over my skin. "I always see you."

"I was worried when Arlo wasn't in his room. It was cute to see him wanting to lift weights. Did he come and ask you?"

He grunted. "Yeah. There are some kids at school picking on him for having spaghetti arms. I told him there was nothing wrong with his arms, but he still wanted to make them stronger."

He went quiet.

I guessed where his thoughts had gone. "Mon amour, you can't break little kids' fingers for picking on him."

"Can't I?"

I grinned. "Non, but I'll let you collect him from school this afternoon so you can glare at them."

"Done."

Gasping, I clutched my chest and teased. "You are willing to walk away from your babies to pick Arlo up? The boy has crawled into your heart."

A squeal escaped me when he pinched my ass. "Stop being a smartass or I'll take you over my knee again."

"Mon amour, you are just asking me to act up."

His chuckle swept over my skin before he kissed my neck again. "Move aside before you burn everything."

I huffed but handed the spatula over. Cooking was boring, and I did like watching Blaze do it a lot more than doing the activity myself.

Arlo walked back into the room, dropping his bag to the floor.

"You packed your homework?" I asked.

"Oui," he replied with a smile.

My belly fluttered. He was such a sweet child. He and his brother. Both made our lives that much brighter. Even though I was Blaze's ray of sunshine, we were now being blinded by the light these boys brought into our world.

"Breakfast's ready. Sit at the table," Blaze called.

I had already set the table earlier, so I walked to my spot, kissing the top of Arlo's head as I passed.

My brows shot up when Sawyer stumbled into the room.

"Chéri, what are you doing up?" I looked to Arlo. "Did you wake him?"

He looked at me, away, then back. "No?"

Sawyer chuckled. "He did, but I told him to do it before I left for work last night."

"Why?" I asked.

Sawyer took the seat opposite me as Blaze placed the tray of food down in the middle.

"Because this is important," he said and then nodded at his brother.

Blaze sat at the head of the table asking, "What's up, kid?"

Arlo blew out a breath and met Sawyer's gaze. His brother nodded again, smiling softly. Arlo licked his lips nervously. "Well, I was hoping... I mean, if you'd both be okay with it, that is, if I can.... Would I be able to call Blaze, Dad, and you, Henri, Papa, like they do in France?"

My ears rang from how hard my blood pumped through my veins.

He wanted to call me Papa.

Me.

My eyes welled, and a sob escaped before I buried my face into my hands.

"Henri?" Arlo cried.

"Oui," I whimpered. "I am your papa." I grabbed his shoulder and tugged him against me for a tight hug. "I love you, Arlo." I looked through my watery gaze over to his brother. "And I love you, Sawyer." I kissed Arlo's head. "Mon amour," I sobbed.

I heard Blaze clear his throat. "Kid, it'd be an honor if you called us that." I glanced back to see him swallowing thickly. "Fuck," he clipped. "Kid, come here."

I released Arlo, and he jumped up to go to Blaze, who scooted back on his seat and pulled Arlo onto his lap. Blaze wrapped his arms around Arlo, dropping his head down.

"Sawyer, chéri, are you really all right with this?"

Blaze lifted his wet gaze to look at Sawyer when the kid said, "He asked me if I thought it was okay. I do. Of course I do. In the years we had parents, they weren't any good." I caught Arlo shaking his head as his brother went on. "Not like you two. I was scared to believe you both could care about us in ways where... where we could become the family we have. But you've proved you care like that in so many ways, and you keep proving it with the love you show both of us." He gave us a soft smile. "This is the best family we could ever have. We love you guys."

Arlo lifted his eyes to Blaze, gripping his tee. "We do." He looked over at me. "We really do love you and Dad."

"Christ," Blaze bit out, hugging Arlo to him again. I got up and walked around the table, curling my arms around Sawyer.

"We love you both so much," I told them.

"We know," Sawyer said.

A knock sounded on the door. I straightened, and Sawyer quickly jumped out of his seat. "I'll get it." He stalked off to answer.

I glanced to Blaze. He stood, too, picking up Arlo, who laughed, before placing him on his feet. "You two eat."

Arlo and I took our seats and started piling our plates. "Your... dad..." Emotions clogged my throat as such a sweet feeling filled me when saying that. "He will pick you up from school today."

Arlo swallowed around a mouthful. "Cool. Will he be out front?"

"Yes." *Waiting to scare some children.*

"Firecracker," Blaze called. "Arlo, get in here."

Arlo grinned and grabbed a piece of bacon to eat on the way. He ran off, and I made my way more slowly, pausing on the threshold of the living room.

"A puppy?" I cried, hands pressing to my cheeks, eyes widening.

Loyal stood next to Blaze while Sawyer and Arlo were crouched on the floor with a little golden retriever bouncing around between the boys.

Sawyer stood. "I got him for you. Well, for everyone really. A family dog. And since Loyal overheard you talking to Blaze, last month, about how cute it would be to have a puppy to complete the family, he told me, and surprise. I didn't just pick randomly. I did some homework about the best pet for a family and learned this breed is good." He blushed. "I hope I didn't overstep. I just wanted to surprise you both."

Loyal shifted. He wanted to reach out to Sawyer no doubt.

"It's the most precious gift someone could ever give. You took all the hard work out of picking and helped us. He'll be the perfect family addition," I told Sawyer, smiling wide.

Sawyer relaxed. "I'm glad you like him."

"What are we gonna name him?" Arlo asked.

"We will watch him for a while and all make suggestions. I am sure we will find something," I said.

Honestly, I couldn't be happier. I was filled up to the brim with love for the people in my life. I would do anything to protect this, and I knew my big, beautiful beast would do the same.

"He is weeing," I cried, rushing over to pick him up and running to the back door while pee went everywhere with a laughing Sawyer and Arlo rushing after me.

Still, even with the pee accident, I knew our family would have a wonderful life together.

Even when there would be bad days, I believed the good days would outweigh them by miles. Not only did I have the love of my life at my side, but Blaze would do anything to make sure we had everything we desired. He also knew I would do the same too.

We would fight together to keep this home happy and safe, and no matter what might arise, we would come out stronger in the end.

Read on for a look inside a paranormal romance between four guys 🤭

In a blink, my life changed, now I just had to work out if it's for the better.

Micah Grey has always thought he's a normal, yet quiet and awkward guy. Just someone who's trying to survive living in his trailer and dodging his mother's debt collectors.
But then it all changes when a power within him surfaces and his eyes are thrown wide open.
Humans aren't the only ones who walk the Earth.
Not only that, Micah has to attend a college where he'll learn how to use this telekinetic ability, a power he apparently should have got when he was young, not at twenty-one. One he thinks is weak, and has some professors and peers questioning why he was admitted in the first place.
Throw in the knowledge of new roommate's: Cade, who seems to hate him, Zeke, who's nice and understanding, and Hyde, who's quiet and yet scary at the same time.
Micah's not sure if he'll survive this new change, but he's finding he wants to because he can't deny the connection he's feeling towards his roommate's.

icah

As I PICKED up the dirty dishes from a table, I couldn't help but overhear the waitress, Tanika, serving a new group sitting in a booth close by.

"Welcome to Danny's. Can I start anyone with drinks?"

"Can you tell me why your boss would hire a freak like that?"

Already, I knew they were talking about me. The guy's voice sounded familiar, one I probably pushed to the back of my mind from my high school days of being bullied. I didn't need this crap on top of the fact I was feeling like hell.

My head throbbed, and a headache wouldn't be far away.

Tanika harrumphed. "Sorry, who are you talking about?"

"Can't remember his name, but he used to slink around high school like a loser. I see he still dyes his hair that weird color. What a fucking loser."

I had always liked my dyed light blue hair. At first, I dyed it to try and get people to notice me, as I was tired of feeling alone. It failed. But now I did it because *I* liked it, and it made me feel different from others. Something special.

"I'm guessing you're talking about Micah." From Tanika's tone, I could tell she was pissed. From the first day we'd worked together two years ago, Tanika had been protective of me. Even though we were twenty-one, she'd taken me under her wing, accepting my quiet nature.

A tornado of worry formed in my gut.

Tanika and I hadn't gone to the same school. She didn't know I'd been the loner. The kid who lived in a trailer park with a drugged-out mother. The kid who got beat on for just being around. The kid who was nothing and no one to anyone.

God, I sounded pathetic.

I reminded myself that I got out of that trailer. Got away from her. It didn't matter that I was in my own trailer on the other side of town. It was still all *mine*.

Who cared that people didn't like me because I was quiet, and that made me seem strange? Or because I was timid¾thanks to my mother¾and book smart?

Only, I wasn't smart enough to gain a scholarship and go to a college far away. Instead, I was stuck in this hellish town, working three jobs just to keep my head above water in case Mom's debt collector paid me a visit when Mom didn't have the funds needed to pay off her gambling debts. It had happened before, quite a few times, and the reminder of my fear from the first time, when Lax, her debt collector, held me at knifepoint as he screamed at Mom to pay, had me setting aside what I could as a "just in case." I'd only been seven then, but it'd been embedded in my mind since.

Really, I didn't even have time for community college.

Would Tanika think differently of me from the guy's words?

"Yeah, that's the one. Shit, he was such a—"

Tanika threw her notepad in the guy's face. A woman beside him yelled in complaint, but Tanika ignored everyone while she pressed her hands to the table and leaned into his face.

Happiness floated through me from Tanika's actions, but I had to stop this. Usually, I wouldn't involve myself in confrontations. I hated fighting or talking, really. But this was Tanika. A friend. My only friend.

"Take your fucking foul mouth and ugly face out of this diner before I kick your ass."

The guy smirked with a glare. "You're getting defensive over *that* guy?"

"He's more of a man than you'll ever be." The warmth from her words had me straightening and flicking my light blue hair from my eyes. Tanika swung her arm back, and I moved quickly over to her, taking her elbow in hand and spinning her around until she was at my back.

"Leave," I told the guy. I still couldn't remember his name or face, just his voice as one of many who taunted me.

He smirked. "Are you going to make me?"

Fiery anger spread through me¾a feeling I wasn't used to. But I was older, and I *didn't* have to put up with his words.

"I will if I have to." It may have been fake bravery, but I honestly thought that if push came to shove, I would stand up to him now because I had someone at my back I cared about, and I didn't want Tanika to think she was alone in her fight to have my back. I'd be by her side, as she was the first person to *want* to know me.

I clenched my shaking hands, wishing he'd just disappear from in front of me. I wanted him gone. I wanted him... to hurt. My gaze flicked to the salt and pepper shakers on the table before I moved my glare back to him.

I stumbled back into Tanika's hands. Blinking rapidly, I watched as the guy rubbed his forehead and throat.

The shakers had forcibly flown across the table and smacked into the guy before shattering, leaving salt and pepper, plus glass, all over him.

"Oi, what the fuck is going on over here?" Ivan, the owner of the diner, strode over and stopped beside Tanika and me, throwing his hands onto his large waist.

Tanika gently shoved me aside. "They were saying shit about Micah, and the table tipped when he went to stand, spraying salt and pepper over him."

That didn't happen.

Did it?

It did.

Right?

Glancing at the other couple, I saw they stared dumbfounded at their friend. The shock on their faces told me I couldn't point the weirdness in their direction. They hadn't done anything.

How did the shakers move?

Pressing my fingers to my lips, I hid my snort under my

breath. I was overthinking it. There was nothing strange or special about what just happened.

"Get out, now." Ivan pointed toward the door.

"That's not what happened," the guy yelled. As he stood, salt and pepper rained down all over the floor from his body.

Ivan crossed his arms over his chest. "Yeah? Then tell me what happened." I caught Tanika poke Ivan in the side.

"*He* did this." The guy threw a hand my way.

Tanika mimicked Ivan's stance and snorted. "He wasn't even close to the salt and pepper."

The woman climbed out of the booth, as did the others. "Jon's right. He made them move across the table."

Tanika and Ivan laughed loudly. Tanika even bent at the waist to slap her thigh. She straightened, wiped under her eyes, and shook her head. "Did you hear that, Ivan?"

Ivan chuckled again. "I did."

My head throbbed again, and a new pain burned in my stomach, which had me gripping it.

"You think he used his mind to move things across the table?" Tanika shook her head. "You're crazy."

"Are you on drugs?" Ivan demanded. "I don't allow junkies in my diner. You need to get the fuck out of here."

Jon went red in the face. "I'm not on drugs or a damn junkie. It's that freak you have working for you."

"Sure," Ivan drew out. "Look, take your shit magic trick and work it on someone else. You ain't getting my worker in trouble for something you did."

"I didn't—"

The woman beside Jon touched his arm. She shook her head. "It's not worth it."

Jon clenched his jaw before he dropped a sigh and started for the door. As he went by me, he gave me a new look. This one held fear, and I wasn't sure why. I hadn't done anything, and he was wrong if he thought I'd somehow moved those shakers.

"Thanks, guys," I said, facing Tanika and Ivan, who were both staring at me. I tucked the long strands of hair behind my ear. I needed to cut the front of it. Though, it was good to have it longer to hide behind. Yeah, I would probably leave it.

Why was I thinking of my hair?

To distract myself, maybe? To stop focusing on the pulsating behind my eyes and the way my stomach wanted to revolt?

"Are you feeling okay, Micah?" Tanika asked with a furrowed brow. Her mirth had quickly changed to worry.

How had she read me so quickly? Besides my body acting up, I felt like Ivan had turned the heat up in the diner.

Wiping at my brow, I nodded. My hair dropped forward into my eyes again. "Yeah, I'm fine." I gestured toward the door where Jon and his friends had just walked through. "Sorry about that situation."

Ivan slapped a hand on my shoulder. "Don't stress, kid. I know you wouldn't cause trouble." He smiled, but it was a little strained. "You sure you're good, though?"

"Yes. I only have an hour left anyway." My head pulsed again. Maybe I was coming down with something.

"All right. Let me know if you want to shoot off early. Tanika, keep an eye on him."

"You got it, boss." She saluted Ivan's back as he made his way into the kitchen, then bumped into my hip. "You know

Ivan won't care if you need to get out of here. Or I can call in Jassy early."

"No, really, it's just a headache." Their kindness nearly brought tears to my eyes.

She grabbed my arm and gave it a squeeze. "Let me know if you need anything."

Nodding, I moved back to clear the table and take the dishes to the kitchen. Maybe when I said I only had Tanika as a friend, I was wrong. Ivan was also one. He took a chance on hiring me and had also stuck up for me before.

It just annoyed me that my past couldn't stay in the past where it belonged.

I'd been lucky enough in the last two years that no one else who'd haunted my days in high school had come into the diner. It had been bound to happen. I just wished it hadn't been tonight. I was already freaking out about seeing Lax, the debt collector, since the scene of Mom coming into the diner earlier was still fresh.

The door opened, and I happened to glance that way. Mom spotted me and stalked right up to shove my shoulder.

"I need money." She scratched at her arm and glanced all around her in jerky motions.

My heart beat franticly as I told her softly, "I won't have anything until after my shift."

The panic in her eyes set my pulse to race. But in a blink, she changed and scowled up at me. "You useless piece of trash." She itched at her arm again, at the scabs. "Why the fuck did I give birth to you? I should have aborted such a waste of space. Hopefully, *they'll* take care of you for me." And with that final note, she stormed from the diner.

I wanted to stand up to her, or more so to Lax like I had

Jon, but Lax worked for someone with a worse reputation in town, which made him scarier than anyone I knew.

Hate pumped through my veins over how weak I sounded and acted. I ground my teeth together as I walked back out into the diner. My head hammered again, but it wasn't the worst pain I'd had. I'd put up with beating after beating whenever Mom had a boyfriend over with a violent streak. There were also the times I got my ass handed to me at school, usually after I'd found enough courage to smart back with a comment.

Those beatings had worn me down to a point where I didn't see a reason to fight back or say anything. When I did, they only got worse.

Sighing, I picked up another set of dirty dishes and forced those depressing thoughts from my mind.

I had survived.

I was surviving on my own two feet and away from her.

One day I would get away from here. One day I would think back to these situations and laugh at them because I'd be rich, smarter, and worth something.

My future *would* be better.

My stomach twisted and my lunch threatened to show up. I placed the bucket down on the table I'd been cleaning and sucked in some deep breaths. I flicked my hair away from my eyes and glanced at the clock on the wall. There were still another twenty minutes to go. I had to make it for the money.

Sucking in a breath, I picked up the bucket, cringing when my stomach clenched.

"Hey," Tanika said from my side so suddenly, I jumped. She smiled apologetically. "Sorry. Look, I think you should get going. It's not long until your shift ends, and I'm sure Ivan will still pay you for it."

Shaking my head, I rubbed at my stomach. "Then I feel like I'm cheating him." My head picked that moment to throb painfully. I closed my eyes and sucked in a sharp breath.

"That's it." She took my arm in one hand and the bucket in the other. My gaze flared at her strength. How could she carry it with one hand, especially since I'd found it so heavy with dishes?

Tanika marched me out into the kitchen, where Ivan was laughing at something with his wife, Flora. Once they saw us, they stopped.

"Micah's leaving a little early," Tanika announced.

"Micah, are you all right? You do look a little green." Flora approached and rested her hand against my forehead. "And clammy."

Taking her hand from my skin, I patted it to show my appreciation for her concern before letting go. Flora was a sweet soul, but I wasn't close to her as I was Tanika, and I didn't enjoy people touching me. I'd only grown used to it with Tanika, as she was super affectionate, and over the years, she'd gotten me used to it.

"It's just a headache and a slightly twisted stomach. Nothing I can't handle. I can still finish my shift."

They all shared a look. Flora's lips thinned in worry while Ivan's brows dropped in confusion. About what, I didn't know.

"Tanika will walk you home."

No!

"No, I'll be fine." Quickly, I undid the apron, pulled it

over my head, and stalked to the cubby where I stashed it before I grabbed my wallet and keys.

If Tanika accompanied me home, and Lax showed, he would see her and somehow drag her into something horrid. I didn't have a doubt about it at all. I couldn't let that happen.

"I'll get going. See you all tomorrow night." I opened the back door.

"Micah, wait. I'll come." Tanika tried pulling her own apron off but got stuck in it.

"No, stay. No one's here to take both our shifts. Bye." I waved lamely and quickly stepped out, shutting the door behind me.

In a rush, I started my walk home. I kept glancing over my shoulder to check Tanika wasn't there. Thankfully, she hadn't followed. It wasn't until I neared the trailer park that I realized I'd forgotten to pick up my pay.

"Shit," I muttered.

A whistle sounded, startling me. "That's a naughty word for a guy like you, Micah."

Stuff me in the ass with knives.

Anything would be better than facing Lax when he realized I didn't have any money for him.

Turning slowly, I caught Lax moving out of the shadows and into the light of the streetlight. Four other guys followed him. Usually, he had about ten guys with him. Maybe he noticed I didn't put up a fight and told the others to go deal with someone else.

God, I'm weak.

"Lax...." My head throbbed as I wiped my sweaty palms on my pants. "I, ah, wasn't feeling well at work. I left early and forgot to get my pay. Can I give what Mom owes your boss tomorrow?"

Lax laughed. The others quickly joined in when he shot them a look.

Tension tightened my shoulders as I drooped them more, trying to make myself invisible but knowing it wouldn't work.

My stomach clenched and my head pulsated.

Slowly, I rubbed at my temples.

"Aw, look, guys. Poor little Micah has a headache."

More laughter rang out.

My stomach warmed in anger. I was sick of this. Sick of going from one messed-up situation to another. Sick of being weak. Sick of all the self-loathing, and the "I wishes," and the "I should haves."

"Hey, I'm talking to you." My shoulder got shoved. I stumbled back, lifting my gaze to Lax. "You go back to work and get me the goddamn money." He looked down at his hand. "Why the fuck you wet?"

I knew I'd been sweating from the pain, but I hadn't realized how much.

"Jesus." He wiped his hand on his jeans. "Just go back and get the money."

"No." My tone was soft but snappish. It even surprised me. If my head wasn't crying out for aspirin, I would have patted myself on my back.

Lax crossed his arms over his chest. "No?"

Nodding, I rubbed at my forehead.

"You're not listening again," Lax yelled, and I flinched, snapping my gaze up to his livid red face.

"Lax, please. I'm not well."

He leaned in and snarled in my face, "I don't give a fuck."

My head rocked back from the force of his punch that followed. Blood sprayed from my nose. Covering it, I stepped back.

"Go back to work and get your money. Last fucking time I tell you, else I'm sending the boys into your trailer."

They would take everything.

Pain stabbed at my temples and stomach. I took another step back.

Lax's jaw clenched. "Right, guys, teach him a fucking lesson, and I want his keys."

"No," I cried out, moving back further. The trailer was all I had. "No!" I yelled, throwing my hands out in front of me.

His people suddenly flew back from where they'd been standing and landed on their asses; groans filled the area.

Lax wasn't the only one with wide eyes. Slowly, he looked at me. "What did you do?"

"N-nothing."

He started for me. I backed up over and over and didn't stop until a new voice, a voice I knew, said, "Stop right there."

Ivan and Tanika moved out from within the trees. Lax looked to them and back at me before he ran at me.

"Stop." I threw my out hand to the side, and Lax shot the same way my hand moved.

Dumbfounded, I looked down at my hand as I heard Lax drop to the ground with his own groan. It was then I noticed the pain in my head and stomach had vanished.

"You're all right," Tanika said from right in front of me.

I saw her shoes first, then lifted my gaze to hers. She smiled softly. "Hey, it'll be fine now."

"Did... did I do that?"

She patted my shoulder and nodded. "Yep. Bit of a late bloomer, but that was all you."

"What? How.... I...." I shook my head and looked over to Ivan, who helped Lax to his feet. I called out quickly, "He's armed. He's always armed."

Tanika curled her arm around my shoulders and steered me toward the trailer park. "Don't worry about him. Ivan will have it covered."

It was fine to say don't worry, but fear still formed a pit in my gut.

I looked over my shoulder to see Ivan leading Lax over to his guys. Surprise shot through me¾Lax moved willingly. He didn't put up a fight, didn't say anything, just walked beside Ivan like I hadn't just thrown him across the ground.

But I had.

Somehow, I'd moved him. I just didn't know how.

Facing forward and with my heart in my throat, I stared down at my hands again. I swallowed thickly.

Excitement and fear churned inside me.

Glancing at Tanika, I wondered why she wasn't freaked out. "Did you see what happened?"

"I did." She stopped at my trailer.

Wait, how did she know where I lived?

When she looked my way, she laughed. "Don't worry, I'm not a stalker. Open up, and I'll give you some answers while you pack."

My head jerked back in shock. "Pack?"

"Well, yeah. There's a place where you can learn how to use your powers."

"Powers?' I whispered.

"Yep. I don't know if you'll have more, but it looks like you have telekinesis."

As I tripped up the steps, all I could think was that I didn't want to faceplant. I put my hands out to stop my fall but found myself flying backward into Tanika. She grunted before I was suddenly weightless again and my butt hit the ground.

Tanika stood beside the door, grinning.

I glanced to my doorway and back to her. "How... you were behind me."

She knelt beside me and placed her hand on my shoulder. "There's a lot you need to learn, young grasshopper."

CHAPTER TWO

Once seated at my very small table with Tanika opposite me, I stared at her and tried to get her words to sink in.

"Do you need me to tell you again?"

Nodding, I pressed my hands to my stomach. There wasn't any pain, but it wouldn't quit flipping around.

Tanika clapped, causing me to jump. She winced. "Sorry." She laced her fingers together and cracked her knuckles. "Okay. The supernatural world is real. There are shifters, vampires, witches, warlocks, and other different types of people with powers. The humans know nothing about us because we live in harmony among them all. Besides, like the humans have their own governments, FBI, cops, and armies, we're the same and have our own that oversee everyone and everything with rules and restrictions." She tapped her chin with a finger. "Hmm, what else was there? Right... there's a college close that will help teach you how to manage your powers. It's a good idea to go so nothing happens where you could accidentally use telekinesis in front of humans and get in trouble for it from the Interspecies Law Enforcement." Her nose scrunched up as she thought about more to load me with, but I worried my head was about to explode.

There were shifters... vampires... witches.... Was Iron Man real?

A yip escaped me when my door opened suddenly. My pulse only slowed a little when I saw it was Ivan stepping in.

"How's things going?" He stopped by my fridge and leaned his shoulder into it. The trailer and fridge groaned under his weight a little.

Tanika studied me, and since I didn't say anything, she shrugged. "I think he's freaking out."

Ivan snorted. "Understandable since he didn't grow up knowing."

"You did?" I blurted, gaping at him.

"Yeah, Micah. I was born a vampire. Flora is a witch and my bonded."

My brows dipped. "Bonded?"

Tanika shook her head. "We'll explain about that later. What we really need to do is get you to Tovenaar."

Information was my forte, and Google had always been a friend when I was bored and wanted to know things. Which was how my brain quickly supplied that *tovenaar* was Dutch for magician. *Ironic.*

Snorting to myself, I shook my head. "What about Lax? I can't just leave. He saw me do what I did." Something I still couldn't believe.

Ivan waved. "It's been taken care of."

Pushing my hair from my eyes, I gripped the strands and stared at Ivan. "You killed them?" I whispered.

Ivan and Tanika started laughing. Tanika smacked my

arm and shook her head. "God, that.... No, Ivan didn't kill him. Vampires have mind mojo. Lax and the others will be off somewhere getting high or something."

Ivan nodded.

"But... his boss could send him back to look for me."

"I've erased you from their minds. I know their boss. He's another vampire. I'll talk to him about your mom's debts being her own, not yours. You live here alone, right? Is there anyone... ah, special you need to talk to before disappearing for a while?"

Lax's mob boss was a vampire? A shudder raked over me while my mind spun from the fact that vampires were real.

"Wait, do I seriously need to leave?" The thought of vampires was replaced with anxiety as it ate my insides. This was my trailer. *Mine.* I couldn't just walk away from it and expect it to still be here when I got back. There were squatters who frequented the trailer parks at night looking for a dry place to sleep, and if they noticed someone wasn't taking care of this place, they'd move in.

Tanika nodded, her hand resting on my arm on the table. "It's for the best. You need to learn about your powers, have control over them."

"But I have work and my trailer."

"Ivan will take care of the trailer. He'll keep it safe. Good news: you'll still have your job. Right, Ivan?"

"Yep. Tanika goes to the same college, and you know she works only night shifts with me. You'll still have a job if your classes aren't too much. If they are, I'll keep a job for you when you get a handle on things. Micah, Flora and I'll have your back. This is a shock to all of us, kid. It wasn't until you started to feel sick, and with the incident at work, we knew a change was coming for you. We're going to help where we can. You've got enough to stress on your plate with only now learning of our world. Don't worry about things back here. Take care of yourself and learn about your power, kid. It's a good one."

It was?

Wait... I had a power? Ivan was a vampire, and I was supposed to go to a magic school to learn control of my new trick?

Did I knock myself out and was now living in my mind?

Quickly, I pinched myself, then hissed when it hurt.

"It's all real, sorry." Tanika nodded.

"How did this happen? My mom doesn't.... She's never shown any powers."

Ivan shifted on his feet. "Could come from your dad's side. You know him?"

Shaking my head, I scrubbed a hand over my face. "No. She never spoke of him. If I tried to ask about him, she'd get angry and...." I brushed my hair away as it fell in my eyes while I stopped those thoughts from surfacing. "She'd just get angry. I don't have a name or any type of information about him."

Ivan's jaw clenched. "I'll go to her and find out what I can. Let you know."

My head jerked back in confusion. "Find out?"

Ivan tapped his temple. "Got powers to read, alter, and erase things in human's minds."

"Right, um, vampire."

It was too hard to believe. Never would have I guessed my happy yet intimidating boss would be a blood-sucking vampire.

"Are you sure—" I jumped back in the seat and gawked as Ivan snarled and flashed his fangs before the iris part of his eyes bled red.

Tanika patted my arm. "He won't hurt anyone other than someone who harms the people he cares about." Ivan straightened. His fangs disappeared, his eyes changed back, and he nodded at Tanika. "Like humans, there are ones in our community who hold evil intent. Which is why we have our own special forces to uphold the law against those who act with malice."

"Okay. I.... It's all a lot." I bit my bottom lip before I sucked it into my mouth and nibbled on it.

I *had* a power.

Ivan was a vampire, and Tanika¾

"What about you? What, ah, I guess it's not polite to ask what a person can do or if they shift into an animal or drink blood?"

Ivan snorted and Tanika cackled. She shook her head. "Just be careful who you ask. Do you remember when I was behind you after you tripped, but then you fell through me because I didn't realize that your slim, short body could be heavy?" I nodded. "I phased through you."

My gaze dropped to the table. "Phased, meaning the ability to pass through physical matter? Also known as intangibility?"

"Exactly."

Lifting my eyes, I stared at Tanika. "You could always do this?"

"Yes." She smiled. "My mom has the ability. Dad is a spellcaster. Others call them mages. He can call up any spell and cast it without actually knowing it beforehand."

Wow.

Seriously, it felt like my mind had just opened another door, floating with new questions and possibilities of "others" in the world.

Now, I was one, and they wanted me to go back to school to learn to master telekinesis.

School and I were never friends.

Swallowing thickly, I glanced at my hands and then the glass on the table. I held one out to it, but the glass didn't move. "Are you sure I have this power?"

"Like I said, both Tanika and I could feel a change in you tonight. It's why we followed you home. Those salt and pepper shakers didn't fly off and hit that guy on their own. You did that, Micah."

"You also threw those assholes out there." Tanika thumbed outside. "If you're doubting having the power, don't. We've seen it and now can feel the power inside you. It's like a lock has been broken, and your power has come through."

Staring at the glass again, I moved my hand to the side, but it didn't shift the glass or water in it.

"It's not in your hands, kid. It's in your mind."

"My mind? And I *have* to go to school to learn to use it properly?"

"Yep." Tanika nodded. "Once there, you'll register in the supernatural community. Your name will go in a registry, and the information will be sent to the government. Whenever someone who isn't in the know about our world suddenly manifests powers or is turned, the government needs to know. It's like being born and having a birth certificate. This will be your certificate when you join Tovenaar."

A rock formed again in my stomach.

"If I don't get registered or go to the college?"

Tanika looked to Ivan. He gave me a sad smile. "If anyone from law enforcement finds you and senses your power, they'll question you to make sure you are registered. Anyone who isn't is taken before the government and questioned. There's also a chance your mind will be read. If they find out Tanika and I knew about you and didn't come forth with the information of someone new, we'd get fined tens of thousands of dollars. If your powers get out of control and you hurt people because of it, it would be worse for you and also us. Sorry, kid."

No way would I want to be harmed or Tanika and Ivan to lose money because of me or worse. I knew I wanted to learn about this power. It was only the thought of school that had me twisted inside.

Turning to Tanika, I said, "And you'll be at the school?"

"I will be. I still have things I need to learn about my power, but I'm also doing a degree there for botany. Plants and trees have always interested me."

My heart skipped a beat as hope flooded me. "There are other things you can learn?"

"Heck yes, there's so much. Even the human courses are provided because our kind still need a job in the human world if you can't get something on our side."

"I...I.... What do they have?"

She smiled softly. "How about I help you pack, and you come and find out yourself?"

Glancing at Ivan, I caught his smile and nod before I looked back to Tanika. Straightening my shoulders, I nodded. "Okay."

Standing, I shifted around the table and went to move past Ivan, until he clasped me on the shoulder. "Welcome to our world, Micah. I'll leave you in Tanika's hands, but if there's anything you need or have questions for me, please call. You have my number. I promise to keep an eye on things here while you board at school until you find your feet. If you want to stay longer in the dorms there, I'll still watch over your place. No matter how long."

A sudden urge to hug him overcame me. He'd been in my life for two years. The thought of not seeing him and Flora for a while saddened me. Even though I'd been quiet and kept to myself around them, they'd been a part of my life when I was starting to stand on my own and helped support me without even realizing it.

Quickly, I wrapped my arms around Ivan and hugged him tightly before I stepped back. I made sure my hair covered my eyes as my face lit with affection.

"Thank you... for everything."

His hand landed on my shoulder. "Aw, kid, it's been a pleasure. Even if you don't want to come back to this area, make sure to pop in and see us."

"I will." I nodded.

"Good." His hand dropped away, and he went to the door as he called to Tanika, who was already in my room. "Tanika, see you at next shift."

"You got it."

When Ivan had gone, I went into my room and saw that Tanika had already found my big duffel bag and was loading it with my underwear. My face heated.

Quickly, I went over there and grabbed some boxers from her hand. "I'll do those."

She snorted. "I'm not the type to swoon over someone by touching their underwear."

Licking my dry lips, I didn't comment because I was uncomfortable with the conversation. I willed my face to stop burning since it easily showed my inexperience around women *and* my underwear.

"Micah." Tanika's tone was light.

"Hmm?" I kept packing, turning my back on her to grab my winter clothes. I didn't have many things and knew there would be room left in the duffle bag.

"Have you ever been with anyone?"

"Tanika," I rushed to say, a harshness to the word.

"It's okay. That's answer enough. Do you like guys or girls?"

An embarrassed, slightly panicked noise dropped from my lips.

"We're friends, right?" She must have caught my nod. "I'm gay. I like women."

Why did we have to speak about this?

When I didn't say anything and continued packing while she now sat on my bed, she said, "Earlier, Ivan mentioned Flora being his bonded." I nodded and flicked my hair out of my eyes, pausing packing. "Well, bonded sort of means that there's someone, or a few someones, out there in the world who.... Shit, how do I explain this? I mean, it might happen with humans, but the divorce rate is too high for it to show they've found their bonded."

Taking a step back, I bumped into the wall. "Are you saying having a bonded is like marriage for us?"

Her brows pinched. "Sort of. But more intense. Look, I'm not saying you'll meet your bonded, who, in human terms, is your soul mate, but there is a chance it could happen, and I needed to warn you."

"How do you know?"

"That's the tricky part. My parents are bonded; you should see how sickly cute they are together. The love you have for your bonded can't be ruined or broken because they were made for you, made to complete you.... I'm getting off-topic. From what Mom said, you don't really know you're bonded until you have sex, actual penetration." Fiery heat burned my cheeks. "That's when the bond forms. I mean, she said she was deeply attracted to Dad, but she also thought Mel Gibson was good-looking."

It was simple then. I wouldn't have sex with anyone. I didn't want to risk finding a bonded after a sexual encounter and have them disappointed in who they got stuck with for the rest of their life. Knowing my luck, it could happen. Even my own mother didn't want me.

Though¾ "Can a human be a bonded partner for someone like us?"

She shook her head. "No."

At least, if I did find my libido, all I would have to do was sleep with a human to make sure I didn't accidentally marry someone.

"Thanks for telling me." And since I was about to embark on this next step, something that still twisted my insides and caused my hands to shake, I could open up a little to show I did trust her. "To answer your question, I think I'm asexual."

"If you are, that's cool, but that might change at Tovenaar."

I wanted to take this conversation and throw it out the

window. My heart hadn't stopped racing since I'd arrived home, and there was a chance I'd pass out soon if I didn't shut her up about this, at least.

"Can we, um, move on?"

Tanika winked. "Got it. You're shy. It's cute." My face burst with heat. Tanika grinned. "Though, I'm kinda bummed you didn't find me attractive at least."

Groaning, I threw a T-shirt at her. "Shut up."

"Okay, okay." She laughed. "Let's finish this and get you to school. It's already late, but don't worry your pretty little head. The dean is used to people showing up at all hours."

Nodding, I grabbed the last few items I needed and packed them.

As I looked around, sorrow stabbed at my chest. I wouldn't be seeing this place for a while. I wouldn't be working for Ivan either. Not now, at least.

"Ready?" Tanika called from the front door.

Grabbing my duffle bag, I flung it over my shoulder and steadied my feet when the weight of the bag nearly took me to the ground.

Was I ready? No. Definitely not.

Even though all I wanted to do was hide under my bed for the rest of my life, I pushed my feet forward. I did it for my inquisitive mind, for Tanika and Ivan.

CHAPTER THREE

Tanika took me back to the diner where her car was parked. Ivan and Flora had already closed up shop, so I didn't have to say goodbye to them again. Thank goodness. If I had, it would have been a struggle to leave. It was like the diner and the owners were my safety net¾an everyday routine I enjoyed.

I was more than grateful for at least having Tanika at my side for this journey.

In the car and on the road, I glanced out the window, nibbling at my thumb nail while bouncing my leg up and down. My stomach fluttered at the thought of something new in my life, and I didn't like it. At least I didn't feel sick like I had before.

"Tanika, do you know people coming into their powers late? Did they feel sick beforehand?"

"I've heard of the cramping in the gut and the headaches. If it wasn't for the way you kept wincing and sweating or with what happened with that jerkoff, I wouldn't have considered it, since you're already twenty-one."

Panic boiled my blood. "Wait. Tell me there are others at *twenty-one* coming into a power?"

Her lips thinned and brows pinched. "I haven't met anyone until you."

Groaning, I palmed my face and tugged at my hair. "I'm still a freak, no matter if it's with the humans or-or us."

"Hey, no, don't say that. There could be a perfectly good reason why your power didn't come out until now."

Tears threatened, and I shot my gaze back out the window as I thought of all the situations where my power could have come in handy in my life.

Why now?

It wasn't like I had just turned twenty-one; I was closer to my next birthday. It didn't make sense. Then again, this whole night was something out of a fantasy story.

Rubbing at my chest with one hand, I bit at my thumb nail again on the other.

"Micah, please, don't worry. You'll fit in. We'll find out why it's happened now, and if we don't, you'll have the chance to learn about your power and other things. It hasn't escaped my notice that you love to read and research."

"Sorry, it's...."

"A lot to take in. I get it."

It was, and all in a short amount of time. I worried if there was any more, my brain would fart before overloading, and I'd collapse to the floor in a heap.

Please don't let that happen.

"We're nearly there. You'll feel a bit of pressure when we

pass through the protective barrier around the college. It keeps out humans and anyone with harmful intentions."

Clearing my throat, I straightened, looked out the front window, and rubbed my hands up and down my thighs.

It was dark, and I couldn't really see anything other than the woods. "I guess we'll see if I do actually have a power." If I was still classed as human, I wouldn't be able to pass through.

"You do have a power. You just need time to adjust and have control of it. It's what we're here for. For you to learn." She shot me a wide smile.

I managed a small shaky one back before facing the front again.

A slight pressure built around me before there was a pop that had my ears ringing. I stuck a finger into each of them and wiggled them around.

Tanika laughed. "Yeah, I forgot about that part."

Licking my dry lips, I focused out the window as a large building came into view. When we got closer, I noted the building was bigger than I thought. I'd looked at colleges before, and they'd intimidated me with their sizes¾worried I'd get lost.

They were nothing compared to this, though. My stomach rolled with unease.

Tanika pulled to a stop out front of two large wooden doors and turned off the car. "I'll move it later. Let's get you inside first."

"Do you room here also?" *Please say yes.* At least I would have someone I knew around all the time.

"I do. I only go out into the human world to work. You can buy anything you need to survive here on campus.

There's a few shopping areas for food and clothes scattered around."

A shopping area. No human school I knew of had one of those.

"You ready?" Tanika asked.

"No." It was the truth, but knowing I wasn't ready for this crazy new step in life wouldn't stop me from learning. "But I'll try."

Tanika rested her hand on my arm for a moment. "That's all you can do. I promise it's not as scary or daunting as it seems."

Yeah, right. I had to tighten my butt cheeks to make sure I didn't crap myself as I climbed out of the car. There was also a chance that my heart was going to beat out of my chest and fall to the ground, and I'd die. Maybe that would be better for me, though... but then I wouldn't know if this development was going to be something better for me and my life.

Sighing, I swallowed thickly as I scrubbed a shaky hand over my face and went to the rear passenger door to take out my bag. Once I had it in hand, I closed the door and faced the entrance again.

There were ten front steps I had to take before my life was altered forever.

Ten steps.

I could do this.

Glancing to a smiling Tanika, I drew in a breath and nodded. Tanika took my hand, and together we made our way up to the door with my pulse in my throat. Shock radiated through me when Tanika didn't knock but pushed a door open and walked in, dragging me behind her.

"It's not locked?"

Tanika grinned, and when the door closed with a bang behind us, I spun and found two men standing just inside the closed doors. Two hulking men in black uniforms. Strapped around their waists were belts with weapons hooked onto them.

"The college has security everywhere. Most of the time you don't see them. But these two lugs are just two out of many who rotate with others for the front door detail. Isn't that right, Mike and Lesley?" Tanika pointed to the men when she'd said their names. Mike was a bald man with a body that even The Rock would be proud of. Lesley was only a little smaller. Where Mike's eyes were narrowed, Lesley's weren't, and they held warmth.

"Girl, how was work?" Lesley asked. Mike grunted and leaned back against the door, crossing his arms over his chest as he surveyed the entryway.

Honestly, it was an impressive space.

The roof was high and arched before it smoothed out flat. There was a grand staircase in the middle, but off to the left held elevators. To the right of the room, there was a massive desk beside us. Behind that was an office, and down along that side held other rooms. To what, I didn't know.

"Work was same old, but can you reach the dean? I have a new student." Tanika smiled over at me. I managed to lift the corner of my lips before taking in the tiling of the floors. The pattern was old, the decorative style mosaic. "Lesley." Tanika took my hand again, causing me to jolt from my thoughts. "We'll wait in his office."

She started to pull me along until I paused and glanced at Lesley and Mike quickly. I dipped my head. "It was nice meeting you both. Um, thank you." A blush rushed to my face. Why did I thank them?

Mike nodded and Lesley smiled widely. "Always good to meet a new student. Good luck with it all...."

"Micah," I blurted quickly before turning toward the office. This time I dragged Tanika along with me.

Thank you? I seriously said that, and I still couldn't understand why my brain spat those words out.

Since I didn't know exactly where I was going, I paused at the front desk and let Tanika take over the lead. As soon as Tanika had us in a spacious office, I sat on a chair and buried my face in my hands. Tanika snorted, then laughed lightly. "You're like one of those people who say, 'You too,' after a waiter says enjoy your meal."

I was. I really was.

"My mouth moves before my brain catches up some-times." Straightening, I glanced at her as she sat beside me in another chair. "You have to know I'll be... I won't... I doubt I'll make friends. I'm not the most social person to begin with, and if I could, I would hide in my room twenty-four seven. You may risk your status here by spending time with me."

Tanika rolled her eyes and shoved my shoulder. "Please. We're friends. Nothing you say or do will take that away. You're stuck with me."

It was nice of her to say so, but we'd only been around each other at work, and there I could keep to myself since I collected dirty dishes, so I usually hid away in the kitchen. Tanika hadn't seen me in a school situation. She didn't know how awkward I really was.

"Just know, it's okay if you change your mind."

"You may not know this, but I'm stubborn. I said it before, and I'll say it again. You're my friend, Micah. Nothing you're worrying about now will break that."

"Okay," I muttered and took my first look around the room.

Both sides held bookshelves with a heap of stacked books. My hands itched to reach out for the knowledge they would, no doubt, hold. But the fear gripping my stomach stopped me. Which was good, since it was the dean's office, and if I was in his position, I wouldn't want a stranger touching my things.

A desk sat in front of our chairs. On it was a computer, papers, and more books. The chair behind it was one of those expensive but comfortable chairs. I had an urge to sit in it to see how comfortable it was.

When the door opened abruptly, I swung around with my hand out and a scream in my throat. Whoever it had been flew through the air and landed with a bang outside the office. Tanika scrambled up, as did I, and we raced out into the main office area.

A boy, around eighteen, blinked up at me from the rubble of what used to be a desk.

Gasping, I raced to his side and dropped to my knees. "I'm so sorry. I didn't mean it." With my arm under his back, I helped him sit. A whimper escaped me when wood and dust dropped off him. I could have really hurt him.

Flicking my hair over my eyes, I glanced down to my knees. "I'm so sorry, again. If you like, you can tell the dean. I... I um, only discovered I held a power tonight." Wide-eyed, I shook my head. "But that means nothing. I shouldn't have reacted that way."

"Micah—" When Tanika didn't finish, and it seemed like she'd cut off whatever she was going to say, I glanced over to see she stood with her hand behind her back and lips thinned with her dancing eyes off to the side. I looked there and found Lesley and Mike.

"Sorry," I blurted out to them. "I didn't mean to hurt another student—" Tanika made a noise in the back of her throat, but I ignored it. "I'll explain it to the dean when he arrives, and... and I have a little bit of money." I didn't. Well, I would have a little if I'd picked up my pay from Ivan before I left.

Lesley smiled as Mike walked off. "It's fine, Micah. I'm sure the dean won't mind. Will you, sir?"

The boy laughed. "Accidents happen." He patted my hand. "Don't worry. I shouldn't have startled you." In a blink, he stood in front of me and held out a hand my way.

Wait....

Slowly, I took his hand and was standing next to him in the next moment.

Holy hell on earth. He was strong to pull me up like that.

Wait....

"Micah, wasn't it?" the guy asked with a soft smile on his face as he brushed himself off. At least he wasn't holding a grudge or wanted to seek revenge. Some of the tension eased from my shoulders.

"Yes?" I said hesitantly, aware it sounded like a question more than anything, but my mind was busy trying to work out if what I suspected was true.

But it couldn't be.

He was young and.... Okay, I had nothing else, but he had to be a student and not the dean, right?

Once he was done brushing off his clothes, his smile brightened even more, and that was when I saw his fangs.

Lesley cleared his throat. "Sir, I'm going back to the doors.'

He nodded and waved him off. "Yes, yes, everything is fine." Once Lesley dipped his chin our way and disappeared, the guy faced me again and held out his hand once more. I took it, and he shook. "Micah, it's nice to meet you. I'm the dean at this college, but you may call me Sebastian."

Tanika snorted. "No one calls him Sebastian. It's always Dean because he's as old as dirt."

The dean shot Tanika a scowl that had me backing up a step. Sebastian noticed and started laughing. "Relax. I won't hurt anyone for the fun of it. They really have to peeve me off first."

I shifted my gaze to the broken desk and back again.

Sebastian, which I felt was fine to use in my mind only, chuckled and gestured toward his office. "Let's head in there and get to know one another." He started forward. "I see you've already made one friend. I wished it had of been anyone else. Tanika is...."

"Special, amazing, brilliant?" Tanika grinned. With her hands on my shoulders, she guided me back to my chair since I was utterly stunned by the new events.

Sebastian scoffed as he sat behind the desk. He really was the dean. Though, he was only a little taller than I was, so he looked tiny in his seat.

Not that I would tell him that.

"I was going for annoying, Tanika." He leaned back in the chair.

"Pfft, please. I'm awesome, and you know it." Tanika also sat, and I sensed both their eyes on me. I glanced out the corner of my eye and did find Tanika looking at me. "I only give the dean hell because he's good friends with my father and has been around since I was a baby."

I nodded and swallowed the lump in my throat. The dean cleared his throat. "Micah, can you tell me the events leading up to you realizing you hold a power?"

Straightening, I flicked my eyes from Sebastian to Tanika and back again before dropping them to my lap. As I explained, I switched from gazing at the books around me to picking at a loose thread in the bottom of my T-shirt.

"Micah?"

"Yes, sir?"

"Either Sebastian or Dean is fine." When I nodded, he went on, "From this night on, your life will change. Here you will learn to manage and control your power. If you wish, we can also enroll you into other courses that might interest you and help toward your future profession."

Excitement bubbled up inside me, and I shot my gaze to the dean's.

He smiled. "I thought that may interest you since you can't stop looking at all the books." He stood and moved over to the bookcase on the left. As he took some from the shelves, he went on. "You'll have the day off tomorrow, and we'll work out the areas you want to learn alongside the things you *need* to learn." He moved back and dropped the books on his desk. "In your free time, you can also go over these¾" He tapped the books. "¾alongside the texts you'll get for classes. They'll help you understand your new world more." He glanced at Tanika. "Tanny, can you get Micah a welcome pack, please? They're in the office beside us."

Tanika popped up from her seat. "Sure thing."

My heart fell to my feet when she left the room. My nerves had been all right with Tanika here, but now that she was gone, I bounced my leg up and down while biting my thumbnail and looking everywhere but at the ancient vampire in front of me.

Tanika had said he was as old as dirt. It meant he would be powerful, right?

"Micah, what's your last name?"

"Grey, sir—I mean Sebas-Dean." Darn it all. I was useless at speaking when nervous.

A soft chuckle sounded around in the room. "Micah, do you understand you'll be safe here? There won't be anyone to take your money, and everything you own will be yours. No one will take another thing from you."

How did he know that about me? I didn't say anything about Lax or the trailer I lived in.

Could he read minds?

"Tanny spoke to me telepathically. She just wanted to look out for you."

Okay, so he could speak to people in their minds.

Yep, just an average day for me. My knee bounced harder.

"I know." I nodded. Licking my dry lips, I forced a question from myself. "Will I, ah, be…. Will…. Is it strange that I'm older and starting here?"

"You're not the first, and I doubt you'll be the last to come into a power later in life. What we do in your situation is see how much you can learn about your power in the first few months, and if we think you can move up a year, you will. Some can master their power quickly, some can't, and if that happens, please don't think badly of it. It means their power is a strong one."

"Okay." I nodded.

The dean wiggled his mouse to bring his computer to life. "Now, let's see where we can put you."

Dear Reader, thank you for taking a chance on Henri and Blaze!

Keep an eye on my social pages because Romania will be coming next.

Website
Facebook
Instagram
TikTok

Hawks MC: Next Generation

Coyote

Ruin

Texas

Swan

Diamond MC

Country

State (novella)

Death

Torch

Polished P & P

(MM romances)

Wreck Me Forever

Never A Saint

Working Out West

Up in a Blaze

Romantic Comedies

Fumbled Love

Bumbled Love

Making Changes

Making Sense

Why choose fantasy titles under L. Rose

A Torn Paige

A Lost Paige

A Final Paige

Within the Darkness

Infinite Bond

Protected by the Shifters series
(MM romances)

Protected by the Bear Shifter

Protected by the Tiger Shifter

Protected by the Fox Shifter

* 9 7 8 1 7 6 3 5 5 9 7 7 6 *